PRAISE FOR ADAM MITZNER

Dead Certain

An Amazon Charts Most Sold and Most Read Book
and Authors on the Air Finalist for Book of the Year

"*Dead Certain* is dead-on terrific . . . It's an entertaining and riveting work that will more than hold your interest."

—*Bookreporter*

"Consistently compelling . . . Adam Mitzner is a master of the mystery genre."

—*Midwest Book Review*

"There are several twists and turns along the way . . . creating a big amount of tension . . ."

—*The Parkersburg News and Sentinel*

"[*Dead Certain*'s] leading coincidence, which is quite a whopper, is offset by an equally dazzling surprise . . . It packs enough of a punch to make it worth reading."

—*Kirkus Reviews*

A Conflict of Interest

A *Suspense Magazine* Book of the Year

"A heady combination of Patricia Highsmith and Scott Turow, here's psychological and legal suspense at its finest. Adam Mitzner's masterful plotting begins on tiptoe and morphs into a sweaty gallop, with ambiguity of character that shakes your best guesses, and twists that punch you in the gut. This novel packs it. A terrific read!"

—Perri O'Shaughnessy

"Mitzner's assured debut . . . compares favorably to *Presumed Innocent* . . . Mitzner tosses in a number of twists, but his strength lies in his characters and his unflinching depiction of relationships in crisis. This gifted writer should have a long and successful career ahead of him."

—*Publishers Weekly* (starred review)

A Case of Redemption

An American Bar Association Silver Gavel Nominee for Fiction

"Head and shoulders above most . . ."

—*Publishers Weekly*

A
MATTER
OF
WILL

OTHER TITLES BY ADAM MITZNER

ADAM MITZNER

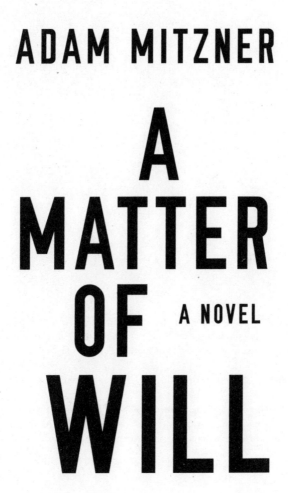

A MATTER OF WILL

A NOVEL

THOMAS & MERCER

Text copyright © 2019 by Adam Mitzner. All rights reserved.

Published by Thomas & Mercer, Seattle

www.apub.com

Amazon, the Amazon logo, and Thomas & Mercer are trademarks of Amazon.com, Inc., or its affiliates.

ISBN-13: 9781503905139
ISBN-10: 1503905136

Cover design by Shasti O'Leary Soudant

Printed in the United States of America

To my family—Susan, Rebecca, Michael, Benjamin,
Emily, and Onyx.

"We are our own devils; we drive ourselves out of our Edens."

—*Goethe*

Will Matthews had never seen a dead body. Not even his parents' bodies—he'd chosen not to view them before their burials, knowing that witnessing them that way would haunt him. But now he was staring straight into the lifeless eyes of a corpse lying in a pool of blood on his balcony.

A part of him couldn't make sense of it. As if it were a movie, the ending of which had veered unexpectedly away from the foreshadowed climax, he wanted to press the rewind button and watch the last few minutes unfold again to see what he'd missed.

Of course, if he had a rewind button for life, he would have pressed it sooner than now. Maybe when he first met Samuel Abaddon. Even earlier than that, truth be told.

What filled Will with even greater panic than the sight of the dead body was the knowledge that this wasn't the end of his story. Far from it. There were choices to be made, and the resolution was still uncertain.

Most terrifying of all, Will couldn't discern whether he should write himself as the hero or the villain in his own autobiography. He had a feeling that the decision he was about to make would set him irrevocably down one path or the other.

The one thing—maybe the *only* thing—he knew for certain was that once he made his choice, there would be no turning back.

WINTER

1.

"The devil I understand, but what's with the other one?"

The question was confusing on so many levels that Will didn't know quite how to reply. Or if he should say anything at all.

The query had been posed by a well-dressed man of about forty, with the clean-cut features of a movie star and the distinguished graying temples of a college professor. The fact that he wore what appeared to be a very expensive suit, probably Italian, meant the man wasn't in academia, however. Banking, most likely, although that was Will's profession too—and he wasn't nearly as well attired.

Business suits were not unusual at Madison Square Garden on a weekday, especially in the box seats only a row up from the ice. The man hadn't even loosened his tie, though, and that made him stand out, its perfect dimple telling the world that he was never not working. By contrast, Will had jettisoned his tie on the subway, and he'd taken off his jacket and rolled up his shirtsleeves the moment he found his seat.

The question was the very first thing the well-dressed man had said to Will, even though they'd been watching the game side by side for nearly an hour. Will found it a little disquieting that the stranger's first foray into conversation—at a hockey game, no less—was to pose a metaphysical quandary concerning the existence of good and evil.

"I'm sorry. Were you talking to me?" Will asked.

He'd been so distracted by the question that he had momentarily forgotten about the game. It was as if everything else—the crowd, the clicking of the players' skates on the ice, the slapping thwack of the puck—had been silenced while the man engaged him.

"That's right. I understand all about the Devils. There's this local legend in South Jersey about a kangaroo-like creature with the head of a goat, bat-like wings, and a forked tail that supposedly stalks the Pine Barrens and makes this bloodcurdling scream. So it makes total sense that a hockey team from Jersey would be named the Devils. I mean, you're not going to name them the New Jersey Tomatoes just because they hail from the Garden State. Am I right about that?"

Will didn't respond. Though he heartily agreed that the New Jersey Tomatoes made for a lousy hockey team name, he assumed the man's question was rhetorical by the fact that the man didn't pause.

"But what the hell was the thinking behind calling a hockey team from New York City the Rangers? As far as I know, there were never any rangers in New York. That's a Texas thing."

Will had been a Ranger fan his whole life—his allegiance handed down from his father, who had talked of Rod Gilbert, "Steady" Eddie Giacomin, and Jean Ratelle, the stars of the team in the 1970s, with the type of reverence usually reserved for biblical figures. Which meant that Will knew every last bit of trivia about the Blueshirts, including the answer to the man's question.

"It's actually a play on words," Will said, turning to look straight at him. "The original NHL team from New York was called the Americans. Then, in the mid-1920s, a guy named Tex Rickard established a new hockey team to play in the original Madison Square Garden. He called his team Tex's Rangers. Not the cleverest of puns, but still. Anyway, the Americans folded during World War II, but the Rangers here have been going strong ever since. The 'Tex' part of their name didn't stick around for very long, thank God."

The man considered the explanation carefully, as if waiting for a better one to come to him. Then he said, "I'm not sure God should be thanked in any way, shape, or form for the Rangers, my friend. If anything, you should be cursing him for the fact that you've only won a single Stanley Cup in the last seventy-five years."

"This is our year," Will said.

The man looked hard at Will. "I see that you're a man of loyalty and commitment. That's a rare find in our troubled times, especially for someone of your generation. A sad fact but true, I'm sorry to say. So rare that I make it a point, whenever I find such a man, to buy him a beer. And I'll tell you, I can count on one hand how many such beers I've purchased over the years."

Will knew the man was blowing smoke, but he appreciated the effort at camaraderie. The truth was that Will wasn't rare in any way. If anything, he was certain he fell into the dime-a-dozen category. Or worse, his life was a cliché. A twenty-seven-year-old from the Midwest who dreamed of hitting it big on Wall Street. He would have been glad to live as a cliché, but he had a nagging fear that he was about to become a cautionary tale instead. If things didn't change in a hurry, he would be the twenty-seven-year-old Midwesterner who had failed to make it in the Big Apple and been forced to slink away with his tail between his legs and nothing to show for his efforts—no job, no money, no girl, and no dreams.

Without waiting for Will to accept his offer, the man flagged down one of the Garden's hawkers. A kid lumbered down the aisle to the front row, a tray of twenty-four enormous cups of beer strapped to him like a backward backpack.

"Give me two," the man said. He turned to the woman on his other arm. "Make that three," he amended, even though she hadn't indicated she wanted a beer. In fact, Will realized he hadn't yet heard the sound of her voice.

Will had noticed the woman as soon as the couple had taken their seats. She could be described as drop-dead gorgeous without a hint of hyperbole. Rita Hayworth in *Gilda*, which Will knew about only because of the first poster used to hide Andy Dufresne's tunnel in

Shawshank Redemption. She was as tall as her companion—taller than Will, and he was a shade under six feet. Some of that had to do with the woman's heels, which had caught Will's eye because wearing stilettos to a hockey game was hardly *de rigueur.* Neither was her low-cut little black dress. It was her hair that had captivated Will, however. Torrents of deep red curls. The kind you knew weren't out of a bottle. She was closer to Will's age than to her companion's, but gave off a vibe like she'd never once dated anyone near her own age. She was the type who dated college boys in high school, and in college went out with her professors.

"That's thirty-three, with tax," the beer boy said.

The man handed him a crisp fifty and said, "It's all for you."

Then, turning toward Will, he raised his cup in a toast. "To the Devils."

Will hesitated, wondering if "a man of loyalty and commitment" should toast a rival team, but then he decided that playing along would be good manners. He brushed his cup against the man's, after which they both took a slug of beer. Out of his peripheral vision, Will saw that the woman had placed her cup on the ground without imbibing.

The man extended his hand. "Samuel Abaddon," he said. His grip was firm, but not so strong he was trying to prove anything.

"Will Matthews."

"Mr. Matthews, this is Evelyn Devereux," Samuel Abaddon said.

"Eve," she said, extending a delicate hand to Will. "Sam always likes to be so formal."

Will took Eve's hand in his, surprised by its softness. He wondered if it was because her skin was truly that supple, or if it had just been such a long time since he had experienced a woman's touch that he was no longer familiar with the sensation.

"Pleasure," he said, which wasn't something he normally said when introduced to someone, especially a beautiful woman. He felt almost compelled to kiss the top of her hand, but when she broke their connection, he was extremely thankful that he hadn't.

"As I'm sure you've surmised, Will, Sam here is one of the last great romantics. He thought that a hockey game was an appropriate Valentine's Day date."

Will had momentarily forgotten it *was* Valentine's Day. Even though this was yet another Valentine's Day he was spending alone, this year it had been to his advantage. He had obtained his ticket by fluke. Arthur Bargonetti, to whom he had only ever said a passing "How you doing?" in the hall, said he'd come into possession of just one ticket for tonight's game and couldn't use it on account of the holiday. Will assumed that Bargonetti had offered it to half a dozen people who'd turned it down for the same reason before Dateless Will became its lucky recipient.

"I think Will here had the right idea. He's flying solo tonight."

Eve shot Sam a thin smile. "Another crack like that, my dear, and you'll be flying solo tonight too—if you catch my meaning."

Will *definitely* caught her meaning. Even though he considered himself the biggest Ranger fan he knew, he had no doubt that if he had been in Sam Abaddon's shoes, he would have made different plans for the holiday.

When Will focused back on the ice, he saw that the Devils had a two-on-one breakaway. The Devils' center was streaking up the middle of the rink. After crossing the blue line, he deked; that provided just enough space to slide the puck into the right-hand corner, beyond the Ranger goalie's outstretched glove.

The crowd let loose a monstrous roar. Even in the Garden, the Rangers' home ice, the contingent of Devils fans was sizable. That made some sense, because it was actually easier to get to the Garden from the Port Authority or Penn Station, the public transportation entry points for New Jerseyites, than it was from most locations in New York City.

"You can't stop the Devils," Sam said. "We'll get you every single time."

A few minutes later, the siren ending the second period blared.

"Another round, my friend?" Sam asked.

Will had barely made a dent in his first beer. Peering over, he saw that Sam's cup was empty. Protocol required Will to pick up the tab now, which meant he couldn't decline buying another beer for himself too.

"On me, Sam," Will said.

Will raised his hand like a second grader, trying to get the attention of the beer boy. Between the second and third periods was of course prime time for beer sales, and the hawker had turned his back to them to service a group across the aisle.

"Christopher, my man," Sam called out.

The beer boy—who *was* apparently named Christopher—turned around. When he did, Will searched his uniform for a name tag, but the huge button he wore said only **$11,** TAX INCLUDED.

Will reached into his pocket and extended two crumpled twenties.

"How many?"

Will waited a beat, deferring to Sam to ask Eve whether she wanted another beer. But Sam didn't say a word.

"Eve, are you having another?" Will asked.

"No, thank you. As someone once said, I pride myself on keeping my wits about me while all others are losing theirs."

She said this with a knowing smile, leaving no doubt in Will's mind that she knew she was quoting Kipling. Her head was cocked in Sam's direction, suggesting that her companion was prone to overindulgence.

"Two, please," Will said.

With the beers in hand, Sam said, "While we wait for the Zamboni to do its thing, why don't you regale Evelyn and me with the Will Matthews story?"

"Not too much to tell, actually."

Although a modest man of accomplishment might have said the same thing, in Will's case it was 100 percent accurate. There truly *wasn't* much to his biography.

"Come now," Sam said. "Every man is the protagonist in the novel that is his life. It's all in the way you tell it. I'm certain you have a truly compelling origin story. Start with where you were born."

Will felt uneasy about being put on the spot, but shutting down his new friend would lead to a very uncomfortable third period. "A small town in Michigan."

Sam held up his right hand, fingers tight together. Someone from another state might think he was swearing an oath, but a Michigander like Will knew that Sam was making a map of the state with his hand, asking Will to point out from where in the "mitten" he hailed.

"Top of the middle finger," Will said. "Cheboygan."

"Ah, the old sewing needle," Sam said, referencing one of the two theories for the translation of the city's name.

"I take it you've been," Will said.

"As a matter of fact, I spent some of my formative years just a stone's throw from Cheboygan. My father was stationed at Alpena when I was in middle school, and for a year of high school."

"Yeah, that's about an hour away."

Will was about to ask where else Sam had lived, but Sam was already on to his next point. "So you're a man from a hardscrabble river town just south of the Canadian border. Let me guess . . . your mother was a seamstress. And your father . . . I want to say that he's a ferryboat captain, but that seems too on the nose. I'm going to go with local shopkeeper."

Will chuckled. "No, on either count. My mother worked in a clerical job for the college, Northern Central Michigan. My father sold insurance, but he passed when I was still a boy."

"I'm sorry," Eve said, which surprised Will because he hadn't thought she was listening.

"Thank you. It was a long time ago."

"My father died only a few years ago," she said. "I'm still not completely over it, to be honest."

Will could tell that she was being sincere by the look in her eyes. They were filled with unmistakable sadness.

"And your mother? Is she alive?" Eve said with a hopefulness in her voice.

Ironically, Will felt a twinge of sadness that he was going to disappoint Eve with his answer. "No. She passed last year."

"Oh, you poor dear," Eve said as she put her hand on top of his.

"You live the life you're given, I guess. It's not ideal, but others have had much greater hardship, so I really can't complain."

"Well said," Sam intervened. "How did a boy from Michigan develop an affinity for the Rangers?"

"My father's family was originally from upstate New York. He was a huge Ranger fan, and he made me one too."

"What took the old man to the hinterlands of northern Michigan?" Sam asked.

"My mother. She grew up there. Third generation."

Sam showed a Cheshire cat grin. "The backstory is now firmly established, and more than a little intriguing. Your old man was clearly a hopeless romantic who followed a woman of unsurpassed beauty to her ancestral home, only to die tragically, leaving behind his namesake to make his own place in this world."

The namesake reference surprised Will. He was certain he hadn't told Sam that his father was also named William.

"How'd you know that I was named for my father?"

"You go by Will, not Bill or William. So I'd wager ten to one that your father went by the latter. Am I right about that?"

Will nodded. He turned to Eve, wondering what she was making of Sam's display. She smiled in a way that suggested she was sympathetic to Will's plight. He wondered whether she'd once endured a similar game about her own biography.

"And now, on to young Will," Sam said. He rested his chin on a thumb, the other fingers balled into a fist—like he was mimicking the Rodin statue. As Sam studied his subject, the Devils and Rangers retook the ice, but the crowd's cheering did nothing to disrupt his concentration.

"You're too well mannered to be a lawyer and not dressed stylishly enough to be in any type of creative field—no offense. Yet your shoes are shined, which tells me that you work in a place where that type of thing matters."

"I'm in wealth management at Maeve Grant," Will said quickly, for fear that Sam's guess wouldn't be flattering.

Will was accustomed to people being impressed whenever he dropped the Maeve Grant name into conversation. Needless to say, he always omitted that he was still in the broker-training program. He also kept to himself that he was on the verge of being fired.

Sam acknowledged the name drop with only a slight nod. Then he said, "Wealth management . . . Aren't we all?"

"Is that what you do too, Sam?" Will asked.

"No. I was speaking figuratively, whereas I can only assume that you were being literal."

"Leave the poor man alone, Sam," Eve said. "He's probably sorry he sat down next to us at all."

In truth, Will was not only enjoying himself, but saw serendipity in the encounter. The key to survival at Maeve Grant was bringing in new clients. In the firm's version of the *Hunger Games*, trainees who missed their quota for two consecutive quarters were fired. Will stayed late every night, determined not to go home without opening a new account. And yet, even though he worked twice as hard as his fellow trainees, he'd missed his numbers last quarter. This quarter was looking even worse.

If something dramatic didn't happen fast, he'd be out on the street in six weeks. No other New York City firm would touch him after he washed out at Maeve Grant. That meant he would have to leave the city. But for where? He had no family in Cheboygan, or anywhere else for that matter. In short, his very existence depended on bringing in a client that would allow him to make his second-quarter numbers. And now he was sitting next to a man in a finely tailored suit, a $50,000 timepiece on his wrist, accompanied by a woman who could be described only as a trophy wife.

"Not at all," Will countered smoothly. "But why don't you tell me about the two of you. Are you married?"

This elicited a deep laugh from Sam. Eve, however, only managed a tight smile.

"Oh no," Sam said. "Evelyn and I, we're . . . I don't think there's quite a word for what we are, to tell you the truth."

"*Yuanfen,*" Eve said.

She pronounced it with inflection, as if she was fluent in whatever language she was speaking, which was the last thing that Will had expected from Eve. He had already assumed that she was from somewhere in the sticks and traveled on the currency of her looks. It made him wonder whether there was more to her—and therefore to Sam for being with her—than met the eye.

"Yes. Very good. *Yuanfen.*" Sam's pronunciation was stilted.

"I'm sorry, I don't speak . . . whatever language that was," Will said.

"It's Chinese, and there isn't an exact English equivalent phrase," Eve said. "It denotes a relationship that is touched with destiny."

Will nodded. He was beginning to think that meeting Sam might be *yuanfen* too. If he played his cards right, Sam Abaddon could be the answer to his prayers.

2.

Gwen Lipton went to law school with every intention of saving the world. She imagined herself at the ACLU defending reproductive rights, or maybe protecting the voting franchise in the Deep South. But then she graded onto the *Law Review* at Columbia, and law firms started climbing over each other to offer her a $180,000 salary as a first-year associate.

Her father had spent his entire career at Martin Quinn and strongly encouraged her to follow in his footsteps and pursue a career in the private sector, "at least for a few years." When she initially demurred, he said, "Think of it as an unpaid internship, except with lots of money. You're going to have a brand-name law firm on your résumé forever. Public-interest shops are thrilled to have someone with law firm training, but it's a one-way street because Big Law only hires out of law school or clerkships. After two or three years, you can go save the planet if you find that law firm life isn't for you."

Taylor Beckett was Gwen's first choice. There were other top-tier law firms in Manhattan—Cromwell Altman, Windsor Taft, Cravath— but Gwen was drawn to Taylor Beckett's commitment to pro bono work and eschewal of tying bonuses to billable hours. It was the best of both worlds, she thought. She could do well, and also do good.

She was now entering her third year of this supposed career pit stop. It had been long enough for her to learn that all of her assumptions about Taylor Beckett had turned out to be wrong.

For starters, she was certainly not doing anything to better man-. kind. So far, every one of her paying cases had involved a corporation accused of some type of wrongdoing—either by prosecutors or regulators or a rival corporation. The facts were always extremely complicated, involving millions, if not tens of millions, of documents. In her three years, those cases that had ended had been resolved by way of settlement, without any admission of wrongdoing—hundreds of millions of dollars paid as a "cost of doing business."

Worse still, the promised pro bono work turned out to be even less fulfilling. Hers involved representing inmates who claimed they had been denied their constitutional rights by prison policies. Her clients were, as a matter of law, always in the wrong. Meaning that all her work did was siphon money away from the correctional facility's actual operating budget, which might have been used to help inmates but instead was spent on lawyers.

And despite the rhetoric the firm spouted at recruits, billable hours were still very much used to determine bonuses. The only difference was that, at other firms, lawyers exceeding certain thresholds automatically received preset bonuses, whereas at Taylor Beckett you could work nonstop and still not max out your bonus. Which was not to say that Gwen was complaining about her pay. Last year, her base salary had been $210,000, and she was given a $40,000 bonus on top of that. But the reason that Taylor Beckett could afford to pay her that princely sum was because they charged clients $675 for every hour she worked, and last year she'd worked 2,458 of them. After her two weeks of vacation—she was entitled to four but could take only two due to work demands—that calculated out to be just a shade under fifty hours per week. And that was billable time only. She spent at least another ten hours a week on administrative matters.

Or as her friends put it, she worked *all the time*.

A week earlier, a headhunter had called. They called about once a month on average, and more than weekly in January and February, after year-end bonuses had been paid and for many associates the prospect of putting in another year like the last one was at its most daunting. Usually Gwen said a quick "no thank you," but this time she stayed on the line long enough to hear about a job that paid "in the low six figures" but was strictly nine to six, with no weekend work.

"I think I'm not ready to make a move just yet," Gwen said after hearing the spiel.

"Okay, but don't wait too long," the headhunter replied. "You're at your most marketable right now. You've got Taylor Beckett on your résumé, and you've stuck it out long enough that employers will know it was your choice to leave. But you're not going to be seeing much in the next few years there that you haven't already seen. Meanwhile, you'll be working longer hours each year, and it really ratchets up in those last two or three before the partnership vote. With no guarantee that you're going to make partner, of course. In fact, as I'm sure you know, the odds are very much stacked against you."

The headhunter's warning sounded to Gwen a lot like her mother's concerns that if she didn't start paying attention to dating, she'd wake up at thirty-five, all the men her age would be dating twenty-seven-year-olds, and she'd be forced to marry some forty-five-year-old divorced man with kids, or a Peter Pan who all of a sudden decided he needed to reproduce in order to maintain the family name.

In both cases, Gwen wondered if they were right.

After all, it was 9:00 p.m. on Valentine's Day and she was in the office. She had been invited to a friend's Galentine's Day party—a gathering that was supposed to be an evening of female empowerment but that Gwen suspected would degenerate soon enough into the attendees bemoaning their failures to find men—but she'd had to cancel at the last minute to finish a brief. It was not due until late the following week, but the partner in charge had just this morning demanded to see it first thing tomorrow.

Even worse than the last-minute artificial deadline was that her phone started ringing, and the caller ID told her it was George Graham, the assigning partner at the firm. A less-welcome caller than Graham Gwen could not imagine. He only ever spoke to her for one reason: to give her more work.

"Hi, George."

"I call bearing gifts, Gwen."

Gwen braced for the reveal. George wasn't empowered to give out bonuses, so more work was hardly cause for celebration.

"You're being assigned to Toolan."

The Toolan case was the hottest criminal case in the country. It involved the A-list movie director Jasper Toolan, who was accused of murdering his wife after engaging in a torrid on-set affair with his leading lady, Hannah Templeton. Prior to being ensnared in scandal, Hannah had been considered America's sweetheart, thanks to her television role as a high school sleuth, which lasted until she was nearly thirty. *Beautiful Agony* was to be Toolan's masterpiece—and the vehicle to transform Hannah's squeaky-clean image so she could snag adult parts.

The movie released at Cannes and earned the coveted Palme d'Or award, although Toolan's arrest had put an end to any wider distribution, at least for the moment. As for Hannah Templeton, her real-life role as someone who led a man to commit murder—*allegedly*, as the press was always careful to note—certainly erased anyone's thoughts of her as a doe-eyed ingenue.

The head of Taylor Beckett's litigation department, Benjamin Ethan, had already been defending Toolan for nearly a year, through a plethora of pretrial motions and various delaying tactics that were standard operating procedure for defense counsel when a client was out on bail. Now, with trial less than six months away, Ethan must have decided he needed reinforcements beyond the ten-person team he already had working on the case.

Gwen understood why Graham would think he was bestowing a great gift—the Toolan case was high profile, a rare chance to engage in criminal law, as opposed to the *Fortune 100 v. Fortune 100* contract disputes that Taylor Beckett usually handled. There was a strong likelihood that it would go to trial, which was a rarity at the firm because nearly every case ended in a settlement. There was also the opportunity for face time with the firm's undisputed superstar, Benjamin Ethan.

But Gwen was excited for an entirely different reason. Earlier in the year, Ethan had given an internal presentation about the case. He was careful not to divulge any information that was not yet publicly known, but he was clear on one point: he had no doubt that Jasper Toolan was innocent of the charges.

"And I'm not using the lawyer dodge that I think he has a triable case. Or that the evidence does not establish his guilt beyond a reasonable doubt," Ethan said. "I mean it the way regular people mean it. He. Did. Not. Kill. His. Wife."

Gwen had made her peace about representing corporate bad actors—the tax frauds, the air polluters, the ones who exploited their employees. But for the first time in her legal career, she could actually now ply her craft in furtherance of the cause of justice. Representing a man wrongly accused was the noblest calling the law had to offer.

"Thank you, George. That sounds great," Gwen said.

And she meant it. Perhaps being assigned to the Toolan case *was* a gift after all.

3.

After the game, Sam insisted that Will join them for dinner. Will had expected Eve to suggest that a night other than Valentine's Day might be preferable, but she assented with a smile, although Will couldn't be sure whether the expression conveyed her consent or the resignation that her objection would not have mattered to Sam.

Their destination, according to Sam, was "a steakhouse around the corner." On further inquiry, Will learned they were heading to Wolfgang's, which was located at Thirty-Third Street and Park Avenue, four avenues away from the Garden. It would have taken about twenty minutes to get there by foot, although Eve's stilettos made it obvious walking wasn't in the cards. Will had assumed a taxi ride was in his future, but it turned out that his new friends had a Lincoln Navigator, complete with driver, waiting out front.

Wolfgang's was located in what looked like a subway station, even though it was at street level. The ceilings were vaulted and tiled in blue and white.

"For my money," Sam said, "this is the best hunk of beef in the five boroughs. Now, some people will tell you it's Luger's, but this place was started by their head waiter, a guy named Wolfgang Zweiner, and he does it better than they do. Not to mention that you don't have to hike out to Brooklyn for the privilege."

It was past ten, but the restaurant was full, the bar area standing room only. The population skewed heavily male, nearly every one of them in a suit.

Will wondered when the kitchen closed and if they'd even be seated given the late hour. That concern vanished the moment Sam was embraced like a long-lost brother by a man he called Wolfgang.

"You picked quite the night to show up without a reservation," Wolfgang said. "And you're a party of three?" he added, looking over at Eve and Will.

"We just came from the Garden," Sam said by way of explanation. "Our friend here had the misfortune of underestimating the power of the Devils to emerge victorious, so we took pity on him. He's hoping to drown his sorrows in a magnificent piece of your dry-aged beef and some superior juice of the grape."

Wolfgang was a dapper man, outfitted in a dark navy suit with a red silk pocket square the exact same hue as his tie. His mustache was a shade grayer than the hair that still remained on his head.

"For anyone else, Sam, there'd be no room at the inn. But for you, my good friend, allow me to find a nice table."

Not more than a minute later, Wolfgang set them up at a quiet four-top in the corner, far away from the kitchen and the noise of the bar area. A bottle of champagne in a silver ice bucket was already chilling beside it. Sam popped the cork like a man who'd done it countless times. After pouring for Will and Eve, he filled his own flute.

Holding his glass aloft, he said, "Now what's the line from *Casablanca* again . . . ? Oh yes, 'to the beginning of a beautiful friendship.'"

"Cheers to that," Will said, touching his glass first to Sam's and then to Eve's.

Eve smiled, and Will got another glimpse of the greenest eyes he'd ever seen. Once again, he couldn't believe Sam had chosen to spend the night in his company when he could have been alone with Eve.

The waiter rushed over. "Mr. Abaddon, so nice to see you again. I see that you're enjoying the champagne, compliments of Mr. Zweiner, but would you also like to see the wine list?"

"No need, my friend. A bottle of the Screaming Eagle, 2010."

"Excellent," the waiter responded. "And for dinner?"

Without even a nod to Will or Eve, Sam proceeded to order: the steak for two, "black and blue," the hash browns, "very well done," and every nonstarch vegetable on the menu, which he explained was on account of Eve being a vegetarian, although he said the word as if it were some type of disease.

The waiter once again told Sam his selections were excellent, then retreated to implement the command. A minute later, he returned with the wine. After the tasting ritual was completed, the waiter poured a full glass for each of them.

"To the Devils. Long may they reign," Sam said with a smirk.

This time Will felt their camaraderie had been established well enough that a rejoinder was appropriate. "And to those that will defeat them in the end," he said with a similar grin.

They each took a sip. Will was not much of an oenophile, but he recognized that this wine was not in the same league as anything he'd ever drunk before. It was incredibly rich, almost a meal by itself.

"That's some seriously good juice, don't you think?" Sam said.

"It's very good," Will confirmed.

As Sam took another swallow of the wine, Will considered the best way to segue the conversation to business. He had already surmised that Sam was the kind of man who would respect the direct approach. Still, he had to ease into the topic a little bit, so as not to appear too desperate.

"What do you do for a living, Sam?"

"You might say that I am a collector of things of great value."

"Like art?" Will asked.

"Among other things," Sam replied, looking at Eve to punctuate the point that he clearly included her among his possessions.

"Always nice to be treated like an actual, living human being with a brain," Eve said.

"A joke, a joke," Sam said, actually looking a bit chastised. "Apologies if I offended you, my dear."

The source of Sam's income was irrelevant to Will. As was this moment of bickering between Sam and Eve. All that mattered was that Sam had capital to invest.

"Are you in the market?"

Sam chuckled, almost as if to himself. "I make it a rule never to discuss business with anyone I don't want to spend time with outside of work. So think of it this way: by getting to know each other, we are discussing business."

———

Sam held his hand into the air, and the waiter rushed over. "Antonin, if you'd be so kind as to provide us the check?"

As soon as the waiter returned, Will seized the opportunity. He grabbed the bill out of Antonin's hand. "Allow me, Sam. I can charge it back to my firm as a business expense." Will grinned at Sam. "Assuming, of course, that I passed your test about being someone you wouldn't mind spending time with outside of work, and you allow me to pitch you Maeve Grant's products and services."

Without waiting for an answer, Will opened the case. He almost had a coronary right there on the spot. The bill, before tip, was $12,516. The Screaming Eagle alone had cost twice what Will earned in a month!

He tried to get his eyes to focus, thinking he must have read it wrong, misplaced the decimal point. But even after a series of blinks, the bottom line didn't change.

Sam grabbed the check from Will's hand. "That's very generous of you. Or maybe I should say, of your employer. But this is my treat."

Will breathed a sigh of relief. Maeve Grant would never have approved the expense. Not to mention that he didn't have nearly that much spending power on his credit card.

"Thank you, Sam. Tonight was truly an extraordinary evening."

"It was at that," Sam said. "And yes, Young Will, you did pass my test as someone who I'd be more than happy to spend time with outside of business."

It was music to Will's ears. Enough for him to even give silent thanks to the Devils for bringing Samuel Abaddon to him.

4.

The Maeve Grant Tower had opened only a few weeks before Will joined the firm eighteen months earlier. In short order, the building had become a recognizable feature of the New York City skyline. Not due to any architectural significance, but because it was a good 30 percent taller than its neighbors, which made its placement on Park Avenue look like some type of mistake. At ninety-five stories, it was the third-largest building in the city, behind only the Freedom Tower and the Empire State.

Will entered the lobby at 6:30 a.m. He knew if he arrived much later, he'd likely be unable to get to his desk before his boss, Robert Wolfe, made his 6:45-sharp phone call to ensure that Will was in and ready to work—even though the official start of the day wasn't until 7:00.

Even on his busiest mornings, when Will's head was crammed with earnings information he needed to impart on cold calls, he always stopped for a moment to look up at the lobby ceiling. It was nine stories above him and was actually the glass bottom of an aquarium that served as the focal point of the restaurant on the tenth floor, which was, aptly enough, simply called The Tenth Floor. It was the most expensive eatery in Manhattan and, from what Will had been told, made the typical high-end places like Wolfgang's seem like McDonald's by comparison.

When he'd first joined Maeve Grant, Will had assumed it would be only a matter of time before The Tenth Floor became his regular lunch spot. Not only had that not come to pass—in fact, he had never once been there—but now he realized he would be denied the privilege of continuing to even look up at the place from the lobby if he didn't make his numbers this quarter.

Maeve Grant's wealth management business was located on the twenty-ninth through thirty-fourth floors. Those spaces didn't at all resemble the grandeur of the lobby. More than anything else, Will's workspace reminded him of a rat maze. Gray industrial dividers formed eight-foot-high walls for cubicles as far as the eye could see. Only Maeve Grant's biggest producers, like Wolfe, merited a windowed office.

Will's cubicle was at the perfect center of the floor. Like the middle seat on a plane, it was the least optimal location. Every sound seemed to collect there; he was too far from the exits to be able to leave unnoticed; and one of the large screens displaying stock tickers hung right above him, which always made Will flinch whenever he stood, because it hung down close to his head.

Brian Harrold was Will's next-door neighbor in the cube maze, and also his closest friend. It was a damning reality because he and Brian weren't truly friends; they lacked the intimacy that Will believed would cause the term to have any substantive meaning. They were much more akin to "work bros," knowing little about each other beyond the careful construction each had built for public consumption. But the title still fit because Will didn't have any other friends at the office. Or anywhere else, truth be told. The hours at Maeve Grant left little time for a social life—except for the occasional dates with women he met online, few of which had progressed past a second.

When Will arrived that morning, he could hear Brian pecking furiously at his keyboard. "Fucking Footsie!" his cube neighbor shouted.

"What are those limey bastards up to now?" Will said, knowing that Brian could hear him through the divider, which didn't extend all the way to the ceiling.

"Screwed up my YTD is what," Brian replied. "The one hundred is down again."

Like Brian, Will had also begun mimicking the jargon and mannerisms of the muckety-mucks at Maeve Grant. As a result, Will knew that he often sounded just as ludicrous as Brian sounded now. Brian's year-to-date results—the YTD he referenced—probably showed, at most, a modest five-figure profit, which would be considered loose change for most brokers and a rounding error for the big dogs. Besides which, the London market—the FTSE, or Footsie in Wall Street speak—had been volatile since New Year's, so the fact that it was down again was hardly an earth-shattering event.

Like virtually all the other members of their trainee class aside from Will, Brian was an Ivy Leaguer, a graduate of Yale, with a degree in history. He hadn't known a derivative from a mortgage-backed security when he started, even though he had "summered"—that's the term he used, as if the season could be made into a verb—at Maeve Grant between his junior and senior years of college.

When Will had asked Brian about the summer program, Brian answered him with a joke.

"This guy is on his deathbed, right?" Brian began. "And the Archangel Michael or whoever tells him that he has a choice after he dies: he can go to heaven or to hell. So the guy says, 'Can I visit each before deciding?' And Michael says, 'Sure, why not?' And he whisks the guy up to heaven. It's certainly nice enough there. Everybody sitting on clouds, playing their harps, that kind of thing. But the guy thinks it's a little boring, so he asks to see hell. Michael takes him to the underworld, and it's amazing. There are people dancing and drinking, and everybody is having just the best time. He figures it's a no-brainer, right? The guy tells Michael he definitely wants to go to hell. Okay, so fast-forward a few months. The guy finally dies, and he gets his wish. But when he gets to hell, everyone is suddenly miserable. They're doing the worst type of drudgery, and the devil is cracking the whip on them nonstop. The guy is confused, so he says to one of his fellow toilers, 'I was here just a few months ago, and it was great. Everybody was partying and drinking and having fun.' And the guy looks at him and says, 'You must have been visiting during the summer program.'

"Oh, I almost forgot," Brian said. "You got a good one last night. I had to sneak peeks at my phone when Sarah went to the bathroom, because all hell would have broken loose if I checked a hockey score on Valentine's Day. But except for the Rangers being on the wrong end, seemed like a good game to watch from the luxury boxes."

Will found Brian's reference to the game comforting. There had been moments since he woke up when he thought he might have dreamed the entire evening's revelry. But this was tangible proof that he had, in fact, watched the Rangers lose to the Devils. That left only his interaction with Sam and Eve as potential figments of his imagination.

"Yeah, it was great," Will said. "There was this guy in the seat next to me with this absolutely stunning redhead, and we got to talking. Then we all went out for dinner after."

This tidbit had apparently piqued Brian's interest, because Will heard him get up and walk the four feet to the threshold of Will's cube. "You were picked up by a married couple?" Brian said, with a tone that suggested this scenario was the plot of a porn film he'd recently seen.

Will grinned. "Get your mind out of the gutter. It wasn't like that . . . but the guy was pretty rich, and so I was thinking he might be a potential client."

"What makes you say that? The rich part, I mean."

"He ordered a twelve-thousand-dollar bottle of wine for dinner."

"What the fuck?"

"I know, right? It was so . . . crazy. The guy doesn't say a word to me for most of the game. Then, out of nowhere, he starts on about how great the Devils are. The next thing I know, we're at this steak place having this lavish meal. So I offer to pick up the tab like a hero, figuring that Wolfe will let me charge through three hundred bucks in the name of business development. But when I look at the check, it's for over *twelve grand*. I almost threw up. Without missing a beat, the guy says it's his treat."

"You need to reel that whale in, my friend. You should call him right now."

"Yeah . . . There's one small flaw in my master plan for world domination. When I woke up this morning, I realized that I have no way of contacting him."

"He didn't give you a business card?"

"A lot of the night is blurry—a twelve-grand bottle of wine packs quite the punch—but I don't think so. I certainly didn't have one in my wallet or any of my pockets. I'm not even sure what the guy does for a living. I thought his name was Sam Abaddon, but I'm not getting any hits about a guy with that name in finance or art or who lives in New York City. I even tried googling his girlfriend, but she has a French-sounding last name, so I'm not sure I'm spelling it right."

"Yabba dabba? Like what Fred Flintstone says?"

"What?"

"Didn't Fred Flintstone say 'yabba dabba doo'?"

"Not *yabba dabba. Abaddon.*"

Brian laughed. "Your whale sounds more like a Swedish rock band."

Will could appreciate how strange it all seemed. It didn't make too much sense to him either, and he'd lived it. Or at least he thought he had. Maybe he had hallucinated everything.

"I guess I'm just going to have to wait for him to track *me* down," Will said.

"Yeah, I'm sure that's going to happen," Brian replied as he headed back to his cube.

5.

At least according to the expression, digging ditches was supposed to be the worst way to make a living. "It beats digging ditches" was the standard refrain in response to any employment complaint. Will, however, suspected that ditchdiggers had their own comeback: "It beats cold-calling."

Will could scarcely imagine a more soul-sucking way to spend his day than asking strangers to give him money to invest based on promises that were predicated on little more than wishful thinking. Still, until he had a book of business under his broker number, he was expected to fill his day by contacting the people on the call list the firm provided and wresting from them whatever money he could.

On his first day, he and the other trainees had been given a script for these calls. The instruction was to follow it verbatim:

> "Am I speaking to [INSERT FULL NAME OF CLIENT]?
> Excellent, and a very good [MORNING/AFTERNOON/
> EVENING] to you. My name is [INSERT YOUR FULL
> NAME], and I'm a vice president in the wealth-manage-
> ment division at the international investment bank Maeve
> Grant, which, I'm sure you're aware, is one of the most
> respected institutions on Wall Street. I'm going to spend
> all of a minute and a half with you, because ninety seconds
> is enough time for me to provide you with an opportunity
> that may very well change your entire life."

At this point in the script, the broker was supposed to engage the customer by saying something like, "How does that sound?" Will had learned from repeated experience, however, that letting the customer answer an open-ended question invited a hang up. So he always plowed forward:

> "Plain and simple, Maeve Grant has the inside track on a block of stock that we're making available to a select few highly qualified individuals. Let's be honest. We're all in this to make a buck, and Maeve Grant wouldn't itself control a large block of this company's stock if it wasn't highly confident of a huge return. So why wouldn't you want to be along for the ride too?"

The script was "true," which in Wall Street terms meant it was not demonstrably false. Will *was* a vice president, although every single broker at the firm held at least that title, even the trainees. There were four levels of vice president above his rank, and the big producers were managing directors. It was also true that Maeve Grant was one of the most well-respected names on Wall Street, although that reputation was largely due to the strength of its investment-banking department, where the billion-dollar corporate deals were struck.

It was when he got to talking about the stock he was selling that the script became even more unmoored from reality. Will had very little reason to believe that a few hundred shares of whatever corporation he was pitching were going to change anyone's life. Nor did he have any basis from which to conclude that Maeve Grant actually was highly confident that the security in question would generate a huge return.

But he reasoned that such a statement was hardly different from the outsize claims made by car manufacturers about the performance features on the latest model of a sports car, or by some diet company about its ability to help someone lose twenty pounds. Or that anything that was advertised, for that matter, was going to change anyone's life. And there was nothing unethical—and certainly not illegal—about claiming it *might* in order to make a sale. Indeed, it was the first rule of sales: you sell the sizzle, not the steak.

———

The market took a beating that day. The Dow was down over 300 points, and the S&P lost almost 2 percent. The international markets had not fared much better.

"Jesus," Brian said when the bell rang on the trading floor, signifying the end of the carnage.

Will rubbed his face. Today's results put him that much closer to being out of a job.

To add insult to injury, he saw Robert Wolfe approaching.

Each trainee was assigned to a more senior broker and given a small share of that broker's business to manage, while spending the bulk of his or her time cold-calling for new clients. Will had been paired with Wolfe, one of Maeve Grant's biggest producers—and an even bigger asshole. Will wondered why a man named Wolfe would want to consciously look like one, but his boss either didn't get the joke or reveled in it, because he wore his hair past his collar and sported a thick beard that he groomed to perfection. On top of that, he was a caricature of what a Wall Streeter had looked like circa the 1987 crash. Today, that meant he was sporting a blue shirt with a white collar and cuffs, and the yellow braces holding up his pants perfectly matched his tie and silk pocket square.

"You really took it up the ass today, Matthews," Wolfe said without any preamble.

"Tough day all around in the market," Will replied.

"Not for me. I saw the correction coming and shorted some tech and transportation as a hedge."

Will was certain that was a lie. Wolfe began each day with an email to his team, which included four brokers and Will, his sole trainee, touting the opportunities he saw in the market. The subject line was always "The Wolfe Pack," which Wolfe undoubtedly thought was witty. Today's missive hadn't recommended shorting anything, nor had it counseled caution.

The one business lesson Will had learned from Wolfe, however, was that kissing up to the boss never hurt. "I wish I'd done that."

"Yeah. Well, as I always say, if wishes were Porsches, we'd all have one."

Wolfe did say that a lot. Will assumed that Wolfe had heard the Scottish proverb "If wishes were horses, beggars would ride" somewhere, changed it so that it wouldn't be obvious he was plagiarizing, and been passing it off as his own wisdom ever since.

"Today's the midpoint," Wolfe continued. "And I got to say, you're going to need a goddamn miracle to survive."

The first quarter lasted ninety days, but because this February had only twenty-eight days, the actual midpoint date had been the day before. Still, close enough. Maybe even Wolfe had found better things to do on Valentine's Day than take the time to tell Will he might well be looking for new employment in six weeks.

"I know it," Will said. "I'm doing everything I can think of to make my number. I'm cold-calling nonstop, studying the charts, watching your trades, reading everything I can find. With the market down, though—"

"I'm going to stop you right there, Matthews. There's only one guy to blame for your shitty ROI. And his name isn't the fucking market. It's Will Fucking Matthews."

ROI—return on investment. It was one of only two things that mattered in wealth management. Will knew that Wolfe was about to mention the other.

"And your AUM is also in the crapper."

Wolfe pronounced *AUM* like it was a word—*OM*—which made him sound like he was doing a meditation chant. Everyone else articulated the letters of the acronym, which stood for "assets under management."

"I had a meeting with a guy yesterday who is strongly considering opening an account."

"Is that right?" Wolfe said, his ironic disbelief front and center.

"Like you always say, no one is a client until the money's out of his hands and into ours. So we'll see."

Wolfe looked down at Will with a squint. Will knew that meant his boss had deduced he was blowing smoke. On the bright side, Wolfe's disgust caused him to leave the cube.

As soon as he was sure the coast was clear, Brian poked his head into Will's cube. "Goddamn Wolfe. It's like that guy has made it his mission in life to screw with you."

"He's nothing if not an inspiring mentor," Will said, his words dripping with sarcasm.

"Forget him. Let's go get drunk," Brian said.

Will's stomach lurched, a reminder of the night before. "As inviting as that sounds, I have a date."

"Show me. I need to get a look at the girl who's hot enough to make Will Matthews stop cold-calling before midnight."

For all Brian's professional polish, he acted like a horny fourteen-year-old when the topic of the opposite sex came up. But Will certainly didn't mind getting a second opinion on what he was about to get himself into that evening. He turned away from Brian and pulled out his phone. A few swipes later, his date was smiling on the screen.

"Okay . . . that could work," Brian said as if the woman were something he was considering buying. "Good hair, decent smile. Hard to tell from just the face, though. And it's a bad sign if there's not a bathing suit pic."

Will wouldn't have said that out loud, but he believed it too. After all, this was internet dating. He wouldn't have even reached out to her if she hadn't had a bathing suit pic among her array—and if she didn't look good in it.

He decided to satisfy Brian's interest a little. Another double click and there she was in a red one-piece, standing on the deck of a boat.

"Healthy rack," Brian said.

Will laughed. "I'll be sure to tell her you said that."

6.

Gwen was well versed in the basic facts of the Toolan case from following online articles and what she had watched on cable news. It had already been given the moniker "Trial of the Century," and people were calling it O. J. all over again.

The prosecution's case was based on the oldest story in the book: rich man kills his wife to be with his much younger mistress and avoid the costs of a divorce. The defense's rejoinder was also a tried-and-true one: distraught wife kills herself after her husband tells her he's leaving her for his much younger mistress.

Jasper Toolan was not yet fifty, but he had already laid claim to two of the top ten highest-grossing movies of all time. *Beautiful Agony* was his opportunity to burnish his reputation with an Oscar and enshrine his name in the same small club as Spielberg, Coppola, and Scorsese. Enter Hannah Templeton, the movie's femme fatale. The love triangle's last cast member was Jasper's long-suffering wife, Jennifer Toolan.

The late Mrs. Toolan was something of an unknown quantity, largely because she hadn't been a Hollywood type—the reason the family had lived in Manhattan, not LA. She didn't have a Wikipedia page, and even Google revealed little more than the fact that she'd been married to Jasper. Gwen could find no reference to where Jennifer had been born; where she'd gone to school; or what, if anything, she'd done before becoming the great man's wife.

The answers to these questions, and undoubtedly to many more, would be doled out to Gwen over time as she worked the case. That process was about to begin, which was why she and the other fourteen members of the Toolan team were assembled in a conference room, awaiting the arrival of Benjamin Ethan.

Gwen had taken the empty seat beside Jay Kanner, the junior partner on the case. Kanner was what happened to someone after half a million billable hours. He was in his midthirties but looked a decade older. He didn't have a hair on his head, the dark circles under his eyes were large enough to have their own postal code, and his jowls sagged like a basset hound's.

"Welcome aboard," he said. "Ready to join the circus?"

"Is that what I've joined?"

"It's certainly different than any other case I've ever worked. I'm the number-two guy on it, and I've never even met the client. How's that for weird?"

"I'm a third-year associate. I've never met *any* client."

That was not entirely true. There were her pro bono clients, of course. And Gwen had met a corporate client once or twice, but that person was usually no one more important than a junior lawyer in the client's legal department. She had never met a general counsel or a CEO—or anyone with clout. And in her three years at the firm, this was the first time she'd ever represented a paying individual. Taylor Beckett's fees were cost prohibitive to anyone other than corporate behemoths and multimillionaires.

The door swung open, and Benjamin Ethan strode into the room. He immediately took his seat at the head of the long conference table.

Ethan looked every inch the part of hired gun for the rich and famous. Tall and thin, with floppy blondish hair that was seamlessly turning gray, he had the handsome-WASP look down pat—aided in no short measure by round tortoiseshell glasses that had been out of style for at least a decade and a boxy Brooks Brothers suit that might have been raided right out of the *Mad Men* wardrobe closet.

Despite herself, Gwen felt a little giddy to be in his presence. The legend of Benjamin Ethan was etched deeply in the firm lore of Taylor Beckett—how he'd been president of the *Harvard Law Review*, clerked on the Supreme Court, and then made partner more quickly than anyone before or since. He'd risen to national prominence when he won an acquittal for Lawson Graves, the New Jersey governor accused of corruption back in the early 1990s. Ethan had reportedly been on Barack Obama's short list for attorney general and later for White House counsel, but for reasons that were unclear, at least to Gwen, he'd never entered public life.

Gwen scanned the faces of her colleagues. To a person, they seemed as starstruck as she was. She realized just how pathetic that made them all, but at least she was not alone.

"Thank you all for coming. A special thank-you to the new faces. Jay will distribute the hot docs to the newcomers, which will include a chron. First things first. I want to remind you all that we are representing an innocent man. Let's be clear: our job would be the same even if we weren't, but the fact that we *are* on the side of the angels here means something to me, and I hope to you too."

Gwen nodded along. For the first time since she'd arrived at Taylor Beckett, she was actually excited about her work.

"You newcomers haven't read about this in the press, but Jennifer Toolan was a very troubled woman. We will introduce evidence at trial that she was under the care of a psychiatrist, and had been for years. Also that she was taking a pretty healthy dose of antidepressive medication, and that she had at least one suicide attempt in the past."

Gwen had not heard about any of this; it went a long way in explaining the defense. If Jennifer Toolan was already at risk for suicide, it made sense that her husband's leaving her for a beautiful, much younger woman could have pushed her over the edge.

"All of that, of course, is for trial," Ethan continued. "The reason we're here now is because we plan on filing a motion in limine to exclude from evidence any statement that Jennifer Toolan made that our client was physically abusive."

A motion in limine was a request for a judge to exclude certain evidence. It was reserved for pieces of evidence important enough that their admission at trial might change the entire legal strategy. Both sides needed to know how the court would rule before trial began.

"No mystery what's going on here," Ethan continued. "The prosecution has very little evidence, and so its strategy is to paint Jasper as a bad guy. Play up the cheating with Hannah, his former alcoholism, and probably other stuff we haven't heard about yet—and then hope to whip the jury into enough of a lather that they convict. A key point in that strategy is for them to rely on the fact that, in 2017, Jennifer Toolan filed a police report claiming that her husband had struck her. Although you might not know it if you only read certain publications, the undeniable fact is that the next day—not even twenty-four hours later, but more like first thing the following morning—Jennifer Toolan went back to that same police station and *withdrew* her complaint. She told the officer on duty that she had made a mistake in filing it in the first place and took back her statement that her husband had ever lifted a finger toward her."

Gwen had read about both the alleged assault and the subsequent recantation. She considered herself enough of a Me Too person to believe a woman who claimed to be the victim of spousal abuse. At the same time, it was logically inconsistent to say that the same woman might be lying when she later said it hadn't happened. While she knew that Jennifer Toolan might have changed her story solely to protect her husband's career, she was also mindful that others suggested it was very Hollywood to make false abuse allegations for leverage in a later divorce proceeding.

"We have other strong grounds to keep out of evidence any reference to a claim of abuse. First, an abuse claim is not relevant to a murder charge a year later, and whatever probative value it has is outweighed by the prejudice. But almost more important, there is a hearsay problem here. Jennifer Toolan is not able to testify, and therefore her prior statement off the stand is inadmissible. Lastly, admitting the police report would deny Jasper his right to confront the witness giving testimony against him, namely his wife. Your job, therefore, is to find case support for each of these points."

When Ethan had finished, Kanner said, "After this meeting, I'm going to give you each individual research assignments. I want a summary of what you've found by end of day tomorrow."

There were groans all around about the tight deadline. Gwen, however, didn't mind at all. A deadline the next day meant she could spare an hour that evening to keep the date she'd scheduled, although she'd have to be careful to limit her alcohol intake.

7.

There were a number of reasons that Will liked to take his first dates to Tao. For starters, it was around the corner from his office, at Madison Avenue and Fifty-Eighth Street, which meant that the time commitment to get there was minimal. The drinks were strong. The bar area was dimly lit but spacious enough that you could usually find a seat, and not so loud that you had to shout to be heard.

What he liked best about it, however, was that it had a built-in conversation starter—the restaurant had been featured in an episode of *Sex and the City*. Although his dates had by and large been in elementary school when the series went off HBO, he'd never been out with a woman who *hadn't* binge-watched it and seen at least one of the movies. His usual MO was to casually mention that one of the episodes featured a scene at Tao. His date would invariably ask which one, and he'd reveal that it was the one where Samantha met her girlfriend. From there, the conversation could turn to other *Sex and the City* episodes, different television shows or movies they liked, or lesbianism—all of which were fine by Will.

Will arrived at Tao fifteen minutes early. He preferred to see his date before she saw him, kind of like the way soldiers tried to capture high ground before a battle. Another of his first-date maneuvers: he liked to have a drink in hand by the time his date arrived. That way he could tell her what he was drinking and whether it was any good. Then he'd offer a taste. If she accepted, it meant that she was at least willing to share some of his germs.

As with cold-calling—and everything in life, Will thought, if he was waxing philosophical—the first thirty seconds were the most important. All that would follow was built upon the foundation laid in that brief window of time.

Gwen entered the bar a few minutes after seven, which had been their appointed meeting time. Will recognized her instantly, which wasn't always the case with online dates. Better still, he liked what he saw in the flesh. She was olive complexioned, with black hair and large eyes. Although she was wearing lawyer clothing, he could still tell the swimsuit picture was accurate.

Gwen looked around the bar for a face she recognized. He lifted his arm and waved, and she immediately smiled. Will knew that smile meant nothing beyond the fact that she had spotted him. It was the expression that immediately *followed* that indicated whether she was happy to have done so. He wasn't entirely sure what he discerned on her second take, however. He thought he saw another smile, but it might have been the tail end of the first.

She made her way through the crowd to the sofa he occupied. He scooted over a bit, and she sat down beside him. They shook hands.

"Nice to meet you, Gwen."

"And you too, Will. You look just like your picture."

"That's the way pictures work, right?"

"You know what I mean."

"Joking. Yes, I do. And I breathed a heavy sigh of relief when you walked in too. Can I get you a drink?"

"What are you having?"

"I normally go with something standard—a scotch or bourbon— but they had an exotic drink menu, and . . . the next thing I know, I'm holding what they call a Ruby Red Dragon. It's actually pretty good. Grapefruit-y, if you like that."

Without missing a beat, Gwen grabbed the glass. "Do you mind?" she asked, but it was clear from the sparkle in her eyes that she knew Will wasn't going to put up any resistance.

"No. By all means."

She took a long swallow. Before she could pass judgment on his drink, a waitress appeared.

"Can I get you anything?" she asked.

"What do you have that's better than what he's drinking?" Gwen said with a smile aimed at Will.

The waitress recommended a vodka-based drink called the Lotus Blossom. As soon as she walked away, Gwen said, "God, I haven't been here in ages. You know, it's like one of the few restaurants that was featured on *Sex and the City* that's still around."

"Really?" Will said. "I didn't know that. I've seen a few episodes, but I can't say I'm much of a fan."

"I know. Guys aren't allowed to like *Sex and the City*. They'll take away your man card or something. But considering that you're a financial guy, you might be interested to know that Tao generates more revenue than any other restaurant in the country."

"Is that right?"

"Actually, it might be the Vegas Tao, not this one. But this one I think is tops in the city. You can look it up later and text me if I'm wrong."

"Aren't you a lawyer, not some restaurant trivia specialist?"

She smiled again. Her profile pic didn't do it justice. Gwen had a killer smile.

"I'm a third year at Taylor Beckett, in the litigation group. I had this case last year that involved lost profits at a restaurant. One of the things we had to do was analyze the profits of neighboring restaurants, which is how I know that the owners of Tao are making real bank."

Will realized that he was smiling now too. It was also the real kind, not the plastic first-date smile he usually wore. On first impression, he liked Gwen. That upped the ante of this date considerably.

He asked about her life, and she recited what was on her profile. It sounded like a rote speech she'd given dozens of times, which made Will wonder just how many dates Gwen actually went on.

"Do you like being a lawyer?" he asked.

"Sometimes. Sometimes not. The hours have been just crushing lately, and so that's no fun. And I got a new case today, which is going to require that as soon as I leave you, I head back to the office. It's a big one too. The defense of Jasper Toolan."

Will was impressed. That *was* a big case.

"So, can you provide any insider information about it?"

"Probably as much as you can about whatever stock Maeve Grant is selling these days. Which is to say I could, but I'd be disbarred for it. So I won't."

"Damn."

"What about you? How's life at Maeve Grant?"

"If you'd asked me last week, I would have told you that it was miserable. Then yesterday, I met this potential new client. I think there's a chance that it's all going to turn around for me."

"It sounds like we both had professional triumphs this week. Cheers to that."

She held her glass up for a toast. He clinked his tumbler to hers.

"I had this feeling, even when things were really looking grim, that something was going to happen that would make everything okay. Do you get those too?"

She laughed. "No. I'm from New York City. I just assume the worst all the time. That way I'm hardly ever disappointed."

He laughed with her. "Well, I suppose that bodes well for your pre-conceived impression of me. Maybe it's because I'm a Midwesterner, but I try not to get caught up in that New York City always-wear-black and see-a-movie-star-on-the-street-and-it's-no-big-deal vibe. When I was a kid, we had a dog, Poochie. Don't ask—I named him when I was really little. But my point is that my dad used to always say, 'Be like the dog.'"

"I'm afraid to know where this is going," Gwen said.

"No. It's good. You know when you come home, how happy your dog is to see you? Jumping up and down like it's the greatest thing ever, even though it happens every single day?"

"Yeah."

"So be like that. That's what he meant. If you're happy to see someone, show them. Believe the best in people, like the way your dog believes in you. Your dog never thinks you're going to leave him, or forget to feed him, or ever treat him badly. He knows that you're a member of his pack."

Gwen laughed. "Your dad should start his own religion."

Will laughed too. "My father died a long time ago, but maybe I'm the . . . Is Paul the disciple who spread the word? Because I've tried to be like the dog ever since."

"I'll take your word on Paul. I'm many years removed from Sunday school, I'm afraid. And I'm sorry about your father."

Will nodded to accept the condolence. "Sadly, my mother too. Last year."

"Oh, now I'm really sorry. I was going to complain about mine being divorced."

Will wanted to remove the unintended pall he'd created. "Why don't we get all the first-date stuff out of the way right now?" he cheerfully said. "Like a speed round."

Gwen's eyes lit up. "I love that idea."

"You said you were a city girl?"

"Yep. Upper East Side. I always wear black and never go up to a movie star I see on the street. In fact, there were two movie stars' kids in my high school class."

"I'd ask who they were, but then I'd seem too much like the star-struck Midwesterner that I am. Born and bred in Northern Michigan. A tiny town near the Canadian border called Cheboygan."

"I've actually heard of that."

"No you haven't. You've heard of the one in Wisconsin. The cheeseheads over there spell it incorrectly—with an *S* instead of a *C*. Anyway, the Wisconsin one is the big city—they must have fifty thousand residents. Whereas in my town, we had fewer than five. Next question. Any siblings?"

"Three. I'm the oldest. Julia is the baby. She's in school in Arizona. Carson is the middle, and he's . . . I truly don't know what he does to support himself, to be honest, but he lives in Colorado and does a lot of skiing."

Will got the distinct impression that Gwen came from money: Upper East Side upbringing, brother who was a ski bum.

"I'm an only child," he said. "It's actually a family tradition. Both my parents were only children too."

"That's so weird. So you don't have any uncles or aunts?"

"Or cousins. So no family whatsoever, I'm afraid. But I have come to have faith that the best families are those we make for ourselves."

"That is a very 'be the dog' outlook," she said. "I like to think that's true too." After a moment, she continued. "I only have one real dating deal breaker. Are you a gamer?"

"Like in playing video games, or with women?"

"Actually both. I assumed that you'd lie if you actually are a gamer with women, and I take some comfort in the fact that if you were, you'd probably know that the correct word is *player*. But I really meant as in video games. I say it because my ex could spend *hours* gaming, and it drove me insane. Although I will say I'm an excellent shot thanks to *Call of Duty*, can probably fly an airplane courtesy of *Flight Unlimited 3*, and don't even get me started about my driving skills, thank you very much, *GTA*."

"Good to know. But to answer your question, I'm not a gamer. I never have been, but I will now insist on driving when we're in a car together. Although I will most certainly defer to you if we're ever in a combat situation."

"Deal. So I'm all good now. Any other questions for me?"

"Just one. Is Gwen short for Gwendolyn or Gwyneth, or is your name just Gwen?"

"Guess."

Will knew he was being put on the spot. His answer didn't matter nearly as much as the reasoning he cited to support his conclusion. "Gwendolyn."

Her smile told him he was right. Granted, the odds were only three to one, but Gwen seemed impressed nonetheless.

"Lucky guess, or have you been stalking me?"

"I like to think it was an educated guess."

"So educate me."

"Well, my dear Watson, I figured you're too old to be named after Gwyneth Paltrow, because she didn't actually become famous until the mid-1990s. Also, I assume that your parents, being sophisticated Upper East Side types, wouldn't name their offspring after some actress. That narrows it down to Gwendolyn or Gwen. I've never understood why anyone names a kid a shortened version of a longer name. So, if your parents loved the name Gwen, the smart play was to name you Gwendolyn and just *call* you Gwen."

"Very good sleuthing, Sherlock," Gwen said. "But, sadly, you're wrong at nearly every turn."

"It's Gwen?" Will said, surprised he'd misread her initial expression as confirmation that he'd guessed correctly.

"No, it's Gwendolyn. But your deductive reasoning is flawed. The sad truth of the matter is that my hypereducated parents named me after a TV character. They loved this show called *The Wonder Years*. The girl character was named Winnie Cooper, but her full name was Gwendolyn. So they named me Gwendolyn and called me Winnie. Which, obviously, I hated. So when I was able to assert my own nickname, I became Gwen. I can't say I like it that much more, but at least I'm spared from being called Pooh all the time."

"I like that you named yourself. My father's name was William, as was his father's. Our family doesn't do juniors or Roman numerals, so my father was William Matthews and I was Will Matthews, for short. When my dad died, some people back home started calling me William, like it was a title I had ascended to or something. But it always kind of creeped me out. So, I think I'm going to be Will well into my old age."

"But what will *your* son be named?" Gwen asked.

Will hesitated for a moment, as if he was thinking. In fact, the correct answer had immediately come to him.

"Whatever my wife wants."

Gwen laughed. "Good answer, Will Matthews."

The waitress came over and asked if they wanted another round. Will was hoping that the answer would be affirmative, but Gwen set him straight without a second thought.

"I need to get back to work. And researching legal cases while drunk can be even more fatal than drunk driving."

"Just the check, please," Will said to the waitress. Then to Gwen: "I'm going to head back to the office too. More cold-calling, unfortunately. Just in case my new client doesn't actually materialize."

"Aren't we the two most pathetic twentysomethings out there?" Gwen said.

"If only there was something we could do about it," Will replied.

"If only," Gwen said with a sexy smile. "Maybe that should be the first topic of our second date."

Will liked the sound of that very much.

8.

The next day began well, on all fronts. Gwen texted that she was free the following night, which meant two dates in three nights. The market was also doing its part to bring Will happiness. Yesterday's losses had all been recaptured, and Will's cold-calling had resulted in two new accounts. He doubted that one of them would ever fund, as it seemed that the woman he'd reached was giving him her information solely to have someone to talk to. But the other one might actually be looking for a place to invest.

The one dark cloud was that he hadn't yet heard from Sam Abaddon. This was another way that investing was like dating: if they didn't call in the first two days, they weren't going to.

But he shook away the negativity. Sam *was* going to call. It was just a matter of when. Everything was breaking Will's way, and that meant that he was going to reel in the whale too.

And then, as if his very belief had made it happen, Will's phone rang. The caller ID said the number was blocked, but somehow he knew it was Sam.

"Is this Young Will Matthews?"

"Sam! I was hoping I was going to hear from you. I actually wanted to reach out myself, but I didn't have your contact information. I tried googling you, but I must have the wrong spelling of your last name or something, because nothing came up."

"Then it's a very good thing that I remembered the correct spelling of *your* name. I thought that, the fact you're a Rangers fan notwithstanding, we could do some business together. Am I right about that?"

"Yes, you are definitely right about that. The way it starts is for me to open an account for you, which means I need to take down some information. And then—"

"I'm stopping you right there, Will. That's not the way *I* start. The way I start is by taking my new wealth manager to dinner. I'll be out in front of your office at seven sharp."

With that, the phone went dead, leaving Will with only one thought: *How much will Sam deposit? A few thousand? A hundred grand? Dare I hope—a million?*

———

As had been the case after the hockey game, they were chauffeured. Sam was in the back, and like before, he looked to still be on the clock—dark-gray flannel suit, power tie perfectly dimpled, crisp white shirt, collar standing at attention.

Will was disappointed not to see Eve. Of course, her presence at a business meeting would have been out of place. He took solace in the fact that Eve's absence meant that Sam was serious about opening an account.

The car headed for the RFK bridge, which meant that they'd be leaving Manhattan for dinner. The driver followed the signs for JFK Airport. For a quick second, Will wondered if this was going to be like one of those scenes in a movie when the man whisks his date off in a private jet for dinner. But about a mile before the turnoff to the airport, the car turned onto Lefferts Boulevard.

They came to a stop in a strip mall. Will might have thought that Sam was pulling his leg—surely a restaurant he had traveled an hour to dine at wasn't located in such unimpressive surroundings? Three things made him hold his tongue: a sign above the place that said **DON PEPPE**, a line in front of the establishment, and the fact that Sam didn't strike Will as the kind of guy who joked about restaurants.

"They won't take a res," Sam said as they alighted from the car, "so people line up to get in."

Even from his limited interaction with Sam, Will had already surmised that his future client was not one of those people who lined up to get in *anywhere*. As a result, Will wasn't the least bit surprised when Sam headed straight for the door. Sam didn't even flinch when one of the poor saps standing in the cold shouted out, "Line's back here, buddy."

Will quickly followed Sam inside, fully expecting a sharp contrast from the restaurant's exterior. But the interior design was equally unimpressive. Don Peppe's was an open space with about fifty tables. The ceiling was low, and the walls were beige, with framed horse-racing memorabilia the only artwork. It took Will a moment to make the connection, but then he realized that the Aqueduct Racetrack was nearby.

A large man approached. His white shirt strained against its buttons, and his black tie made it just to the beginning of his protruding belly. He could have been an extra in *The Sopranos*, and Will wondered if he had a colorful nickname like Fat Johnnie or Tony the Butcher.

"Mr. Sam," he said as he and Sam kissed each other on both cheeks. "So nice to see you today."

"Will, say hello to Vincent LoRossi."

Will merited only a handshake, which was fine by him.

"Give me thirty seconds," LoRossi said. "A table just asked for the check."

As promised, within a minute, they were seated. Before anyone even brought them water, a bottle of red wine without a label was plopped on the center of the table. The waiter poured it into two tumblers—the kind you'd drink orange juice out of at breakfast.

Sam said, "They have two types of wine here. Red and white. Both come cold. They know I think white wine is an abomination with any form of meat and that I always order meat. So we're drinking red."

The waiter cracked a smile at Sam's comment. "What can I get you, Mr. Sam?"

They hadn't been given menus, but blackboards located around the room listed food choices with prices. Will was quickly reading through them so he'd be ready to order when his time came. It turned out that there was no need, because Sam said, "Lorenzo, my friend, we're going to start with the baked clams. Then bring us the fried peppers with the veal Don Peppe."

Not a single item that Sam had ordered was listed on any of the blackboards.

Sam raised his wineglass. "Cent'anni."

Will knew what that meant from the opening scene of *The Godfather*. Part two, if he recalled correctly. *A hundred years.* Although it was not clear to him what exactly Sam wanted to continue for the next hundred years, Will touched his glass and drank the chilled red wine.

"How's Eve?"

Will immediately regretted posing the question. He actually hadn't meant to mention her. Unfortunately, his nerves had gotten the better of him, and he'd just blurted it out.

"She's good," Sam said. "She liked you. And I take it that, like all red-blooded men, you liked her too. But don't like her too much. Will you do me that favor? Because if you did . . . well, I'd have to kill you."

Will smiled awkwardly at the joke. Sam, however, remained serious for a telltale second before he smiled at the approach of a waiter carrying a plate full of clams. At least a dozen were on the platter, each roughly the size of a quarter, and the breadcrumbs on top were burned to the same degree but made slightly different patterns. The smell of garlic wafted up, making Will's eyes tear slightly.

"For my money, these are the best clams in the world," Sam said. "It's because of their size. It allows them to retain their flavor, so the topping doesn't overpower the clam. You go to Umberto's, and the clams there are the size of your fist. And don't get me wrong, I'm not leaving any of them on the plate either, but these . . . *Marone*." Sam said the word with an exaggerated Italian accent and his fingers pinched together.

They each ate a few in silence. Will couldn't disagree with Sam's assessment. He'd never had a baked clam as good.

"You've been very patient, Young Will. Let's get down to business, shall we?"

Once you had a client on the hook, the cold-calling script flipped. You wanted to let them speak, so Will offered only a silent nod.

"I'm always on the lookout for guys who I like, and I like you. I'll tell you straight away—I'm not the smartest guy out there. But I am the best judge of character you're ever going to meet."

"Thank you," Will said, largely because he didn't know what to say. The compliment was more about Sam than him.

"I know you're a young guy, but in my book, experience is the most overrated predictor of success. What matters is hunger. And I can see that in your eyes from a mile away."

"I'm not just hungry, Sam. I'm downright starving to death," Will said with a smile.

Sam laughed loudly. "That's what I want to hear. I'm working on a few ventures at the moment, and they're beginning to throw off some cash. I'd like to invest that return with you and see how well you can manage my wealth."

Will detected sarcasm in the phrase "manage my wealth," but he wasn't about to look a gift horse in the mouth. "That's what I do."

"Good. So the way this will work is that I'd like you to . . . you got a pen, Will?"

Will hadn't come to dinner expecting to take notes, which must have been apparent from the look on his face. Sam handed him a pen out of his breast pocket. A Mont Blanc, of course. Wolfe used one too. It was Brian who had alerted Will to the fact that the pens cost anywhere from $50 to over $10,000, and were recognizable by the white "snowcap" emblem at the tip.

The writing instrument helped with only half the problem. Sam raised his hand, and a waiter—not Lorenzo—ran over. "Carmine, you got something to write on? An order book is fine. Whatever."

The waiter reached into his back pocket, pulling out the pad on which he took dinner orders. He held another one in his hand, so this must have been his backup.

When he walked away, Sam continued, "The accounts should be in the following names: Drogon, Rhaegal, and Viserion."

Will scribbled the names on the pad. It took him a moment, but then he realized why they sounded familiar: they were the dragons in *Game of Thrones*. He wanted to share with Sam that he got the reference, but before he could, an army of busboys descended on their table. Within thirty seconds, all evidence that they'd enjoyed the clams had been removed, and two platters were situated in their place. One clearly held the fried peppers, which reminded Will of a fire due to their bright-red flame and black tops. The other dish, he concluded, was the veal, but only by the process of elimination. All he could see was a mound of chopped tomatoes, onions, and large chunks of garlic.

Sam reached for the veal as if the conversation about business had been completed. Will watched him pull half the platter onto his plate. Will shoveled a quarter of the fried peppers for himself, and then added the other half of the veal.

"Unfortunately, there's some paperwork that needs to be filled out to get the internal approval to open a new account," Will said.

Sam took a mouthful of veal. Will watched him slowly chew, only realizing that Sam had swallowed by the bobbing of his Adam's apple.

"Come to my office tomorrow. I'll give you the particulars concerning the corporate structures, ownership, and anything else you need," Sam said.

"Just tell me when and where, and I'll be there."

"I'm at 666 Fifth. That's between Fifty-Second and Fifty-Third. Thirty-third floor. It's listed under Red Keep. Let's say nine sharp."

Will knew the building, a landmark in Manhattan. It was as well known for its dotted aluminum facade as for its satanic address.

Will nodded, but before he could confirm audibly, Sam said, as if it were an afterthought, "The first deposit, which I expect to make as soon as the accounts are opened, will be in the six-million-dollar range."

Will tried not to choke. *Six million dollars!*

He quickly did the commission analysis in his head. Maeve Grant charged 1 percent of AUM per year. Will took home 25 percent of that. A $6 million deposit meant $60,000 in commissions to the firm, and $15,000 for him.

His salary was $50,000. He'd just gotten a nearly 33-percent raise.

As if people made seven-figure deposits with him on a daily basis, Will said, "That sounds good."

"Into each of the three entities . . ." Sam clarified. "So eighteen mil in total."

9.

The next morning, at precisely 8:55 a.m., Will stepped off the elevator of 666 Fifth Avenue and onto the thirty-third floor. He could only smile at the thought of Wolfe's 6:45 call going to voice mail and Brian's then telling Wolfe, "No, I don't know where Will is."

A sign opposite the elevator directed him to Red Keep, Inc. He walked down the hall until he came to a metal door bearing the same designation.

Will pressed the buzzer beside the door. A moment later he heard a click and then let himself into a large, empty room. Truly empty—it was barren. No chairs, no table, no rug, no receptionist. Just stark white walls and a midnight-black marble floor.

Sam opened the door separating the empty entryway from his office. "Welcome. Come on in."

The difference between the outer room and Sam's office was night and day. Sam was situated behind a sleek steel desk that reminded Will of a jet and that was at least thirty feet from the door. The wall of corner windows behind him captured the city skyline in all its glory. A long conference table sat in one corner, and a separate seating area that could accommodate eight filled the other. A mansion-size Persian rug in gold covered most of the herringbone floor.

It was the kind of workspace that Tony Stark would occupy. Yet the furnishings were not the most alluring thing to catch Will's eye.

That distinction belonged to Eve, who was sitting in one of Sam's guest chairs.

Will extended his hand. "So nice to see you again, Eve. I hope you're well."

"Nice to see you again too, Will."

Sam recaptured Will's attention, saying, "You may not have noticed, but the reception area is a bit barren. One of Evelyn's many talents is that she is a professional decorator, albeit one with very expensive taste. So after you and I complete our business, Eve is going to come with me to an auction at Sotheby's and spend some of my money."

"You can afford it, Sam," Eve said.

"Only if Young Will here is as good as he says he is at managing my wealth."

"That seems a perfect segue," Will said.

Will reached into his briefcase and pulled out a sheaf of papers. After he laid the documents on the desk, Sam removed a Mont Blanc pen from his suit jacket and began to sign where noted by the SIGN HERE sticker tabs, without making the slightest pretense to first read any of it. A moment later, Sam handed the executed papers back to Will.

"I also need copies of the articles of incorporation for each company, as well as something indicating that you have signature authority. Normally it's in the bylaws. Also, some form of identification for you. Driver's license or passport works."

Sam rose from his desk and walked out of his office. Will had not seen any doors from the entry area other than the one that led to this space, but then it occurred to him that Sam might lease other space on the floor or elsewhere in the building that was not connected to his personal office. Perhaps the incorporation documents were stored there.

As soon as they were alone, Eve said, "Ready to wade into the fierce gravitational pull that is Sam's orbit?"

Will laughed, more to mask his insecurity than because he thought it was amusing. It was a question he'd been asking himself too: Was he ready to handle this much money? To venture into the big time? He didn't know for sure. The truth of the matter was that he had scarcely a clue as to what he was getting himself into.

"Any words of advice?"

"You wouldn't take it, even if I shared it."

Will was about to ask what she meant by that when Sam reappeared. In his hand were a few sheets of papers flapping around.

"The articles of incorporation and the bylaws for each of the entities. And a copy of my passport, proving that I am none other than Samuel Richard Abaddon," he said, handing the papers to Will.

Will scanned the documents quickly to see that they were all there and properly executed. Satisfied that everything was in order, he tucked the pages back into his briefcase.

"Excellent," he said. "Thank you. Give me forty-eight hours for the accounts to open, and then we'll be good to go."

As Will and Sam were making their way across the rug, Will said, "I'm going to confess, Sam, that once I knew the proper spelling of your name, I googled you again. Part of the SEC's Know Your Customer rule."

"And what tidbits did you find out about me on the internet?" The look in Sam's eyes suggested he already knew the answer.

"Nothing. And I mean that literally. You have no cyber footprint at all. At least not that I could tell."

Sam smirked. "Then you learned a great deal, my friend. I see no reason to court attention from people with whom I'm unwilling to share that information directly. But, seeing that you went out of your way to check up on me, what do you want to know?"

"For starters, what business are you in?"

"You would think, after all these years, I'd have a ready answer to that question. The truth is that I have varied business interests. The unifying theme is that I exploit opportunities for financial gain."

Will laughed. "You don't think you could be more mysterious about it? I mean, are you in finance, art, real estate . . . ?"

Sam smiled. "All you need to know about my business, Young Will, is that if you do well by me, I'm going to do well by you. Really, really well."

The men shook hands, after which Will said goodbye to Eve with a wave.

As the elevator descended, Will couldn't shake the niggling suspicion that something was odd about the situation. Eve's question—*Ready to wade into the fierce gravitational pull that is Sam's orbit?*—rang in his ears, this time taking on a more sinister tone. Had she been warning him?

Will cast away the thought. He needed to be like the dog. Sam Abaddon was heaven-sent, and like he'd said, all Will had to do to make his own dreams come true was do well by Sam.

10.

The moment Will entered the Maeve Grant office, Brian knew something was up. Will was trying to mask his good fortune with a casual air, but by the way Brian was smiling at him, Will knew his poker face had been nothing of the sort.

"Blowing off the Wolfe's 6:45 call and then showing up two hours late to work? It looks to me like someone got laid last night," Brian said. "The girl with the rack?"

Given the likely things that could cause Will to enter the office with a spring in his step, Brian was playing the safer odds. No way would he have guessed that Will had raked in $18 million in AUM.

"Something even better."

"She has a twin sister?"

Will laughed. "I reeled in my whale."

"That Flintstone wine guy?"

"The very one. Just came from his office, where I had him sign the new-account forms. And get this. He's wiring . . . wait for it . . . eighteen *mil* today."

"Jesus. That's . . ." Brian paused to do the calculation that Will had already done a dozen times. "That's forty-five K. You're locked to graduate. Not to mention that you practically doubled your salary."

"I'm just waiting for the Cage to confirm."

The Cage was the department at Maeve Grant responsible for receiving and distributing customer securities, as well as cash deposits. Officially it was called "Operations," although only people who actually worked in that department called it that.

Years ago, the people in the Cage had actually worked behind bars, like bank tellers. Back then, each customer's stock certificates were physically deposited in a segregated account, much like a bank's safety-deposit boxes. In the early 1970s, firms began holding the vast majority of stock in what is called "street name," which meant that Maeve Grant was listed as the beneficial owner, and actual ownership was signified only by a ledger entry. That meant that bars were no longer necessary—there were no longer physical pieces of paper of value that needed to be locked away—but the nickname nevertheless remained.

"The Wolfe was looking for you. And he didn't seem happy."

That's how Brian referred to Will's boss. Sometimes, when they were out of the office, at a bar or someplace noisy, he'd follow it up with a howl.

"Think how sad he's going to be when I tell him that I've got more than enough AUM to graduate."

"You'll know in about five seconds, because he's making his way over here."

"Good morning, ladies," Wolfe said, his usual greeting when he knew none of the female employees could hear him.

Brian left Will's cube without even offering an excuse, like a frightened kitten whose hiding space had been found.

"I got to tell you, Matthews, I took a deep dive into your numbers this morning. I figured that the reason you were late was because you've finally given in to the inevitable and you were busy exploring all the opportunities that await you in the food services industry."

Wolfe laughed at his own joke, as if the end of Will's career was something he relished.

Will would have preferred to keep his boss in the dark about Sam's investment until the money actually arrived. More than one client had promised a huge deposit only to later think better of it. And unlike the saying about love, losing a big client before he funded was certainly worse than never having had him in the first place. But Wolfe's presence made it impossible for Will to pretend he didn't know about a game-changing event now and then act like he'd earned it two hours later.

"Not exactly. I was actually with a new client. He's going to fund enough so that I'll make my numbers this quarter."

"Ah, the power of prayer."

"No, it's something more tangible. I'm expecting eighteen million to be wired in today."

There were precious few moments—come to think of it, *no* moments—that Will had enjoyed in Wolfe's company. Which made this a first. He watched his boss swallow, at a loss for words. Will knew the moment would pass soon enough, and Wolfe would regain his position as the dominant figure in their relationship. But that didn't mean that the few seconds during which the tables were turned were not pure bliss.

And then Will saw something click inside Wolfe's brain. He literally bared his teeth, looking as lupine as his name denoted.

"No offense, Matthews, but why in the hell would he do that?"

The question was a fair one. In fact, it was one that Will had been asking himself since last night. Still, he wasn't going to give Wolfe the satisfaction.

"I assume because he thinks that I'm going to be able to manage his money. That is what you're training me to do, isn't it?"

"Don't be a wiseass. There are ten billion money managers out there, this guy has eighteen million lying around uninvested, and he decides to invest with twentysomething Will Matthews, who's about to get fired for underperforming?"

Wolfe made no effort to keep his voice down. Which made this a very public flogging.

"We're from the same town back home," Will said, gilding the lily a bit. "So we have that in common. He took a liking to me and, I assume, sees it as a relationship that can grow through the years. My guess is that the eighteen million is part of a much larger portfolio. So he's really just giving me a taste right now. Like a trial run."

Wolfe's eyes burned into Will. "You tell your client that I want to meet him."

Introducing Sam to Wolfe would be, to excuse the quite literal nomenclature, letting the wolf into the henhouse. Right after the hand shaking, Wolfe would tell Sam that *he'd* be more than willing to oversee the accounts at no extra charge, emphasizing Will's inexperience. The moment Sam agreed, Wolfe would demand a fifty-fifty split of all commissions. And that would just be the beginning. In no time at all, Wolfe would be reaching out directly to Sam, telling him about the latest opportunities in the market, giving him a taste of a hot IPO that Will didn't have access to. Before long, Wolfe would be telling the higher-ups at Maeve Grant that the account was all his and there was no reason for him to give half of the commissions to Will.

Will decided his best play was to stall. Although Wolfe would never let up with his demands, Will hoped that, given time, he'd establish a tighter grip on Sam, and that would make it more difficult for Wolfe to elbow his way in.

"The client said he was traveling for the next couple of weeks. That's why I had to meet him this morning. But sure. When he comes back to the city, I'd be happy to schedule something between you and him."

Wolfe's face was a mask of contempt. But he was smart enough to know that calling Will on the lie wouldn't get him anywhere. Not without proof that Sam was still in town, and there was no way that Wolfe could know that. Which meant that Wolfe had no choice but to fold.

"Reach out to him today, Matthews. Put something on the calendar for ASAP."

"Will do."

Wolfe turned to walk away, and Will sighed with relief. He had already planned in his own mind that Sam's "foreign travels" would last well into next month.

"Oh . . ." Wolfe said, as a seeming afterthought, although Will had the distinct impression it was anything but. "I'm going to tell the Cage to freeze all trading until that meeting happens."

"That's not fair," Will said.

Wolfe actually seemed amused by the invocation of justice. "What's fair, Matthews, is knowing your fucking place. I told you I wanted to meet your client, and you're giving me some crap about him being unreachable. Well, here's a reminder that I still call the shots. Even with eighteen million in your column, all it takes is one word from me that I see reputational risk, and Compliance will be so far up your new client's ass that when he swallows, they'll be able to taste his goddamn food."

There were two things that Maeve Grant preached on a daily basis: make as much money as you can, and don't get on the wrong side of a reputational-risk equation. During one of the many interminable orientation presentations Will had endured during his first two weeks at Maeve Grant, an older guy in Compliance with bushy white eyebrows and not a hair on his head otherwise had said, "There are two types of risk in the brokerage business. Losing your clients' money is the less important one. Markets rebound, and money lost can be regained." He waited a beat and then, in a somber voice, as if he were describing a new disease without any known cure, said, "A blow to the firm's reputation, on the other hand, could put Maeve Grant out of business."

If Wolfe decided to raise a stink, Compliance would be duty bound to investigate to rule out money laundering or whatever Wolfe told them he was concerned about. No one welcomed regulatory scrutiny. Which meant that no matter how much of a shine Sam had taken to Will, he'd reconsider entrusting $18 million to a guy who couldn't handle his own boss.

"I'll talk to him first chance I get and put something on the calendar," Will said.

"Yeah, I thought you would," Wolfe said with a satisfied smirk.

11.

Gwen had initially assumed there was little chance of finding any precedent to support the idea of excluding a prior claim of abuse in a murder trial. She based that legal analysis on her viewership of the O. J. Simpson miniseries, in which Marcia Clark (as played by Sarah Paulson) had no problem getting O. J.'s spousal abuse into evidence—for all the good it did her. But after spending a few hours glued to the Westlaw database of legal decisions in cases that had *not* been made into TV miniseries, she was surprised to find that there was actually a basis for exclusion after all.

The case was called *Crawford*. In it, the United States Supreme Court ruled that out-of-court statements about abuse were inadmissible at trial. In layman's terms, it meant that juries would never hear about 911 calls or prior police reports of spousal abuse unless the abused spouse took the stand. And that never happened when the abuser was on trial for murdering the abused.

Two years after *Crawford* was decided, the Supreme Court revisited the issue in two cases decided on the same day—*Davis* and *Hammon*. In *Davis*, the Court held that a 911 call was admissible when the caller was reporting a crime. But in *Hammon*, the same justices ruled that a battered spouse's statement to the police at the scene was "testimonial" and therefore inadmissible at trial if the spouse failed to testify.

Gwen was hard-pressed to figure out a cogent distinction between *Davis* and *Hammon*, but she was already versed enough in the art of persuasive advocacy to know that she needed to argue that Jasper Toolan's alleged prior abuse of his wife was exactly like the facts of *Hammon* and could not have been more different from the scenario in *Davis*. The one very fortunate fact aiding that analysis was that Jennifer Toolan had not called 911. Rather, she had walked into the local precinct to file her complaint. That would be the hook to claim that her statements to the officers were "testimonial"—just like those in *Hammon*—and absolutely nothing like the 911 call in *Davis* that reported a crime.

———

"There she is," Katie Van Slyke squealed when Gwen approached their table. "I was beginning to think you had gone into witness protection or something."

"I've just been busy at work," Gwen said.

Katie was Gwen's college roommate and her best friend, or she had been back when Gwen spent more time with people than she did with her work computer. Even so, Gwen would have canceled their lunch date but for the fact that she hadn't seen Katie in more than three months and feared that if she bailed today, Katie would organize an intervention.

"That was your excuse for missing my Galentine's Day party. And also about New Year's Eve at Rachel's."

It was true on both counts. Another one of their college crowd, Rachel Wood, had hosted a New Year's Eve party. Gwen had planned on going, had been actually looking forward to it, and then had ended up celebrating the ball drop in a conference room at work, putting the finishing touches on a settlement that absolutely had to be dated December 31 for some tax reason but that was actually not completed until 3:00 a.m. on January 1. Then she'd RSVP'd yes to attend Katie's Galentine's Day party, and work once again had reared its ugly head.

"I know you're a career woman now, and that's all good, but I'm worried about you, Gwen. I never see you anymore, and you're always working. Back when you were dating . . . He Who Shall Not Be Named . . . at least there was some fun in your life. Now I'm not so sure."

Gwen had christened her ex with Voldemort's moniker. What once sounded funny, however, now suggested something much more sinister about their breakup than Peter's habitual infidelity.

"I'm good, Katie. No need to worry. Rumors of my spinsterhood are greatly exaggerated. I went on a first date just the other day with a guy I really liked."

Katie's face became animated for a moment, but then the waitress came by to take their drink orders. Katie asked for a glass of white wine by the vineyard's name, while Gwen opted for club soda.

"I have to go back to work," Gwen said by way of explaining her beverage choice.

"So do I," Katie said with a grin. "Back to your date, though. Tell me everything."

Gwen had forgotten how nice it was to share good news. She had precious little of it of late.

"Not much to tell just yet. He's a broker at Maeve Grant. Nice-looking. Our age. From Michigan."

Katie went over Gwen's first date with Will the way lawyers interrogate witnesses—a no-stone-unturned approach that was relentless. In less time than it took for their salads to arrive, Katie knew that Gwen and Will had met up at Tao and that he had attended the University of Michigan, had been in New York for less than two years, and was not actually a broker but a trainee.

"And at the end of the date?" Katie asked lasciviously.

"We shook hands in front of the restaurant. It was kind of awkward, in a cute way. We were both going back to work. I thought he was going to kiss me good night, but instead he shook my hand and said,

'I had a lovely time and I hope very much that you will see me again.' He said it just like that. Like he was the Prince of Wales or something, you know?"

"He sounds like a romantic."

"I guess."

"So, when are you going to see him again?"

"We're actually going out again tonight. But I just got put on this new case, and that may mean that I'm going to have to put my romantic life on a hold for a little bit. It's okay because I'm super excited about the case." Gwen waited a beat to build suspense. "I'm on the team defending Jasper Toolan," she finally said.

Gwen expected Katie to be as excited about her work news as she was about her dating news, but she knew as soon as the words left her mouth that wasn't going to be the case. Katie displayed the same disappointed face that Gwen imagined her mother would wear if she had been part of this conversation.

———

At six, Gwen's evening plans were thrown into disarray by Jay Kanner.

"Benjamin wants more research on the forfeiture section," he said.

As disappointed as Gwen was about the prospect of having to cancel on Will, the fact that she was disappointed—and not relieved—was a first for her in a very long time.

"The prosecution is going to claim that Jasper forfeited his right to confront his wife at trial when he murdered her," Kanner said. "Their argument is going to go something like: *It can hardly be the case that if Mr. Toolan had sent his wife two first-class tickets to the French Riviera for a long, all-expenses-paid vacation during his trial, Mrs. Toolan's prior statements would be admissible, but because Mr. Toolan decided to murder her instead, they are not.* So, we're going to have to counter that."

After hanging up, Gwen returned to the legal database. As if the legal research gods were matchmakers at heart, she found the case law she needed almost immediately: a 2008 Supreme Court opinion called *Giles*. In that case, the defendant shot his unarmed ex-girlfriend six times, once in the back after she was facedown on the floor. To rebut the defendant's claim that he shot in self-defense, the prosecution sought to rely on the girlfriend's statement to police, made only a few weeks prior, that Giles had threatened to kill her. They further claimed that Giles had forfeited his confrontation rights by making his girlfriend permanently unavailable—in other words, the same argument that the prosecution was going to advance in the Toolan case.

The learned justices of the US Supreme Court, however, ruled that whatever Giles's reason had been for committing murder, it hadn't been out of a calculated decision to prevent his girlfriend's harmful testimony. As such, he did *not* forfeit his confrontation rights, and his girlfriend's prior statements of abuse were not admitted at trial.

That settled the issue. Although Gwen couldn't be sure whether Jennifer Toolan had been physically abused by her husband, she was certain that if Jasper had murdered his wife—and she didn't for a second think that he had—it wasn't a calculated decision to prevent his wife from testifying someday about an old abuse claim that she had already withdrawn, and over which he had never even been arrested. Which meant that she had the answer to the forfeiture question.

With her work done, Gwen would be able to get out of there and meet Will for dinner. She realized that even better than feeling disappointed about the prospect of having to cancel on him was feeling excited to see him.

12.

Will lived in what might have been a nice apartment but for the facts that he shared it with four other guys and it had only three bedrooms and one bath. It was in Murray Hill, which had become the newest haven for the city's youngest residents, who had been priced out of the trendier neighborhoods in Brooklyn and therefore found themselves in Manhattan.

The five of them occupied the top two floors of what had once been, at least according to the plaque on the gate, the rectory for St. Gregory's Church. The building was owned by a divorced guy who kept the lower levels for himself and his two young daughters, who visited Wednesdays and every other weekend.

Will had the smallest bedroom, but at least he lived in it alone. The master and the second were both shares that barely fit two twin beds. Will's living quarters—created by a makeshift wall strategically erected in the living room to capture one windowpane—had clearly been configured as an afterthought to accommodate another tenant. He had crammed a queen bed inside, although it meant that the door always hit it, the clearance just short of allowing it to swing its full arc. The room was otherwise empty, allowing enough floor space for a narrow passageway barely wide enough for egress. The closet Will used, as well as the bathroom, were on the floor above him, where the other two bedrooms were located.

The most unfortunate part of the apartment's layout, at least as far as Will was concerned, was that the communal space—the living room and adjoining tiny kitchen—were just outside his thin bedroom wall. Unless the other guys were asleep or out, they were always sitting there, usually watching TV with the volume way up.

When Will arrived home that evening, Cy was sitting on the sofa, watching a rerun of *Bones*, drinking a bottle of Dos Equis.

"Mr. Wall Street," Cy announced.

Will had long since learned to ignore what had become his moniker among his roommates. The other guys worked for different tech start-ups. Even with a gun to his head, Will wouldn't be able to describe effectively what any of their employers actually did or any of his apartment-mates' job responsibilities.

He entered his tiny hovel and picked towels, as well as the last two days' worth of dirty underwear, up off the floor. Laundry day was still a few days away, but in the unlikely event the evening ended in his room, he wouldn't want Gwen to think he was a total slob.

Gwen had already seen him in a suit, so Will thought that a more casual look might work for him tonight. He put on his best pair of jeans, which fit snugly, a black button-down shirt—the sleeves carefully rolled up to just below the elbow—and boots that gave him another half inch in height, pushing him over the six-foot threshold.

On his way out the door, Will again crossed paths with Cy, who was still sitting on the sofa. He noticed two empty beer bottles on the coffee table and a third in his hand. Cy lifted his bottle of Dos Equis to eye level and said with a god-awful Spanish accent, "Stay hard, my friend," and then laughed as if it was one of the funniest things he'd ever heard. Will could still hear the laughter when he exited the apartment.

———

El Rio Grande's shtick was that it had two large outdoor patios with an indoor space between them. One patio was designated as Mexico and the other as Texas, although the same food was served in each. The only discernible difference between the sovereignties was the Texas side displayed the Lone Star State's flag and lots of **DON'T MESS WITH TEXAS** signs, while Mexico took a similar pride in that country's heritage. In February, however, neither patio was open, which made the enclosed restaurant between them particularly loud.

When the guacamole was placed before them, Will decided the time was right to share his news. "That new client . . . he opened an account and wired in eighteen million."

Gwen's face lit up. "That's great. Congratulations."

"Yeah, but there's still a little hiccup. My boss . . . get this, his name is Robert Wolfe, and I swear, he actually looks like a wolf. He's got this full beard and long hair and bleached-white teeth. Anyway, he's demanding to meet with the client before letting me trade."

"Why is that a problem?"

"The short answer is that he's . . . the technical term, I believe, would be an *asshole*. The longer story is that the only reason he wants to meet my client is to steal him out from under me."

"So what are you going to do?"

"I was going to slow-walk it, but that's not going to work. I have little choice but to set up the meeting. But I'm a little worried that might not solve the problem. My boss is definitely the kind of guy who, if the client doesn't go along with his ideas, would think nothing of torpedoing the business altogether."

"How can he do that?"

"He'd go to Compliance and make up some legal concerns."

"Are there any?"

"Other than that it seems a little odd that the guy is letting some-one like me manage so much money, no. But it wouldn't matter. No client is going to wait around while Maeve Grant does a financial colostomy on every nickel they're investing. So just by raising the issue, my boss scuttles the business."

"And he'd do that?"

"Did I mention that the guy's an asshole? I'm certain he doesn't care about Maeve Grant as much as he does screwing me over."

"I think it's going to be okay, Will. You're a dog, right?"

"I'm not *a* dog," he said with a grin. "I'm *like* the dog."

"Exactly," she said, her smile beaming.

Will was fast realizing that Gwen was not like the other women he'd dated. She was whip smart and certainly had more candlepower than he did. That she was probably a notch more attractive too made him worry that he might not be bringing anything to the table, although he assuaged himself with the thought that perhaps he was underselling himself in the looks department. Besides, she must have seen something in him to agree to a second date.

———

The February air was still cold when they left El Rio Grande, but it no longer brought him to a shiver. Will was uncertain whether it was because of the alcohol or the actual temperature, but the fact that he could see vapor form in the air with their words told him that it was just as cold as before, maybe even a few degrees lower.

They made their way east, chatting aimlessly until they reached Gwen's building, a high-rise on First Avenue.

"This is me," she said.

Will waited, hoping for a sign indicating the evening was not over. Gwen leaned in and kissed him on the mouth. He didn't move for a moment, then two, but after the third beat, he stepped closer, so that their bodies were touching, albeit with their winter coats providing a protective barrier. Gwen's hand reached up into his hair, and Will put his hand on her back.

Gwen stepped back then, breaking their seal. When Will opened his eyes, he felt slightly dizzy.

"Good night, Will Matthews. Maybe you'll take me out on a non-school night soon."

13.

The email from the Cage arrived a few minutes after ten. The subject line read Approval.

Will clicked it open.

> Drogon: Account No. 3184242
> Rhaegal: Account No. 7140331
> Viserion: Account No. 2791816

A half hour later, Will's phone rang. By now, "Blocked Number" was synonymous in Will's mind with the name Sam Abaddon.

"I'm downstairs. I need your help with a special project."

Will looked up at the clock. Too early to be plausibly out for lunch.

"I don't know if I can get away."

"I know that you can. I'm not entrusting eighteen million—and soon to be a whole lot more than that—to a guy who needs to ask permission to leave his desk."

It was easy to weigh the risk-reward of the offer. If he left and Wolfe fired him for it, Will could bring Sam over to a new brokerage house. By contrast, if he said no and Sam pulled his business, Will's career was over. Not just at Maeve Grant, but anywhere.

On his way out, Will stopped into Brian's cube. "If the Wolfe is on the prowl . . . just make something up about where I am."

Sam's chauffeur-driven Lincoln Navigator was idling in front of the Maeve Grant Tower. Will climbed into the back to see Sam on the phone. Sam welcomed him with a hearty grin, then held his thumb and index finger close together to indicate the call would be short.

The car began to move into the traffic on Park Avenue, cutting across Central Park at Ninety-Seventh Street. After that they continued heading west, ultimately merging on to the Henry Hudson Parkway.

Sam was talking into the phone about some transaction that was being consummated in yen. Although Will should have known whether 500 million yen was a lot in dollars, he wasn't certain. Finally, as they were driving under the George Washington Bridge, Sam ended the call by saying, *"Denwa de no o wakare."*

He turned to Will. "Young Will, how are you on this fine morning?"

"I'm good. And you?"

"Absolutely amazing."

"Care to share where we're going?"

"Of course. Didn't mean to have you feel like you were being kidnapped. I just had to settle some business with the Far East first. They're a day ahead of us, and this deal has a hard break at COB."

Will nodded, acutely aware that Sam hadn't answered his question about their destination. He decided not to pose it again. By now the signage on the highway indicated they were entering the Bronx.

"I'm having a get-together Saturday night at my place," Sam said. "Mostly business people. I'd like you to come. It'll give me the opportunity to introduce you to everyone at once as the newest member of my team."

Sam paused. He seemingly viewed the invitation to a party in two days as sufficient explanation for why Will was in the back of his SUV driving through the Bronx in the middle of a workday.

"That sounds great. Thank you."

"And bring a plus-one."

"Okay," Will said, hoping—praying, actually—that Gwen was free Saturday night. If not, he'd be squeezing Brian into a dress.

"I suppose a smart guy like you is right about now asking yourself why a party invitation for Saturday night required your immediate presence. And why we're going to the Bronx."

"Not going to lie, Sam. I was wondering that . . ."

Sam smiled and then looked away, as if he was momentarily tongue-tied. If that was the case, it would be a first.

"I want to put this delicately, Will. But . . . well, we're going to pay a visit to my tailor. A fine gentleman named Mario Gazzola. He's the best in the city. In fact, I'd put him up against my guy on Savile Row and the best they have in Milan too. Well worth the hike to the Bronx to see him."

"Your *tailor*?"

"The party is black tie. I should have mentioned that. And forgive me, but I assume that you don't have a tuxedo. And, again, with respect, I further assume that even if you do have one, it would be of a similar quality to your suits."

Will didn't own a tuxedo. Still, he thought his suits were just fine.

"And that's a problem because . . . ?"

"Because, my friend, you can't do an eight-figure deal wearing a suit you bought at Men's Wearhouse for $399."

Two of the suits in Will's rotation had indeed been purchased from Men's Wearhouse—a fact Will kept to himself.

"Mario will set you up with a tux and the accoutrements. That's all my gift to you. I realize I've invited you to the party at the last minute, and I want you to make a good impression as much for my sake as yours. But I'm going to strongly encourage that, since Mario's going to the trouble of taking your measurements, you purchase some additional suits, shirts, and ties. Between the commissions you already pocketed on the initial investment and the money that's soon to follow, you can afford it. Am I right about that?"

———

Mario Gazzola worked out of a third-floor walk-up in an area of the Bronx that Will would have been frightened to venture into at night. The man himself was almost exactly the way Will had imagined him, which was to say a cross between Geppetto and the head waiter at an upscale restaurant. Reading glasses perched on his nose, he had a shock of white hair and wore a blue flannel suit, sans jacket, but with a double-breasted, lapelled vest. A measuring tape dangled around his neck to complete the look.

Will was hardly surprised when Mario kissed Sam on both cheeks and addressed him by the honorific and his first name. By this point, it would have been a shock to Will to see Sam meet anyone by shaking hands.

Sam introduced Will and said, "Mario, I want you to use all of your powers and all of your skills . . . I don't want anyone to see him this way."

Will got the reference. It was the phrasing Don Vito Corleone used in *The Godfather* when asking the undertaker to make Sonny's corpse suitable for his mother to see.

"Of course, Mr. Sam. What would you like?"

"The first order of business is formal wear. The same Loro Piana material that you used for my tux last year. After that, set him up with some suits. I leave it to the two of you to select patterns. The only thing is that the tux is needed for Saturday. My apologies for the short notice."

"Oh, Saturday . . ." Mario said with a note of despair. But then a smile came back to his face. "For anybody else, I would say no. But for you, Mr. Sam, I say, I'll do my best."

The entire process took two hours, which was an hour and a half longer than Will would have predicted. In addition to measuring every facet of Will's body—including his wrist circumference—Mario peppered Will with questions about his style preferences.

Sam answered most for him. Notch or peak lapel? "Peak on the tux," Sam offered immediately. "On the suits, it's dealer's choice."

Number of buttons? "Two," Will said, knowing it was the safe bet.

Vent? "Middle," from Sam this time, after waiting sufficiently long enough to realize that Will didn't have an opinion. Besom or flaps? "Flaps on the suit," Sam offered again, which was a relief because Will didn't know what *besom* meant. Belt or tabs on the suit? Sam selected tabs, based on his belief it created a cleaner look. Pleated or flat-front pants? "Flat-front." Pant break? "Full," Sam said, thankfully, because Will would have said, "Okay," in response.

Grosgrain or satin? "Satin," Will said, because he actually knew what that meant.

"No cuff on the tuxedo, obviously, but what about on the suit pants?" Mario asked.

"Yes," Sam answered. "Two-inch."

"You don't cuff tuxedo pants?" Will asked.

"No, you do not," Sam said. "The rules for a tux are as follows: vest or cummerbund, not both. Black socks—no exception, no pattern. You tie the bow tie. I don't care what Brad Pitt wears at the Oscars, you don't wear a long tie with a tuxedo. The bow tie texture matches the lapels and the stripe on the pant leg, so they're all satin or grosgrain, but you don't mix and match. No pleats, no belt, obviously, because the pants never have loops. Braces—they're not called 'suspenders' when they affix by button—in a solid black or white, no design. Studs also should be simple. Nothing that's a conversation piece. So no Bat-Signal or Monopoly pieces. Onyx, mother-of-pearl, or diamond. You're too young to pull off a silk scarf, so don't try. A crisply folded white pocket square that actually can be used as a handkerchief. And pocket squares are always solids—for suits *and* formal wear. Am I missing anything, Mario?"

"Lace-up, patent-leather shoes. No slippers. I only do besom on the tux," the tailor said.

In addition to the tux, Will selected three suits: a blue chalk-striped flannel, a solid blue wool, and a solid gray of the same material. At Sam's urging, he chose linings that made a statement. He also ordered six shirts—four white, two blue—each with spread collars and French cuffs. Will's initials would be monogrammed on the cuffs with silver thread.

"Thank you, Mario," Sam said when the order was complete. Sam did not take out a credit card to pay but said, "Send the bill to me. I'll settle up with Young Will separately. Please be sure to add a premium for the rush delivery."

———

In the car on the way back to Manhattan, Sam said, "I took the liberty of texting my guy over at Berluti, and he's going to send you tuxedo shoes and a cap-toe oxford lace-up. Same address as you gave to Mario. My treat on both."

"Thank you again, Sam. Really." Then another thought occurred to him. "I'm a ten shoe."

"I know," Sam said. "You're not actually that difficult to size up, Will."

14.

The story Will had just imparted over the phone—about being whisked away from work by a rich man for a new wardrobe—sounded to Gwen like a scene from a movie. As she imagined it unfolding, she realized it *was* a scene from a movie: *Pretty Woman*.

"The reason I'm calling, however, isn't to tell you about my new clothes. It's because I'd like you to come with me to the party on Saturday night."

The invitation to a work function surprised Gwen. "Really?"

"Yes, really. You said you wanted to go out on a non-school night, remember?"

"Yes. I'm not rejecting a Saturday night date. But are you sure you wouldn't prefer to go alone? It'll let you mingle and talk business."

"Positive. At the risk of overselling it, I can safely predict that the food, alcohol, and probably the real estate are all going to be truly something. And, just to seal the deal, I will further guarantee you a great time."

"And what if it's not?" she said, hoping she sounded flirtatiously coy. "If I don't have a great time, what are my damages?"

"Lawyers," he said. "Is there a Latin phrase for *not a chance*?"

She liked his confidence. "Okay. It's a date. Text me the particulars, and I'll be there."

"All you need to know is that I'll come to your apartment at eight. Oh, and it's black tie."

"You're kidding, right?"

"I wish I was, but sadly I'm not. If it makes you feel any better, that's why I had the emergency visit to my guy's tailor. He was betting I didn't own a decent tux. I don't, but still."

"No, it doesn't make me feel any better. And it is something you might have mentioned before I accepted. I consider formal attire to be a material term of this contract between us. Believe me, Will Matthews, you're going to owe me big-time after this."

"I hope so," he said before saying goodbye.

———

That evening, Gwen opened her hallway closet—the one that held her "special" clothes—to evaluate her choices for the party. Much to her abject horror, she realized she'd collected a baker's dozen of bridesmaid dresses. Viewing them on the rack, she knew that almost every one was hideous and never could be worn again. Worse still, the very sight of them was depressing as hell.

She considered it among her worst character flaws, but happiness had a way of frightening her. When things were going well, she became fixated on how quickly they could turn. Which meant that her budding romance with Will was not cause for celebration. It was reason to be wary of storm clouds she could not yet see but was certain were lurking just beyond the horizon.

She heard Will's voice in her head, going on about how she should be more like the dog. There was no reason she couldn't succeed at work *and* be with a man she loved when she came home. And simply because things were going well for her now, that didn't mean danger lay ahead. Perhaps she was still reaching new heights—at work and with Will. Maybe this was just the beginning.

Gwen brushed away her existential thoughts to address the more immediate issue at hand: what she was going to wear to Will's fancy business soiree.

The choice was narrowed down to her go-to little black dress or a statement piece in silver. Gwen had worn the black one to the firm formal last year; it was the kind of dress you'd wear to a work event that everyone was pretending was not a work event. That would have made it seemingly ideal for this event too, but Gwen nonetheless slipped the silver one over her head. The price tag was still attached, attesting to the fact that Gwen had never worn it before. She had purchased it for the same work formal, but during a last-minute fashion show like the one she was currently engaged in, she chickened out and chose the black dress as the safer choice.

Looking at her reflection in the mirror, Gwen remembered why she'd made that call six months earlier. The silver dress featured a V-neck that went down to *there* and didn't permit her to wear a bra.

For all her anxieties, she didn't have any about her looks. Like everyone, she would change things about her body if she could, but even with the reduced gym time required by her work schedule, she was tall enough that an extra five pounds would not make or break her. All of which meant that the dress hugged her exactly as it was meant to do.

Staring at her reflection, she imagined Will beside her, looking handsome in his tuxedo. It was their third date. She couldn't deny she had already decided how she wanted it to end.

15.

The last time Will had worn a tux was for his high school prom. The garment he was donning now bore virtually no resemblance to that one. The tux Mario had constructed felt like a second skin. It moved effortlessly with Will. The satin lapel and leg stripe glistened.

Will had allotted himself forty-five minutes to tie the bow tie—and spent nearly all of it. Although Mario had shown him how in the shop, Will had to resort to a YouTube tutorial because he'd forgotten the steps. After four tries, he was satisfied that both sides were symmetrical and the knot firm, but not too tight.

When Will exited his room, he caught his reflection in the window. This caused him to adjust the bow tie a bit, even though it was already perfect, and to smooth his hair, which also was not in need of any more coiffing.

It was a tragedy that he had to cover the masterpiece of a tuxedo with his sorry excuse for an overcoat, but it was freezing outside. If he were getting right into a cab to go to the party, he might have braved the cold without it, but he had to walk over to Gwen's building first, so he threw it on.

Will had been hoping to be invited up to Gwen's apartment, as perhaps a preview of what might occur later, but the doorman told him, "Ms. Lipton will be right down." Will's disappointment vanished the moment he caught first sight of his plus-one. Gwen was holding her coat over one arm, either because it was too warm in the elevator to wear it or, as Will hoped was the real reason, because it allowed him a full view of her.

"You look . . . beautiful, Gwen."

"Thank you," she said with an appreciative smile. "It's the only dress like it I own. I bought it for the firm's formal last year, but then I decided it was too much for a work event." She laughed, realizing the faux pas. "I'm sorry. I know this is a work thing for *you*. Is the dress okay? I can change into something more conservative if you'd like."

"No," he said, exhaling the breath that had caught in his chest. "It's perfect."

———

Sam's home was in a glass-sheathed cylinder that rose into the sky from Midtown. Gwen and Will stepped off the elevator on the thirty-seventh floor and were greeted by a man the size of a refrigerator. He was outfitted in formal attire and held a clipboard. Will noticed a bud in one ear, which further reinforced that he was tonight's security.

Mr. Sub-Zero took their coats, which he handed to a model-beautiful woman who stood beside him. Will assumed that Sam's apartment had some high-tech facial-recognition software, like the type they used to confirm guests at the royal wedding, because although Will was quite certain they'd never met, the security man said, "Mr. Matthews, so good of you to come. Please make yourself at home. There is a bar area on the north side of the apartment, and there are heat lamps on the terrace, which makes the temperature outside very comfortable."

The man opened one of the pair of large wooden double doors, then stretched out his arm, inviting Gwen and Will to enter.

The space inside was a 10,000-square-foot glass box illuminated by a crystal chandelier the size of a compact car. The apartment was open-plan, affording guests a view of the living room, a dining area, and a kitchen. A setback terrace appeared to wrap around the building.

The most impressive feature, however, was not actually *in* the apartment. It was the Manhattan skyline, captured through the floor-to-ceiling windows.

"Looks just like my place," Gwen said with a straight face.

"Yeah, mine too. Except this is smaller and mine has a better view."

After taking in the real estate, Will turned his attention to the guests. He estimated that fifty people were in attendance; Gwen and he were clearly the youngest among them.

"Can I get you a drink?" he asked.

"Yes, please. In fact, let me come with. I'm worried that if we're separated, given the size of this place, I'll never see you again."

At the bar, Will asked for a scotch on the rocks, because he thought that sounded like what a grown-up would order. Gwen opted for a dirty martini.

Drink in hand, Gwen commented that she was reasonably sure the large painting on the wall beside them was a Rothko. Will decided it was better to share his ignorance with his date than his host, and so he asked what that meant.

"Mark Rothko. He was one of the premier abstract expressionists of the midcentury. To put that in terms Wall Streeters will understand, it probably cost twenty million, at least." Gwen looked at Will with some focus. "What business is your client in?"

"I honestly don't know. He's been a bit cryptic about that."

"Don't you *have* to know? As in SEC Know Your Customer obligations?"

"You thinking of turning me in?"

"Maybe . . . if you upset me in any way."

"I'll be sure to keep that in mind."

"You should. And you also should find out what your client does for a living."

Will felt put on the spot, but he knew Gwen was right. It was strange that he still didn't know the source of Sam's obviously considerable wealth.

"It's not like I have no idea," he said, hearing the defensiveness in his voice with each word. "He's in finance of some sort. And art. And I think a little real estate."

"A jack-of-all-trades, then," Gwen said with a smile that made clear she was unimpressed with Will's explanation.

"No, more like your run-of-the-mill super-rich guy with his fingers in a lot of pies," Will replied.

Gwen looked as if she had a response at the ready, but then Will turned toward the direction of a female voice calling his name. It was Eve, looking as if she were a work of art herself. She wore a skintight red dress. Her hair was loose, and her emerald necklace made her eyes shimmer that much more.

"Eve, allow me to introduce you to my friend Gwen. Gwen, this is Eve. Eve is . . . a friend of Sam's."

He watched Gwen's eyes roll over Eve. He took an odd pleasure from Gwen's obvious *dis*pleasure that such a beautiful woman was on a first-name basis with Will. A bit of jealousy meant that Gwen was marking her territory.

"*Friend* covers a multitude of sins," Eve said. "Come, let's go outside. The view makes you feel as if you're in heaven."

Will put his hand protectively on Gwen's back as they walked onto the terrace. They stood up against the stone railing, and Gwen and he instinctively looked down. He wasn't sure if it felt like heaven, but certainly it made you think of yourself as some type of deity—Zeus on Olympus, perhaps—much more important than the mere mortals below.

Sam appeared from behind and placed a hand on Will's shoulder. "Young Will Matthews has graced us with his presence, I see."

"Quite a party, Sam," Will replied. "Thank you so much for inviting me. This is my friend, Gwen Lipton. Gwen, our host, Sam Abaddon."

Sam smiled at Gwen, then shook her hand. Apparently only restaurateurs and tailors merited the kiss on both cheeks.

"Thank you so much for coming. Now, if you don't mind, I'm going to steal Will for a bit and introduce him to some people he will be very glad to have met. Evelyn, my dear, can you make sure that Gwen isn't too lonely? We won't be terribly long."

Without waiting for Eve's or Gwen's consent, Sam veered Will away.

———

The first introduction Sam made was to a man named Lloyd Fieldstone. He was an older gentleman, probably more than seventy. He wore a white silk scarf of the kind that Sam said Will could not yet pull off.

"Lloyd here owns the equivalent of Rockefeller Center in downtown Moscow," Sam said. "Lloyd, Will is the finest securities man at Maeve Grant. He's going to be handling my investments, and I thought you might need someone of his caliber too. Am I right about that?"

Will was tempted to feign modesty, but the moment didn't present itself, because Fieldstone quickly said, "You have never steered me wrong when the matter involved money, Sam. If Will's your guy, that's all the due diligence I need to perform." He turned to Will. "Do you have a card?"

Will was reaching into his pocket when Sam said, "You're showing your age, Lloyd. Nobody uses business cards anymore. Tomorrow, I'll email Will's contact information. Call him Monday morning to set things in motion." Then he shook Fieldstone's hand. "Will and I are going to make the rounds. Enjoy yourself, old man."

Sam made half a dozen introductions in the next hour, all of which proceeded along the same lines. Rajat Singh was a tall, thin man with a full beard who had several business concerns, mainly telecommunications, on the subcontinent. Dae-Hyun Rhee was pear-shaped and wore oversize eyeglasses. He was from South Korea and in finance. George Kennefick, from Australia, had a blond, middle-aged surfer look to him. His business was oil, although he called it petroleum. His story of meeting Sam involved several women; Sam cut him short before he could retell it in all its glory.

"Speaking of breathtakingly gorgeous women . . ." Kennefick said. "Where's Eve?"

"She's here somewhere."

Sam was being intentionally unhelpful. Sam and Will were looking straight at the terrace. Eve was directly in their sight line. She was hard to miss and still chatting up Gwen. Kennefick could have simply been told to turn around, but Sam had chosen to deny him the opportunity.

"You're not hiding her, are you, mate?"

"Not at all, George. But maybe she's trying to keep her distance from you."

He let loose a loud guffaw. Will had the distinct impression that Sam was not joking, and that meant there must be an unspoken history involving the three of them.

If that was right, Kennefick didn't seem to appreciate the subtext. He put his arm on Sam's shoulder and said, "She's the reason I came halfway around the world to a party. It wasn't to see your ugly mug, I'll tell you that straightaway."

Sam looked at Kennefick's hand the way you might a bug that has landed on you. For a moment Will thought Sam might actually swat at it. Instead, Sam grasped Kennefick by the elbow and said, "Always a pleasure, George. When I see Eve, I'll be sure to tell her that you were asking for her. Until then, though, I need to introduce Young Will here to some other people. Please excuse us."

"Very nice meeting you, Mr. Kennefick," Will said, extending his hand.

At the beginning of the handshake, Kennefick kept his focus on Sam. When he finally met Will's eye, he said, "Very nice to meet you too, mate. Hopefully we'll get to do some business together in the near future."

After that, the names and businesses blurred. All told, in the hour or so he was in Sam's company, Will must have been introduced to a dozen men, each with a successful business in a faraway land.

"I can't thank you enough," Will said after the introductions were complete and the two men were talking alone in the corner of the terrace. "You've literally changed my life. I keep asking myself—"

Sam completed the thought: "Why you?"

"Yeah."

Sam put his arm around Will's shoulder. "There are a million guys trying to suck up to me every day to get a piece of my business. I don't even answer the phone when they call. But like I told you when we met, I see something in you, Will. That indefinable thing that separates the winners from the losers. Call it a gut feeling or intuition or whatnot, but I sense the opportunity for us to do some great things together. And make a lot of money doing it. Am I right about that?"

"Yes. One hundred percent."

Will thought back to all the "meeting Sam" stories that had been shared with him in the last hour. Perhaps someday, he mused, he would be introduced to a younger man at one of these parties and Sam would say, "Will here is in finance, and we met by chance at a Devils game."

Will felt a swell of pride, but then he realized that there was still a battle on the horizon.

"I have a favor to ask."

Sam smiled. "Have I not done enough for you already?"

Will felt one inch tall, but he had to ask for Sam to meet with Wolfe.

He could have lied and told Sam it was a pro forma thing that Maeve Grant required before opening any new accounts. But he figured

Sam would see through that, having undoubtedly had other brokers in the past. Besides, he got the feeling that Sam would appreciate the honesty.

"I'm sorry to even have to ask. But my boss, unfortunately, is a world-class dick. He's demanding to meet with you. He thinks that he'll charm you into letting him put his name on the account as cobroker so that he can grab half the commissions. When I pushed back, he said he'd go to Compliance—" Will caught himself. "I figured it's just easier to ask you to sit down with him, if that's okay. And even if you do, I can't guarantee that he's not going to demand to meet the people you introduced me to as well, if any of them want to open accounts."

Will braced for the worst. In his mind he heard Sam say, *Maybe I misjudged you, Will. I mean, if you can't work out this petty dispute with your boss, I'm uncomfortable entrusting you with so much of my money.*

But instead, Sam smiled as if it was of no concern. "I'm heading out tomorrow morning for a meeting in the UK but expect to be back by Wednesday. Set something up for Thursday. Anytime. I'll make myself available."

"Thank you, Sam. I'm sorry to have to make you jump through this extra hoop."

"It's no problem at all, Will. I'm more than happy to meet your dick of a boss. And don't worry. I'll make it crystal clear to him that *you're* my guy. I'll tell him I never want to see or hear from him again, and neither does anyone I refer. Trust me, you won't have an issue with him again."

16.

Gwen's first impression of Eve was far from charitable. Stunningly beautiful in a way that couldn't help but be off-putting to other women, and a good decade younger than her very wealthy partner, Eve seemed to be the textbook example of a gold digger.

But then, apropos of nothing they'd discussed previously, Eve posed a question that shattered all of Gwen's preconceived notions.

"Don't you tire of being the girlfriend?"

Gwen's surprise was not because the question wasn't on point. In fact, Eve might well have been reading Gwen's mind. Still, the sentiment was usually not so bluntly put. But more important, up until that moment, Gwen had been certain that not only would Eve never tire of being the girlfriend, it seemed like her *raison d'être*.

As she was processing this sudden turn of events, a very handsome waiter approached. "Another glass of champagne, ladies?"

Eve smiled and said, "Yes. Thank you." She removed two from the man's silver tray.

Gwen was reasonably sure that Eve would not have pressed for a response. It was as if raising the issue was sufficient to make her point. But something compelled Gwen to join the issue.

"I'm actually not even the girlfriend yet. This is only our third date."

"The all-important third date," Eve said with a smile.

Gwen could feel herself blush. She pivoted the conversation back to Eve's romantic life. "How long have you and Sam been together?"

Eve took a long sip of champagne. "You know that test that they apply to movies? Whether any of the female characters have a discussion with each other that's not about a man?"

"Yes, the Bechdel test."

"Right. We should do the sisterhood proud and stop talking about the men in our lives. Let's show some interest in each other. So, Gwen, tell me about you."

Gwen suspected that this was Eve's way of avoiding having to discuss her relationship with Sam. Still, she wasn't going to be responsible for setting back the cause of female empowerment.

"I'm a lawyer at a law firm called Taylor Beckett."

"Smart *and* beautiful, then. What type of law do you practice?"

"I'm in the litigation group. Right now, I'm on the team working on the murder trial of Jasper Toolan."

"I've read about that. Fascinating. Did you always dream of someday defending famous men who were accused of murdering their wives?"

Eve said this with a smile, but to Gwen it was no joking matter. "No. I'm sadly a top-notch sellout. I went to law school to help the disadvantaged, but I'm about a million miles away from that now."

"That's the great thing about losing your way, isn't it?"

"What is?"

"You can always find the path back."

"Smart *and* beautiful?" Gwen said with a smile of her own.

"No, just someone who has made her fair share of wrong turns."

"And what do you do for a living?"

"I'm an interior decorator. What's the joke? If you can't change the world, change the decor? That's my life, in a nutshell." Her eyes looked back into the apartment. "Exhibit A."

Gwen considered the space again, now with the knowledge that Eve had decorated it. "Does that mean that you're responsible for the Rothko?"

"In a matter of speaking, I suppose. Which is to say, it was *selected* by me, but of course Sam paid for it."

"It's wonderful."

"I agree. I absolutely adore the way it makes you feel. Almost as if you're at one with color. Of course, beauty is in the eye of the beholder. When I brought it home, Sam said that he thought he could have painted it himself. Right now, I'm on the lookout for a Pollock for him. I'm quite certain he'll find the chaos soothing."

Gwen noticed that Sam and Will had moved on from the others and were now engaged in what appeared to be a serious tête-à-tête. She wondered what type of art Will Matthews favored.

"And here we are, back to talking about the men," Eve said with a laugh. "You try your best to be a feminist, but men have a way of dominating the conversation even when they're not in it."

"You know, I don't think Will told me what business Sam is in," Gwen asked.

"I'm quite certain he didn't."

Gwen knew that Eve wasn't just being flip. "That sounds mysterious."

"I think Sam likes it that way."

The lawyer in Gwen didn't like things that sounded mysterious. Transactions that seemed odd—a wire transfer from overseas, a payment from a shell company incorporated in the Isle of Man, anything that was explained as being done for "tax reasons"—might not be illegal, but were, at the very least, a red flag that something might not be on the up-and-up.

She wanted to believe that Will couldn't possibly be involved in something criminal, but all of a sudden she questioned that assumption. Gwen had met enough brokers to know that many of them lived by the credo that if you weren't engaged in something shady, you weren't trying hard enough. Then again, practicing law had jaded Gwen. She was like the doctor who specializes in genetic abnormalities and was convinced that everyone's got one. Being rich—or in Sam's case, super rich—was hardly a crime. Nor was being private about your business interests.

Apparently sensing Gwen's apprehension, Eve said, "Sam's a hedge fund guy. Nothing that mysterious about it. And like all hedge fund guys, he dabbles a little in real estate. And he likes to own other expensive things."

Gwen was disappointed in herself. It was like watching a magic trick that amazed you and pestering the magician for the secret, only to be told that it was something as simple as hiding the quarter between your fingers to make it seem as if it had disappeared. Although you got the knowledge you had been seeking, what you gave up was clearly of much greater value.

"Don't you just love a man who thinks that good fortune is bound to come their way?" Eve continued. "Like latter-day Jay Gatsbys? Sam's that way, and I have a feeling Will is too. Maybe it's just an offshoot of white male privilege. But Sam really believes that the world will bend to him if only he puts in the work and gets lucky at the right time. Women know that the world doesn't work like that. So we assume that when something is too good to be true, it's not true."

"But that's because we're right, and they're wrong," Gwen said sharply.

"Are we, though?" Eve smiled. "I mean, look around you. Sam's doing okay following his belief system."

"Maybe you're right. There's this joke they tell in law school about how you can tell who's destined to be a lawyer from a young age. We're the people who read the back of the ticket to the roller coaster, where a disclaimer says that you waive any liability by riding, which basically means that the company could shoot you while you're on it and there's nothing you can do. Everyone else is just excited to be on the ride."

"Don't get me wrong, Gwen. Will's very lucky to have someone who's smart and beautiful by his side, looking out for him. Just don't let your well-honed sense of cynicism rub off on him too much. I think his future is going to be very bright. At least from the way Sam talks about him. He thinks Will is truly someone special."

Gwen once again surveyed the room. She couldn't deny that Eve had a very strong point. There they were, among the 1 percent of the 1 percent, and Will was the new golden boy. Gwen had certainly heard her fair share of stories of twentysomethings who had struck it big. They were always risk takers—never lawyers. People who believed in themselves and the possibility that great things could happen. People who were like the dog. And who was more like the dog than Will Matthews?

17.

At midnight, Gwen leaned in and whispered in Will's ear, "Would you mind very much if we left?"

"No. I was thinking the same thing."

Gwen gave only her address to the cab driver. Will was smart enough to keep quiet as the car headed for her building.

The doorman smiled at Will, suggesting he was envious of what awaited Will upstairs. In the elevator, Gwen pressed the button for the twenty-fourth floor. They stood in silence as the car ascended. Will remained mute as they walked down a long corridor that reminded him of a hotel because of the way the pattern on the carpeting repeated every twenty feet.

Once inside the apartment, Gwen took Will's coat and carefully placed it on a hanger in a closet beside the door. She then did the same with her own, again revealing the dress that Will had had trouble keeping his eyes off all night.

"You should make yourself a little more comfortable," she said. "Take off your shoes and tie. You're off the clock now."

She was right. Earlier was work. This was pleasure. He should relax.

"Would you like something to drink?" she asked.

Will very much wanted something to calm his nerves. He had limited his alcohol consumption at the party because he needed to keep some semblance of control, but he didn't mind ceding that to inebriation now.

"Sure. Whatever you're going to have."

"I have a bottle of white wine in the fridge. How's that?"

"Perfect."

Gwen's living room was almost exactly as he had pictured it in his mind. Grown-up looking, which made it a sharp contrast to his living space that still resembled a college dorm, if not a frat house. Her sofa almost certainly had been purchased new, and he suspected she'd selected the fabric from a swatch. An upright piano sat in the corner, and the walls were decorated with framed art.

Gwen joined him on the sofa a minute later, handing Will a glass of wine before kicking off her own shoes. "That was quite the party."

"I know, right? Just your average Saturday night for Will Matthews."

He was determined to wait until they had both finished their wine before making a move. That would serve the dual purpose of relaxing them both while also increasing the sexual tension. At least, that was what he hoped.

"Thank you so much for coming with me, Gwen."

"It was everything you promised and more. On top of which, I got to wear a dress that I thought would hang in my closet forever."

Will felt himself leaning in toward Gwen, as if he could no longer control the timetable he had previously established in his own mind. As they kissed, he sensed Gwen placing her wineglass on the coffee table. A second later, he felt her hand come up to his neck. His hands were on her bare back, feeling the softness of her skin.

Then Will's lips dropped to Gwen's neck, and she let out a light moan.

———

On Monday, Will woke up in his own apartment with a renewed purpose for living. He lingered in bed, reliving the weekend that had just passed—a highlight reel that he wanted to etch into his brain. Shutting his eyes, he again saw the curve of Gwen's breasts, how his hands had covered her nipples as she hovered over him, the way her head lolled back, and how she tightly clenched her eyes shut when she climaxed.

But what he remembered most vividly was her laugh when it was over. The way she left no doubt that she had enjoyed herself. It was the kind of laugh you let go after an amusement park ride, when the thrill has subsided but you remember how exciting it was in the moment.

He couldn't recall ever having a weekend like this one. That both his personal and professional lives could simultaneously be on such an upward trajectory seemed more like a blessing from above than mere coincidence.

His thoughts were no longer about survival at Maeve Grant. Now he was thinking about just how high he could fly. If only a fraction of the men he'd met Saturday night invested with him, he'd be earning in the mid six figures in no time at all.

———

Will arrived at the Maeve Grant Tower decked out in the blue chalk-stripe suit that Mario had sent over with the tux. In the lobby he saw Brian, who jogged to catch up to him. When he did, he looked Will up and down from head to toe.

"Did you get captured by *GQ* or something?"

"A little wardrobe update, that's all."

"Zegna? Valentino?"

Brian prided himself on being something of a fashionista. He owned suits by each designer—purchased on his parents' credit card, of course.

"Bespoke."

Will had just learned the term last week. He was now throwing it around like he was "to the manor born."

"No fucking way," Brian said as they entered the elevator.

"A tailor in the Bronx that Sam Abaddon hooked me up with. It was actually quite the weekend for me. I attended a black-tie event at Sam's penthouse on Saturday night, where I met about a dozen or so potential new clients. Then Gwen and I . . . well, use your imagination."

Brian laughed loudly. "Who the hell are you, and what did you do with my friend Will Matthews?"

Will couldn't help but laugh too. Brian wasn't wrong. He was a new man today.

He felt so confident, in fact, that he decided there was no time like the present to set up the meeting between Wolfe and Sam. As soon as he got off the elevator, even before going to his cube, he headed across the floor to Wolfe's office.

It was empty. The lights were off.

"Is he in yet?" Will asked Maria Murano, Wolfe's administrative assistant.

"Not yet. Must be a problem with traffic."

"I need to set up a meeting between him and my new client, Sam Abaddon. Can you put something on his calendar?"

"Sure." She clicked on the keyboard. "How soon you want to do it?"

"Thursday, if that works for him."

"I think so. He's got some room at eleven."

"Perfect," Will said.

As Will walked away, Maria said, "You look different today. Did you get a haircut?"

———

At nine, a man who identified himself as Clayton Lewis called. Will couldn't place the name at first, but surmised quickly that Lewis must have been an attendee at Sam's party. He wanted to open three accounts and planned to transfer $2 million into each of them.

While Will was filling in the last of his account information, establishing that Lewis's investment horizon was two to four years and that he could tolerate a medium amount of risk in the portfolio, he caught a glimpse of two of New York City's finest entering the floor. The police officers made a beeline to the corner office—the one belonging to the branch manager. Once they were all inside Joe Mattismo's office, they closed the door.

Lewis was telling Will to expect the wire later that afternoon, but Will was only half listening. His eyes were fixated on the closed office door.

By the time Will ended the call, the police presence had caused enough of a stir that Brian had poked his head into Will's cube to ask what he thought was going on.

"I don't know," Will said with a shrug.

Ten minutes later, Mattismo came out of his office. He stood on the desk of his secretary's workstation so that everyone who worked on the floor could see him.

"Everyone!" he shouted. "Gather around."

There was the rumble of a hundred people getting up from their desks and walking toward the corner of the floor. Once everyone was assembled, Mattismo said, "I have some truly awful news. Our friend and colleague, Robert Wolfe, was found dead this morning. It appears that he was the victim of some type of road-rage incident. We don't have all the details yet, but on his way into the office today, he became involved in an altercation with another driver."

Mattismo looked visibly shaken by the news, as if he were reconsidering every driver he had ever flipped off. "I'll circulate more information when I get it, and also about funeral arrangements. But for now, I think it will be appropriate for us all to engage in a moment of silence to remember Robert, and to pray for his wife and three young daughters."

SPRING

18.

The Tenth Floor had become Will's go-to lunch spot. He and Sam met there at least once a week. Warren ran the restaurant's front of the house, and he always greeted Will like he was a soldier returning from battle.

"Mr. Matthews, what a pleasure to have you dine with us again," Warren said while pumping Will's hand with both of his. "Mr. Abaddon has already arrived and requested to be seated. Follow me, please."

The interior of the restaurant was even more magnificent than Will had imagined when he was relegated to staring up wishfully at the space from the lobby. It boasted floor-to-ceiling windows that created glass walls along the northern and eastern exposure. Although Will had never actually counted, he guessed there were at least twenty crystal chandeliers. Virtually every surface was a bright white, with the only color provided by the aquarium, which filled a good portion of the center of the dining room. Will had once thought that nothing could be more beautiful than the way the water shimmered like a rainbow from the lobby. But up close it was even more spectacular, a kaleidoscope of gold, silver, reds, and blues.

Warren led the way to Will's usual table, situated directly alongside the pool. Sam stood as they approached and extended his hand.

"I hope you haven't been waiting long," Will said.

"No, you're right on time. I haven't even had an opportunity to order the wine."

"Go easy on me, please. The 2013 Bond Pluribus we had last week wiped me out. Believe it or not, I actually have some work to do today."

"Speaking of work, let's get a little out of the way while you're still sober enough to hold a pen."

Sam reached for his attaché case, unlocking its ends and then snapping the clasps open. Out came the usual sheaf of papers that often accompanied these lunches.

Will gave the documents a cursory review. He would have studied them more carefully, but experience had taught him that, regardless of the level of attention he paid, he still couldn't fully comprehend their contents. Usually they were filled with dense legal jargon, and sometimes entire sections were in a foreign language. Turkish or Russian, maybe Greek—at least as far as Will could discern, which wasn't very far because he didn't speak any languages other than English. Any questions Will raised were invariably met with Sam nonchalantly saying, "The lawyers insisted on that being there."

Today's document was at least short. Two pages. And it was in English.

At the top of the first page, in all capital letters, it read STATEMENT OF THE BOARD OF DIRECTORS BY UNANIMOUS CONSENT. Will flipped to the last page. The signature block listed Will as secretary of the company, although the name of the company was left blank.

Will had been named the secretary or treasurer, sometimes both, of scores of corporations. "Shelf companies" they were called, because their registration documents simply sat on the shelf, like a book no one had read for years, until called into service. As an officer of the corporation, Will could sign on the company's behalf, thereby eliminating the need for signature pages to be messengered back and forth with Sam. Not to mention that such positions always came with five-figure stipends and didn't require much work beyond attending a few meetings, which were usually held over the phone.

"Which one is this?" Will asked.

Sam looked at the sheet. "Oh, they forgot to fill it in. It's for Stormborn, Inc. Cyprus-based. There was a death of a board member, so we needed to elect a new one. Nothing very important."

"What does it hold?"

"You know, I'm not a hundred percent certain myself," Sam said with a grin. "I'll check and get back to you."

The answer hardly mattered. Will knew that Stormborn didn't own stock in Microsoft or Apple, or any other company he'd ever heard of, or one that traded on any public exchange. It owned stock in another shelf company. If Will peeled back the layers, he'd find more of the same. A labyrinth of holding companies, like Russian nesting dolls, most with *Game of Thrones*–related names, and all of which were incorporated in Cyprus or the Isle of Man or some other tax haven. Will didn't know just how far down he'd have to dig to find that Sam Abaddon was the person with authority over everything, but he thought he'd done the paperwork equivalent of tunneling to China and back and still hadn't.

In Will's discussions with more seasoned brokers, he'd learned that such subterfuge was standard operating procedure for high-net-worth clients. It was perfectly legal to minimize taxes, and in fact tax havens existed solely for that purpose. But whenever Will considered that Sam's businesses might not be solely on the up-and-up, which meant that Will might be aiding and abetting illegal activity, his concerns were assuaged by the fact that Maeve Grant's Compliance department had blessed every deposit and every trade. Or at least no one ever raised a concern with Will, which in his mind was the same thing.

He turned the page and then came to a stop. "George Kennefick?"

"Yeah. The poor bastard. Car crash. He was on his way back from the pub."

"That's the guy from Australia, right?"

Will hoped that he was wrong about the fact that the dead man who needed replacing was the same person who had earned Sam's not-too-veiled contempt after commenting about Eve at Sam's party.

"Did you know George?" Sam said, nonplussed.

"We met at your party a few months back. The first one, at your apartment."

Sam smiled as if he was recalling the party—not the fact that one of his guests was now deceased. "That's right. He did make the trip over for that. Excellent memory, Young Will. Take a look at who gets his job now."

Will turned the page to see who had been elected by unanimous consent to fill the director position. Needless to say, Sam's buildup hadn't left too much mystery in the matter.

"Me?"

"Congratulations," Sam said with a smile. "It comes with a fifty-K salary, and the obligation that you attend a once-a-year conference call that lasts five minutes, if that."

Given the news Will was about to share, the extra $50,000 didn't mean much. Besides, the more pressing issue was whether Sam would actually kill a man for just ogling his girlfriend. Maybe Kennefick's behavior had gone further than leering, and Sam truly had something to be jealous about. Of course, it was still far more likely that Kennefick had drunk too much and driven his car into a telephone pole.

Will had dismissed the timing of Robert Wolfe's death as coincidence. The story everyone at Maeve Grant had heard was that Wolfe's Mercedes was T-boned about a mile south of the on-ramp for I-495. The cops speculated that words must have been exchanged, and unfortunately for Wolfe, the other driver, who'd fled the scene, was either on his way to the golf course or kept his three iron in the car, because all it took was one swing to Wolfe's head and it was lights out.

In the weeks after the incident, the members of Wolfe's team had all been interviewed by two detectives from the NYPD. Will assumed that everyone painted the same picture of their fearless leader, and the cops quickly reached the conclusion that Wolfe was, in fact, the kind of guy who wouldn't hesitate to start an altercation if anyone even dinged his car. And if the NYPD had concluded that his death was a road-rage incident, who was Will Matthews to think otherwise?

After Will told Sam about Wolfe's untimely demise, which was not until a full week after the event, Sam didn't look the least bit surprised that a man he'd just agreed to meet had bitten the dust. Then again, when Will shared the news with Gwen, she didn't register surprise either.

George Kennefick was now the second person in Sam's orbit who had died in a car-related incident. That wasn't entirely right, Will told himself. Robert Wolfe had been in *his* orbit, not Sam's. Besides, Will wasn't even sure that there was any jealousy between Sam and Kennefick. He'd witnessed only a short interaction between the two men, after all. So it was entirely possible that he'd misread it.

"Aren't you just the gift that keeps on giving?" Will said as he pulled out a pen—his own Mont Blanc, a gift from Sam—and scribbled his signature where noted.

Sam relieved Will of the executed papers and tucked them back into his briefcase. Once again, he spun the dials on the catches, this time to lock it. Then he stored the case beside his chair.

"Just had my sit-down with the branch manager," Will said.

The meeting between Will and Joseph Mattismo was a long time coming. In fact, as soon as Will's AUM topped $100 million, which was more than two months ago, Mattismo told him that Maeve Grant would present him with a retention package. It had taken longer than they originally thought, because every time another of Sam's associates opened an account, the value of Will's package increased.

"And?"

"Ten for ten."

Maeve Grant had provided Will with a $10 million loan, payable in ten years, although Will would actually never pay a penny of it back. Not directly, at least. Instead, Maeve Grant would divert 60 percent of the commissions Will earned each year to satisfy the principal and the low interest that had accrued, with the expectation that in ten years, if not sooner, he'd have paid back the loan. When that happened, Maeve Grant would give him another loan based on his projected earnings at that time.

The firm's stated rationale for offering such arrangements to its top-producing brokers was that it was more tax advantaged than a lump-sum bonus, because a loan didn't have to be recognized as income. Of course, the true reason was that it was the ultimate set of golden handcuffs, tying the broker to the firm with the strongest bind there was: money. In Will's case, lots and lots of money. If Will were to leave Maeve Grant's employ, the balance of the loan would immediately become due.

"My, my," Sam said. "Welcome to the world of the multimillionaires. What do you plan to do with your newfound wealth?"

"Find a place to live that I don't have to share with four other guys, for starters."

"I think I can help you with that. Of course, it would come with strings attached. You'd have to be Evelyn's neighbor. She lives on the building's fourth floor, in a place much less grand than the one I'm suggesting you take a look at, believe me."

Sam pulled out his iPhone and began typing. "Today at six work for you?" he asked, lifting his eyes up from the screen.

"For what?"

"To see the place. I just texted the broker. She was pitching it to me as an investment property, but I think it would be perfect for you. It's her exclusive, and it hasn't yet hit the market. Trust me—you're absolutely going to love it."

"How much will I love it? In dollars, I mean."

"It's less than ten mil, that I know. But here's what I was thinking . . . Allow me the honor of putting up the funds for you to buy the apartment. That way, you can present an all-cash offer and lock the place down. If all goes well, you could move in by the end of the week."

Will considered Sam's offer. It was certainly extremely generous. But like the Maeve Grant loan, Will assumed that there would be handcuffs.

"Thank you. That's very unnecessary, but much appreciated. I'll only agree if you charge me market interest. After Maeve Grant processes the paperwork on my deal and the funds come through, which should be within thirty days, I'll pay you back. Plus the interest."

Sam shook his head. "No, I'm afraid that's not going to work for me. I'm going to need more than just the lousy six percent interest to make the deal."

Will was confused. Sam had made the offer in the first place. Will would have been perfectly happy to go to the bank for a mortgage.

"Okay. What then?" he asked.

"The only payment I'm willing to take is the promise that you'll invest the Maeve Grant ten mil smartly. I'm closing a new fund with my friend Sanjay Argawal. Have you met Sanjay?"

Will had met so many people over the last few months that most of the names had blurred together. "Maybe . . ."

"Yes, yes, you did. In Paris. Remember that party we attended? The one at that place with the dead-on views of the Eiffel Tower?"

Will did remember. It had been quite a party.

"Right."

"Sanjay was the one throwing it. Anyway, the fund is a billion-five raise, with a ten million minimum. Five-year time horizon. Projected one hundred percent return, twenty annually."

Sam reminded Will a bit of how he must have sounded back when he was cold-calling. Throwing around projected returns as if the money were already in the bank, as opposed to what it really was: wishful thinking.

"What's the fund?" Will asked, because he feared that rejecting Sam's proposal out of hand would make him seem ungrateful.

"Emerging companies on the subcontinent."

"I'd love to, Sam, really. But if—and I'm sure the fund will be a huge success—but if it goes down at all, I wouldn't be able to pay you back for the loan for the apartment, not to mention make the interest payments. Also, Maeve Grant won't allow it. They require that I keep at least fifty percent of the proceeds of the note with them."

Sam laughed, as if Will had told a joke. Will, on the other hand, had the sixth sense that the joke was on him.

"Look. You know as well as I do that the only reason Maeve Grant imposes that restriction is so they can recapture the float on the money that they are supposedly giving to you. They claim it's yours, but it's still really theirs. So just tell them that a client is threatening to yank a few hundred million under management if his own broker doesn't put some skin in the game. I guarantee you, that'll do the trick. They'll be begging you to make the investment with Sanjay."

"Okay," Will said. "I'll make the request as soon as I get back to the office."

"Good man. Let me tell you another thing, Will. You'll sleep better knowing that your entire net worth isn't in the hands of Maeve Grant. Isn't that what you're always telling me? To diversify? Not to be so at risk from any one sector? It's good advice when you give it to me, and it's even better when I'm giving it to you. Trust me, the last thing you want is for Maeve Grant to have that kind of power over you. Am I right about that?"

Will nodded in agreement. The one thing he was unsure about, however, was whether Sam appreciated the irony in that statement.

Then again, what choice did he have? Turning down Sam's generous offer would be risking everything he had.

19.

Gwen loved everything about being in court. She found just breathing the air in the courtroom to be intoxicating, even when, like today, she was doing so from the back of the gallery. She'd actually had to take vacation time to be there. Even though the proceeding involved Jasper Toolan, only the lawyers needed for the hearing were allowed to charge the client for their time in court, and that didn't include her. She had other assignments on which she could have been billing time, which meant that, as far as Taylor Beckett was concerned, Gwen's decision to be a spectator in the courtroom, even on a matter she was working on in some way, was no different than if she had gone to the movies for two hours in the middle of a workday.

The lawyers who were required to be there included Kanner, the junior partner running the day-to-day, and Doug Eyland, the senior associate on the team, who served as Kanner's right hand. Neither of them would be doing much more than Gwen, however. Benjamin Ethan was the only one who would be speaking for the defense, just like he was the only lawyer who was ever quoted in the press as counsel for Jasper Toolan. No one else on the fifteen-person team ever merited mention.

Toolan was also not present. He could have been, of course. But Ethan was adamant that they limit any news coverage of Toolan as a defendant, so as to keep the idea that he might be guilty out of the minds of potential jurors. As Ethan had told Kanner, who had told

Eyland, who had told Gwen, on its own the hearing wouldn't be newsworthy enough to garner TV coverage, and the newspapers would run the story on the inside pages, likely without a photo. If Toolan himself showed up, however, and they could take a photo or some video, it would become a front-page story and a segment on the cable news shows.

In her nearly three years at Taylor Beckett, this was only Gwen's fourth time inside a courtroom. The first was when she was sworn in as a member of the bar. The second was when she went with a law school classmate to bear witness to *her* swearing in. The only time she'd actually been a participant, if you could call it that, was for a status conference in a case between one of the Taylor Beckett partners and his co-op board, which he was suing because he claimed that the Japanese teahouse built on his downstairs neighbor's terrace obstructed his view of Central Park. Gwen hadn't worked on the case at all, and she had realized quickly that her presence in court was solely to impress upon the other side's lawyer that Taylor Beckett was providing full resources, and the co-op board would be wise to settle before they spent twice the damages in attorneys' fees, which was exactly what the co-op board ultimately did.

At least today had something to do with her work product. The hearing was on the motion to preclude Jennifer Toolan's prior comments about her husband's alleged abuse.

As everyone waited for the judge, the Honorable Linda Pielmeier, to take the bench, Gwen watched the man beside her sketching Benjamin Ethan—or at least that's what Gwen thought he was doing on account of the fact that the prosecutor was a woman and it looked nothing like Kanner or Eyland, although, truth be told, it was a poor likeness of Ethan. Even though Ethan had not yet moved from his chair, the drawing had him standing at the lectern, his hand outstretched in a theatrical flourish.

"Did someone hire you to do that?" she asked.

The man stopped his shading. "No. It's spec work. I come to court when there's a big case and do a drawing. Then I try to sell it to the lawyers, for their office. That's why I always do the defense lawyer. Never the prosecutor. ADAs won't spend a grand for wall art, but the defense lawyers? They do it every time."

Gwen had never been in Benjamin Ethan's office. As a result, she had no idea whether he had a courtroom sketch of himself on his wall. She wondered if some day she'd have one of herself.

As if he'd read her mind, the man handed Gwen his card. "I do commission work too," he said.

She laughed, thinking that she might not ever get to stand up in court. "Thanks."

There were three hard knocks from the front of the courtroom. "All rise," someone in the front shouted, even though everyone was already standing. "The People of the State of New York versus Jasper Toolan, case number 586958, the Honorable Linda Pielmeier presiding."

Gwen watched Judge Pielmeier stride into the room and walk the two steps up to the elevated bench from behind which she quite literally held court. When she was finally seated herself, she said, "Please be seated."

The judge had undergone chemotherapy in the past year, though she was cancer-free now, at least according to what Gwen read. In the stock photos Gwen had seen of Pielmeier, she had black, relaxed, shoulder-length hair. Today, however, she had little more than a dusting of white on top of her head. When she spoke, her voice was forceful.

"Welcome all, including those in the gallery," Judge Pielmeier said with a smile. "Whenever I handle a high-profile case, I always issue the following admonition. No matter how famous the participants, this is still a court of law. I expect everyone—lawyers, parties, and spectators—to comport themselves with that in mind. In other words, I don't want to hear a peep out of anyone I have not specifically requested to address me." She waited a beat. "Good. Now, we are here today on the defense motion to preclude certain evidence. I have read the papers thoroughly, and am familiar with the case law cited by both sides. As a result, I ask that when counsel address me they recognize my preparations and spare all of us from repeating what has already been stated in the briefs. With that word of caution, Mr. Ethan, you may proceed."

In his patrician way, Ethan leisurely made his way to the podium. Gwen barely saw his face in profile before he was ready to make his argument.

"If it pleases the court . . ." he began. He waited for Judge Pielmeier to indicate that she was, indeed, pleased. When she gave a slight nod, he continued. "Mindful that Your Honor is well versed in the facts and the law, I will get right to the heart of the matter. There is no reliable evidence that Jasper Toolan ever laid a hand on his wife. Unless the Court grants defendant's instant motion, however, the prosecution will fill the jurors' heads with innuendo and conjecture claiming that Mr. Toolan had a propensity to violence against his wife, in the hope that this will bootstrap a charge of murder, for which there is also not a single shred of evidence. To be specific, they're trying to prove that Mr. Toolan murdered his wife by relying on the evidence that Mr. Toolan once hit his wife. But he *didn't* hit her, and therefore such a claim cannot be used to consider whether he might have killed her. It is patently unfair for such evidence to be considered because the defense has no ability to set the record straight on cross-examination. That's the rub here, Judge. Because Mrs. Toolan is not here to testify, there's absolutely no way to demonstrate to the jury the truth—that Mrs. Toolan's police report was false, as she herself admitted not twenty-four hours after she filed it. This Court should not allow the prosecution to submit a police report claiming that Mr. Toolan had struck Mrs. Toolan, when the last word on this matter was Mrs. Toolan's unequivocal statement that the police report was false, and her husband had, in fact, never been violent with her. Your Honor has rendered several opinions of significant importance to the jurisprudence of civil liberties—"

Judge Pielmeier interrupted. "Only *several*, Mr. Ethan?"

The gallery laughed. "Forgive me," Ethan said, sounding actually contrite. "The better word would be . . . *numerous*."

"Proceed," Judge Pielmeier said.

"Thank you. Those *numerous* prior rulings, whether they concern due process or cruel and unusual punishment or First Amendment guarantees, have a common nucleus in that they protect against the enormous power of the government unfairly depriving the accused of his or her constitutional rights. A strong argument could be made that a single instance of assault nearly three years ago has little probative value as to whether Mr. Toolan killed his wife. Further, because it undoubtedly unfairly inflames the jury, it should be excluded on that basis alone. But that's not my argument here today. I'm relying on a much more important point: there is not a credible basis to assume that such an assault *ever* occurred. In the place of Jennifer Toolan's testimony, the prosecution seeks to offer a police report Mrs. Toolan quickly recanted, as well as the testimony of women who claimed to be friends with Mrs. Toolan, and who further claim that Mrs. Toolan told them that her husband had struck her. Now, let's be clear. They didn't see any abuse. So they can't testify to anything they know on their own. Instead, all they can say is what someone else said to them. That's classic hearsay, and should be excluded from trial because, bottom line, we have no idea whether Mrs. Toolan actually said anything of the sort to these women. Even if she did, we have no idea whether it's true."

"Isn't that a question for the jury?" Judge Pielmeier asked. "The jury can assess the credibility of these women and choose to believe them or not, just as they do with any witness."

Ethan didn't seem to be at all flustered by the judicial interruption. Without missing a beat, he said, "Your Honor would be correct if it was beyond dispute that Mrs. Toolan was telling the truth to her friends when she claimed she'd been struck. But we can't know that. And that's the problem. Because even in the unlikely event that Mrs. Toolan did, in fact, tell her friends that her husband had hit her, she might have been . . . let's say, less than candid with them. Maybe she and her husband had a screaming fight and she said he raised his hands, just to impress upon her friends that this was truly serious. That's what she herself claimed was the reason she filed a false police report, after all. Or maybe Mrs. Toolan knew that she was heading for divorce and she wanted to strengthen her negotiating position, so she started lying to her friends about spousal abuse in case there was a later trial. The undeniable truth is that there are many reasons that might have caused Mrs. Toolan to lie to her friends about spousal abuse. And that's in addition to all the reasons that her *friends* might lie. Maybe they think they can parlay riveting testimony into a book deal, or a role on one of those *Real Housewives* shows. Or maybe they're motivated by some misguided view that they're helping Jennifer Toolan's memory by lying."

"Mr. Ethan," Judge Pielmeier interrupted, "you're describing the dilemma we face with every witness in every trial. That's why God created cross-examination. You are entitled to question witnesses so the jury can determine whether they are to be believed."

Even though Gwen couldn't see Ethan's face, she imagined he was smiling. Maybe not at the judge, for fear she would take it the wrong way, but certainly to himself. Judge Pielmeier had fallen into Ethan's trap.

"The Court is making my point exactly," Ethan said. "I can't cross-examine Mrs. Toolan, and therefore there can never be a counterpoint to what her friends might claim she said. Put another way, there could be one of three truths here." Ethan raised an index finger, indicating he was going to count them off. "The friends are lying, and Mrs. Toolan would confirm that if she was able to testify." He raised a second finger. "Or Mrs. Toolan did, in fact, tell her friends that she had been hit, but she would have confirmed that she was lying when she said that."

"And number three is that maybe everybody is telling the truth?" Judge Pielmeier chimed in, receiving laughs from the gallery.

Gwen was sure Ethan hadn't cracked a smile, though. "But the fact that we don't know which one of the three it is makes this a serious due process issue, Your Honor. And as you said, God created cross-examination to show the jury that someone might be lying. But I can't show the jury that Jennifer Toolan was lying to her friends, or that her friends are lying now, because Mrs. Toolan cannot be subject to cross-examination. That's why God also created the due process clause—because defendants have a right to confront their accusers."

"Sounds a bit to me like the boy convicted of killing his parents who asks for leniency at sentencing because he's an orphan."

Ethan began to explain how other judges had ruled on the question, even though it meant disregarding the judge's admonition not to repeat the arguments in the briefs. Judge Pielmeier was having none of it. She cut him off ten seconds in, telling Ethan that she now wanted to hear from the prosecution.

The ADA handling the case was Carolyn Vittorio. She was a woman in her fifties who had made a career out of prosecuting powerful men for crimes against powerless women. As far as the Toolan defense team knew, she'd never lost a case.

"The defense is essentially arguing that you can murder your accuser, and then preclude your accuser's claims of abuse from being introduced at trial on the grounds that you've been denied the ability to confront your accuser," Vittorio said. "I don't think anyone doubts for a second that Jennifer Toolan would have loved to take the witness stand and swear under oath that her husband beat and killed her. The only reason she can't is because her husband beat and killed her."

When it was his turn for rebuttal, Ethan recited the section on forfeiture that Gwen had written, almost verbatim. Gwen imagined that it was like a playwright watching an actor recite her words.

After an hour of attorney back-and-forth, Judge Pielmeier thanked the lawyers. Gwen expected that the judge would take the matter "under advisement," which meant that she would issue a written decision at a later time, after reviewing the briefs more carefully.

But instead, Judge Pielmeier sat up straighter and nodded to the court reporter that she was about to speak on the record. That meant the judge was going to rule immediately.

"I find it a very great stretch to say that the reason Jennifer Toolan was killed was to keep her from testifying about her husband's alleged abuse. The alleged abuse took place nearly three years ago, and I do not think that Mr. Toolan had any fear whatsoever of being prosecuted for it. And, unless you tell me otherwise, Ms. Vittorio, I do not hear the People's theory of motive to be that Mr. Toolan killed Mrs. Toolan to avoid her testifying at a trial concerning spousal abuse."

Judge Pielmeier stopped, apparently so that Vittorio could confirm this on the record. With no other choice, the prosecutor stood and said, "No, Your Honor. That is not our theory of the motive for Mrs. Toolan's murder."

"Yeah, I didn't think so. This means that, on the forfeiture issue, the defense has persuaded me that Mr. Toolan has *not* forfeited his confrontation rights. And the constitutional right to confront his accuser would be infringed if I allowed any hearsay testimony that Mr. Toolan ever struck his wife."

Vittorio stood to respond, but Judge Pielmeier waved her off. "I know this one hurts, Ms. Vittorio, but the law gives me little choice. The police report is out. And I'm not going to allow anyone to testify about anything Jennifer Toolan told them. What I will allow, however, is for the prosecution to put on as many friends of Mrs. Toolan as they can find to testify that they *saw* evidence of abuse. If anyone witnessed any bruising or cuts or any other sign of abuse, that's fair game for testimony. I'll even entertain testimony about Mrs. Toolan's demeanor. But the law requires I draw the line to prohibit testimony about what Mrs. Toolan *said*—either to the police or to her friends—unless she is the one saying it and she's doing it under oath and subject to cross-examination, which, of course, she sadly cannot do."

It was a total victory. The jury would never hear that Jennifer Toolan claimed her husband had struck her. At most, they'd hear her friends claim that they thought that might have happened.

As the lawyers left the courtroom, Gwen caught Benjamin Ethan's eye. She hadn't thought he'd even recognize her as one of his underlings, but he smiled and mouthed, "Good job."

20.

There was no greater signifier of wealth than a New York City apartment in which the elevator doors opened directly into the foyer. It immediately told every visitor that the entire floor was yours and yours alone. Will thought about just how often he'd be correcting deliverymen. "What apartment number?" he imagined them asking, to which he'd reply, "No apartment number. Just come to the penthouse."

The real estate agent, Risa Waters, was walking a step ahead. She was eating-disorder skinny, with black, shiny hair and the hint of an accent that seemed to fluctuate between British and merely affected, like Madonna's.

"I don't know if Sam told you, but you'll be spared having to go through any board approval. I know that doesn't seem like much of a perk, but believe me, it truly is. Board review is the ninth circle of hell. To be honest with you, at this price point, there's no way someone your age would make it through. There's always something more the board wants. First it's an all-cash deal. After you agree to that, they want verification that you have another one hundred percent of the purchase price in liquid assets. And if you jump through *that* hoop, they demand that you have five times the purchase price in illiquid assets. The end result is that to buy this place, you'd need to have . . . I don't even know how much, but at least seventy-five or a hundred million to your name. That's why this is such a steal."

The asking price for the "steal" was $9.2 million.

"It has all the five-star amenities," Risa prattled on. "There's no way that a prewar is going to have a state-of-the-art gym or an Olympic-size pool like this building does. There's even a fifty-person movie theater, available for private use for a small fee."

Will had already begun tuning out her sales pitch. He walked over to the French doors that separated the inside from the terrace.

"Amazing view, right?" Risa said. "One of the benefits of being so far west is that nothing obstructs your view of the river. To the east, you get the skyline. If you're any farther east, though, the only view is into the apartment building across the street, and that diminishes your light significantly. We'll go out to the terrace in a second, but I want you to see the actual apartment first. I'm afraid that once you go out there, you won't care if there even *is* an inside."

Will thought about the first time he saw the view from Sam's place, and recalled joking with Gwen that his place had a better view. Even if he bought this place, it still wouldn't be true, but it also wouldn't be a joke anymore.

"The kitchen is top-of-the-line," Risa was saying. "Quartz countertops, a Sub-Zero refrigerator, Viking six-burner cooktop and oven, a Bosch dishwasher."

Will had no idea what the names meant, but he assumed that she mentioned them because they must be expensive. He followed Risa down the hallway and into the master bedroom. Two sides of which were all windows.

"The closets are to die for." Risa opened up two double doors, revealing a space inside the size of Will's present bedroom, lined floor to ceiling with shelving. "I know men don't care so much about closet space, but believe me, women certainly do. So, for the woman in your life, either now or someday, this will be more important than the view or the kitchen. Believe me."

Will had told Gwen he was thinking about buying a place when the Maeve Grant loan came in. She had encouraged him to take the plunge, although he was quite sure she hadn't expected him to go this far down the rabbit hole. They had discussed something in the $2- to $3-million range, which in Manhattan amounted to a 1,500-square-foot two-bedroom in a doorman building. And, if you were lucky, a view of something other than the building across the street.

"The en suite master bath is truly spa quality . . ." Risa said as they entered the bathroom.

Will couldn't remember the last time he'd taken a bath. But he did note that the tub was easily large enough for two.

Upon entering the second bedroom, Risa explained that most childless residents used the room as an office, usually fitting it with a pullout sofa so it could double as a guest room. "There's even one person with this layout who made it a closet. Can you imagine? She gave the walk-in in the master to her husband, and she made this entire room a closet. What a waste of the views, but she had a lot—and I mean, a *lot*—of clothing. But it'll also make a great kids' room someday."

Will very much liked the sound of that. Even though it had only been three months, he very clearly saw his future with Gwen, and that included filling the second bedroom with children. He'd already asked her to move in with him when he acquired an apartment of his own, which had always been pegged to his Maeve Grant money coming in. He imagined that they'd get engaged soon and married sometime next year. Gwen sometimes expressed reservations about having children before she was a bit more established in her career, but she also said that there was no optimal time, and she too saw a future with the patter of little feet. All of which convinced Will that the second bedroom would have a crib in it soon enough.

After reentering the living room, Risa opened the French doors to the balcony. Will followed her outside like an excited child.

Unlike the empty interior, the terrace was fully furnished. Two long sofas faced each other. Their frames were teak and the upholstery a pale yellow. On the other axis two sets of armchairs, in the same style and colors as the sofas, faced each other. A large rectangular coffee table, also in teak, completed the sitting area.

"I'm not sure why this is out here," Risa said, referring to the outdoor furniture. "It's possible that someone in the building had a party or something and they just never collected it. Or sometimes they use marquee space for a modeling shoot. It looks to be brand-new. I'm sure no one is going to claim it, so consider it a housewarming gift."

Will smiled at the thought that, after investing in Sanjay's fund, he might well have to move the outdoor furniture inside so he would have somewhere to sit. He turned to visualize how it would look in the living room. That's when he saw Eve.

"Hello . . ." she said, waving at Will.

She was wearing sweatpants and a T-shirt. Will realized it was the first time he'd seen Eve not dressed to the nines. It just as quickly occurred to him that she looked equally beautiful—if not more so—this way.

He gestured for her to join them outside. A moment later, she was admiring the view beside him.

"Sure beats what you can see out a fourth-floor window," she said with a wide grin.

"It is amazing, that's for sure. But I think it's a little *too* amazing for someone of my means."

"You're moving on up in the world, Will Matthews. Got to have an address that keeps up."

"I don't know . . ."

"You absolutely need to buy it. Apartments like this don't come along very often."

Risa chimed in. "So all you need to do is say yes, Will."

Will looked around the space. It seemed as if his soon-to-be former roommates had been right after all. He was Mr. Wall Street.

21.

The Clinton section of Manhattan was traditionally considered to be bordered by Thirty-Fourth Street to the south, Fifty-Ninth Street to the north, Eighth Avenue to the east, and the Hudson River to the west. It formerly went by the much more hardscrabble identifier of Hell's Kitchen, but since gentrification in the 1990s, including the development of the waterfront property to the west and the construction of the High Line, it had become among the most desirable sections to call home anywhere in Manhattan.

Will's new building was the crown jewel of the neighborhood. A glass-and-steel spire that shot up twenty-seven floors, tapering at the top. The vanity address was One Hudson Yards.

Will was standing in front of the building when Gwen arrived by taxi. Now it finally felt real. Gwen had that effect on him. If dealing with Sam always had a bit of fantasy about it, Gwen brought him back down to earth. That being said, he was about to take her into a different realm. A fantasy for both of them to experience together.

"I thought when you said that you wanted to meet at this address that I'd be standing in front of some hot new restaurant," she said. "So why am I standing in front of an apartment building? And why do you have a bottle of champagne in your hand?"

"So I could carry you over the threshold of my new home, and then we could share a toast."

Gwen craned her neck up to the sky to capture the full height of the building. Then, turning her focus back on Will, she said, "Aren't you the secret keeper?"

"Come. I'm excited for you to see it."

He took Gwen by the hand. The front door was held open by an attendant, outfitted in full regalia, including white gloves and a brimmed hat. Once inside, they were greeted by another doorman in an identical outfit. He opened the next set of doors, which led into the building's lobby, where a third man in the exact same garb stood behind a mahogany podium as if he were about to deliver a speech.

"Mr. Matthews, so nice to see you again."

"Thank you, George. This is my girlfriend, Gwen."

After Gwen and George shook hands, Will guided her toward the elevator banks. The cars were completely mirrored inside, which created something of a fun-house feel. As they ascended, Gwen said, "You need to fill me in a little, Will. Have you already closed on this place?"

"Yeah. Saw it on Monday, closed today."

"How'd you do it so fast?"

"A real Sam special. This is the building Eve lives in; she's on the fourth floor. Sam heard about the penthouse coming up for sale and got me in to see it before it was officially on the market. I made an offer, it was accepted, and I was able to do it as an all-cash deal, so we closed right away."

Before Gwen could say anything else, the elevator doors opened—directly into the apartment. When they did, she gasped.

"We're here," Will said, gesturing for Gwen to step out into his new home. "It's two bedrooms, two and a half baths," Will said, mimicking how Risa had introduced the space to him.

"Jesus, Will. What did you pay for this?"

"It wasn't cheap, that's for sure. The arrangement I reached with Sam was that he'd front the purchase price, and then when the Maeve Grant money comes in, I'll invest it with a buddy of his that runs a hedge fund. As soon as the hedge fund has a liquidation event, I'll pay Sam back."

"Why didn't Sam just make the ten million investment in the fund himself and then let you use the Maeve Grant money to buy this place? Or take out a mortgage, like a normal person?"

"He's in the fund too, so maybe he wanted to limit his exposure. As for why he wanted me to invest, he said it was important that I have skin in the game."

Gwen's eyes narrowed. Obviously, this explanation was not sufficient.

"Gwen, it's going to be fine. Believe me. I got this. And you're going to love the place. After you've seen it, we can talk about the reasons you think I shouldn't have bought it. But, and I cannot emphasize this enough, remember that I already closed, so . . ."

Gwen took a deep breath. Since Eve's admonition at the party, she'd tried her best not to let her cynicism overcome Will's optimism. Still, this wasn't a gift of a tuxedo and some overpriced footwear. This was a full-floor Manhattan penthouse. Nonetheless, Will's request wasn't too much to grant, so she smiled to indicate that she was on board with tabling the discussion until she got a tour of the place.

Will guided her through the empty rooms, trying to remember the buzzwords Risa had used to describe its features. As he'd expected, Gwen was already fluent in the terms bandied about for New York City high-end real estate—Sub-Zero, Bosch, Viking, pied-à-terre, common charges.

She paused at the second bedroom. When Will mentioned that it was easily large enough for two children, she gave him a genuine smile and said, "Is that so?"

The moment they stepped onto the terrace, the wind gusted up as if on cue. Will watched Gwen's hair dance.

"So, what do you think?" he asked.

"It's spectacular, Will. I mean, even the partners at my firm don't have real estate like this. I'm not even sure our *clients* do. In fact, the only apartment I've ever even seen like this belonged to Sam. But fun and games aside, I need some answers. What did you pay?"

"It was a shade over nine million."

"And is Sam charging you interest?"

"Yes, he's charging me interest. Market rate."

"Your monthly expenses alone—interest and condo fees—have got to be in the thirty- or forty-grand range?"

"I haven't calculated it to the penny, but it's something like that. But Sam's deferring the interest payments because I told him I couldn't make the fund investment if I had to pay monthly interest. So all I need to come up with on a monthly basis are the condo charges, which run about five grand. And I set two hundred grand aside so I could buy furniture. Eve is going to take me shopping tomorrow with the expectation I'm going to spend all of it. Then, when the hedge fund hits, I'll pay Sam back."

"What if it doesn't . . . hit?"

"It will . . . but if for some reason it doesn't, Sam will understand that. Especially considering it was his idea to do it this way."

Will was smiling to defuse Gwen's apparent concern, but by the fact that she looked like she had bitten into a lemon, he knew it wasn't working. "Gwen, it's all good. I ran it by Maeve Grant, and they were fine with it."

"Really?"

"Yes, really. I may not be a risk-averse lawyer like you, but I'm not going to jeopardize my job over an apartment. I told them that Sam was rather insistent that his broker invest alongside him."

"And they signed off on . . . your client basically buying you a ten-million-dollar apartment?"

"It's nine point two," Will said with a smile. When Gwen didn't smile back, he said, "Okay, you're concerned. I get that. It's . . . to put it mildly, a bit unorthodox. But the transaction is all documented, so Sam's not *giving* me anything. Instead of JPMorgan Chase holding the mortgage, and me paying them off for the next thirty years, Sam Abaddon holds the mortgage, and I'm going to pay him off in five years. And you're right that if the hedge fund investment goes south, there's going to be a real problem there. But truth be told, it's not much more of an issue than if the New York City housing market crashed, in which case my issue would be with JPMorgan Chase, and they would likely be far less understanding than my biggest client. But to answer your question, yes, I ran it by my office manager, and he passed it along to Compliance and probably Legal too. It came back with everybody's stamp of approval."

That did the trick. Gwen's body slackened. She even smiled.

"Okay, I'm going to be like the dog," she said. "See? My tail is wagging."

She shook her backside in a half shimmy, half twerk gesture. Will pulled her into him.

"Sam and Eve won't be here for another hour or so. What say we christen the place?"

"You don't have any furniture."

"There's a sofa out here."

"It'll be cold," Gwen said.

"Not if we do it right," Will replied.

———

The elevator doors opened at a little after nine. Sam and Eve stepped off and looked sincerely surprised to find Will and Gwen sitting on the floor in the center of the massive, empty living room, a bottle of champagne between them.

"Apologies," Sam said. "I hadn't thought you'd be here yet."

"It is their home," Eve said. Her smile suggested she knew how Gwen and Will had spent the last forty minutes. "I'm so sorry. We promise to buzz up in the future."

Will cast away their concerns with a laugh. "It's fine. Gwen and I decided to come over a little early. I remembered the champagne but sadly forgot to bring glasses, so we've been drinking out of the bottle."

"Then we're just in time," Sam said. "For I not only bring to this party a very fine bottle of Bollinger, but I also remembered glasses. And in Evelyn's bag is some of the freshest beluga you can find outside of harvesting it yourself from the Caspian Sea."

Sam was holding a shiny black shopping bag that lacked any store logo. He handed it to Will. "May you have many happy memories in your new home."

Will retrieved the champagne from the bag, then reached in for the crystal champagne flutes and distributed them. His last withdrawal was a wooden box that was cold to the touch. After flipping open the lid, Will saw a very generous amount of caviar, with a mother-of-pearl spoon and some crackers beside it.

The pop of the champagne startled him. Will turned to see vapor rising from the bottle. After filling everyone's flute, Sam said, "Come talk with me, Will." Turning to the women, he added, "Business, I'm afraid. It'll be but a minute."

He led Will outside, toward the corner of the terrace. There was a chill in the air that Will hadn't recalled when he'd been outside with Gwen earlier.

"Pretty amazing view. Am I right about that?"

Will nodded in agreement. "I can't believe I own this place."

"This is only the beginning, my friend. Bigger and better things still await. But the higher you climb, the more dangerous it is, because the farther you have to fall. That's why, to stay on top, you need to be forever vigilant."

From the corner of his eye, Will saw Gwen and Eve smiling at each other. He wondered if their conversation was similarly weighty and was near certain that it was not.

"My father was an alcoholic," Sam said. "I swear, if it wasn't inside a bottle, he didn't want to know from it. Included in that category was his only child." Sam chuckled. "I was ten when he kicked. Drank himself to death, naturally. I remember thinking that his coffin should be in the shape of a bottle. I'd seen funerals on TV, so I knew that wasn't the way it worked. But my mother always talked about how he wouldn't be at peace until he'd crawled inside a bottle and died there. So I thought . . . well, the things we don't understand about the world when we're kids."

"I lost my dad at that age too," Will said.

"I know. I remember you telling us that the night we first met. It was one of the things that drew me to you, to tell you the truth. It's the kind of formative thing that only those who have experienced it can truly understand."

Will agreed. People sometimes shared with him their own story of loss, but unless your father died suddenly when you were ten, it wasn't the same thing. Will understood that other stories—like Eve's recent loss of her father—were tragic in their own way, but they were also different. The combination of being just old enough to understand and the shock of learning your world could change in a split second and nothing you could ever do would make it right again inextricably molds you right then and there into the man you will someday become.

"And your mother?" Will asked.

Sam smiled. "She was no prize herself. But I give credit where credit is due, and she did manage to fulfill the only true requirement of being a parent: she was able to keep herself alive until I could take care of myself. If sixteen years old meets that definition."

Sam smiled. It was the kind of expression that made clear that he was thinking about something he hadn't yet expressed.

"I'm heading out of town tomorrow," Sam said, changing the subject. "I should be back in three or four days. I'd ask you to join me, but I know you have a date with Evelyn tomorrow to look at furniture."

George Kennefick's fate popped into Will's mind. "I'm happy to put that off, if you'd like me to come with," he said.

"No, that's not necessary. Besides, I'd feel better having you here. But when I return, I'm going to have some important matters to discuss with you."

"About what?"

"I'd like to keep that to myself for a little while longer. It'll depend on how things shake out during my meeting. But believe me, your expected role will be an important part of what I'll be discussing."

Like many of his interactions with Sam, he was left with more questions than answers. But Will knew that further inquiry would not lead to any greater insight at the moment.

"Okay. I'll be here when you return," he said.

"Good. Enjoy your time with Eve," Sam said. "But not too much, okay?"

22.

After the bottle was empty and the caviar consumed, Gwen and Will went back to her place. Gwen was certain that the nights where she hosted would end the moment Will acquired a bed, and she couldn't help but wonder what Will's acquisition of real estate meant for their future.

Three months ago, Gwen had been contemplating getting a cat just so there'd be a live presence when she came home, and now she was thinking about getting married and then soon after getting pregnant. She was terrified by the thought of making that type of commitment, but her fears were outweighed by her excitement about the future, and she owed that entirely to Will. He'd made her less scared about the unknown, more willing to envision a future that might actually exceed her every expectation.

Gwen had never engaged in any long-term planning with Peter, and they'd been together for nearly two years. But Will was not Peter—in so many ways. Not the least of which was that she was in love with Will. Not just a little bit either. The head-over-heels way that she'd always imagined being in love with someone. The way she felt a jolt of happiness whenever she saw his face. Just as telling was the fact that whenever they were apart she longed for them to be together, like an addict needing a fix.

And if that wasn't reason enough for her to cast away the last shred of doubt about her life, she'd soon be moving into a home that Oprah might live in, with a man she not only loved but who was doing his damnedest to shake from her the worst part of herself—the negativity that had seemed to define her for as long as she could remember.

Still, old habits die hard. Gwen couldn't help but notice that Will had been uncharacteristically quiet on the ride back to her place. He hadn't shared what Sam wanted to privately discuss, but Gwen assumed it was business that she wouldn't have any interest in anyway. Gwen had hoped that Will would explain the situation on his own, but when he slid under the covers beside her without having done so, she raised the issue.

"Did something happen with Sam tonight? You've been awfully quiet since he pulled you aside."

"No," he said quickly, but with a smile that might have been construed to suggest otherwise.

"What did Sam say to you when the two of you were on the terrace?"

"Nothing, really. He's going out of town for a few days and wants me to hold down the fort. That kind of thing. Although he did open up about something. He told me that he lost his father when he was ten. That's the same age that I was when my dad died."

"Is that right? About Sam, I mean. I know that's how old you were when your father died."

"His mother died when he was sixteen, so he's got me beat there."

"Makes it a little clearer why he took such a liking to you so quickly, I suppose. I mean, you're from practically the same hometown and then you both suffered the same tragedy. He must see a lot of himself in you, Will."

Will nodded in agreement. "The mention of my dad, I guess, has made me a little introspective about everything that's happened. And what I'm hoping is still going to happen. I wish my parents had met you, Gwen. They would have loved you as much as I do."

"That's a very nice thing for you to say. I'm sorry that I didn't have the opportunity to meet them. If I had, I would have told them that they did a pretty superlative job of raising a son. They'd be so proud of all you've accomplished, Will."

But rather than seeming comforted by that, Will still looked pensive. "Am I missing something, Gwen?"

The question took her by surprise.

"About what?"

"About Sam. I know you think I'm some head-in-the-clouds optimist, always thinking the best of people—"

"Well, aren't you?"

He rolled his eyes. "Yes, I am. But I also like to think I'm not a complete idiot either. And this thing with Sam . . . It's happened so fast and there's still so much I don't really understand about his business."

"Will. You told me that Compliance has blessed everything, right?" When he nodded, she said, "So you're all good."

Gwen recognized that it was an odd change of position for them. Since they'd met, Will had been the hopeless romantic, believing that all he had to do was imagine it and it could come true, whereas Gwen had been looking for danger around every corner.

He shook his head as if he wasn't sure. "I don't know. Sometimes, it just all seems too good to be true. I'm half waiting for it all to come crashing down on me."

That sounded like something *she'd* say. So much so that she felt compelled to play Will's part now, and assure him that everything would be fine.

"It won't," she said softly. "And if you won't take my word for it, allow me to quote the great Willy Wonka. Remember what happened to the boy who got everything he wished for?"

"What?"

Gwen laughed softly. "That's exactly what Charlie said when Wonka posed the question. And the answer is, of course, 'He lived happily ever after.'"

"Is that right?"

"It can be."

"Thank you, Gwen. There's a part of me that sometimes thinks it's not real, and if I didn't have you to share it with, I swear, I'd think I was dreaming."

Gwen playfully pinched him.

"Ouch."

"Not dreaming," she said with a smile.

23.

Will had never heard of the D&D building, which naturally meant that when Eve mentioned that was where they were heading, he had no idea what either *D* represented. It wasn't until he was standing in front of it that he saw the plaque beside the door: Decorator and Designer Building.

In the lobby, a security guard sat behind a desk. A couple who looked to be in their early thirties, with a child in a stroller in tow, stood before him.

"Not open to the public," the security guard barked. He looked past the young family to Eve and Will and broke into a wide grin. "Eve, so nice to see you again."

"Good to see you too, Guillermo. This is my client, Will Matthews."

Eve barely broke stride as she waltzed past the checkpoint. Will followed her into the elevator.

"First stop, sixth floor. Holly Hunt," Eve said.

"Like the actress?" Will asked.

"What?"

"She was in that Batman-and-Superman movie."

Eve laughed. "No. That was Holly *Hunter*. This one is a designer. Hence why she has space in the D&D building. I thought it would be a good place for us to start because her stuff is both contemporary and comfortable. Clean lines, masculine without being cold. Kind of like you, Will."

Once they were in the showroom, Will decided that, for the life of him, he couldn't discern any difference between the merchandise bearing Holly Hunt's name and what he'd seen at Room & Board, except that none of the items before him was adorned with a price tag and Room & Board wasn't shy about indicating the cost of its products. Of course, Will knew that such secrecy only meant that everything he was about to buy would be extremely expensive.

"I'm a believer that you can't have too many individual seating spaces in a room," Eve said. "That's why I strongly discourage sectional sofas. A sofa, no matter what size, only ever seats two. For your living room, because the space is so large, I'm thinking that you'll need two sofas, seven feet each, that will face each other. Then two club chairs, and two armchairs to round out the space. That way you have seating for eight, and that's all you need before it becomes a party—after that, everyone stands."

Eve glided around the showroom, reaching for swatches of fabric and draping them over the arms of the upholstered furniture. Will selected the one he favored, but agreed to go with Eve's choice when she told him that his was a mistake.

Two hours later, Will had spent nearly a hundred grand. What he had to show for that sum was living room furniture that sat eight, and a dining table and chairs that accommodated twice that many.

After Holly Hunt, they ventured downtown. Not to a showroom or even a store, however. Instead, it was the third floor of a brownstone. They were buzzed in and climbed the three flights of stairs, until they stood before an unmarked red door. Before Eve knocked, a man opened it.

"Eve, my darling. So nice to see you again."

He was of Indian descent, with a full beard, black as coal. He was wearing a turban in the tradition of the Sikhs, but a Western business suit—and a finely tailored one at that.

"Ketan, always a pleasure," Eve said, kissing the man on both cheeks. "This is my client, Will Matthews. We're hoping to find some truly extraordinary rugs. Preferably one-of-a-kind pieces that will increase in value."

"You're in the right place. I just got a new shipment in. Spectacular pieces. Many of them fifty to a hundred years old."

Once inside, they entered a space that could have been used as a ballroom for weddings, except for the fact that the floors were covered with piles of rugs. Ketan clapped his hands, and out of a back room emerged two very large men. They also appeared to be of Indian descent, but neither was wearing any head covering, and they were dressed more casually.

"Let's start here," Ketan said, moving over to one of the piles. "These are mainly Tabriz. Some are center medallion, but not all."

The two men each went to opposite ends of the pile and began to turn over the corners of the rugs. Every so often, Eve would ask the men to pull one out, which would require the services of two other men. Will would then take a look at the rug in all its glory and pronounce judgment.

In the end, four rugs made the cut, with Eve's promise to Ketan that they'd be back for more after seeing how the four they were buying captured the light in the apartment. Ketan promised delivery by the next day. After Will handed over a credit card, the transaction was complete.

Ligne Roset was located around the corner, on Park Avenue South. Eve thought he might find a bed there that he liked.

After walking the floor a few times, Will stopped in front of a bed in the corner with a huge blue fabric headboard that resembled the sail on a medium-size boat.

"Very nice," Eve said. "But you need to test it out. European beds don't use a box spring, so there's less support."

Will sat down on the edge and bounced lightly. "This seems fine."

"That's no way to test a bed that you're going to spend half your life on."

Eve plopped down beside him, and immediately lay prone. She tapped the mattress beside her, urging Will to do likewise. When he hesitated, she said. "C'mon. Lay down. I'm not going to bite you."

Will did as he was told. Staring up at the ceiling, he couldn't stop himself from taking in Eve's scent. She didn't smell perfumy, though. There was nothing floral or spicy about her. The aroma reminded him of very ripe cherries.

The next thing he knew, she had taken his hand. Something in Will's brain said he should pull away, but the message didn't run down his arm. To break her hold, he turned, propping himself up on his elbow. Eve's only reaction to his withdrawal was to face him, mirroring his pose, although she did so while flashing a smile that could have launched a thousand ships.

"So, can you see it all happening here?" Eve asked.

———

From first appearances, Sushi of Gari was nothing like the restaurants Sam frequented. In fact, it looked no different from any midprice sushi place that could be found along Second Avenue. The tables were a blond ash wood, and the chairs lacked upholstery.

"Upstairs," Eve said. "We sit at the bar."

Although Will initially thought a bar meant alcohol, he quickly realized that she was referencing the sushi bar. It sat ten. Aside from an oversize man on one end reading a hardcover edition of the latest Harlan Coben, it was empty. Eve took the corner two stools on the other end.

"We're each going to have the *omakase*," she said to the waiter. "We have no dietary restrictions. And sake, please."

"Hot or cold?"

"Cold," she said.

"James Bond drinks it hot," Will said.

Eve laughed at the reference. That hearty, sexy laugh she used when she was actually amused.

"Maybe in the 1960s, when that was the preferred method. Advances in distillation make it more like wine now. Connoisseurs these days ask for it chilled, but not too cold."

"A woman who knows her sake."

"I know a lot of things, Will."

She uttered the line in a Mae West way, suggesting a sexual knowledge. Then again, Eve had a way about her that made everything she said sound sexual. But like that line by Jessica Rabbit—*I'm not bad, I'm just drawn that way*—Will wondered if he was the one imbuing her words with innuendo that she didn't intend.

"What did you order for us?" he asked, an effort to quickly change the subject from things in which Eve held a special expertise. "The Omarosa?"

"You're adorable, do you know that?" Without waiting for an answer as to whether he was aware of his adorableness, Eve said, "It's not Omarosa, like the *Apprentice* woman. It's pronounced ohm-ah-kas-ay. The *itamae*—that means sushi chef—selects what we get. He'll just give us a single sushi piece every so often until we tell him we've had enough. Like a tasting menu. My favorite part of the experience is that you have to eat it one piece at a time. I think all restaurants should serve this way—by the bite. It makes you savor and anticipate."

Every few minutes, the *itamae* did exactly that, placing a single sushi piece in the middle of a glass plate and setting it down in front of them. Each piece was architectural, evoking a Shinto temple, with a base of rice below vibrantly colored fish, a dollop of something exotic on top of it, like a crown of caviar, potato crisp, or foie gras.

"Did you acquire your sushi knowledge from Sam?" Will asked when they had almost finished their second glass of sake.

"No. The opposite, actually. I taught him. And about much more than just raw fish too."

She smiled, once again in a come-hither way. Will recognized that this was going down a path he shouldn't be traveling, and yet there was something about Eve that rendered him unable to resist.

"How are things between you and Gwen?" she asked.

He wondered if she was probing or reminding him that he had a girlfriend. "Good. Really good, in fact," he said.

"The beginning is always the best part. Sam was very romantic when we first got together. Gifts, vacations. Then it slows down, and before you know it, it's gone. And the weirdest thing is that you can't remember when everything turned. You know what I mean?"

Will actually didn't know. He couldn't imagine a time when things with Gwen would be any less perfect than they were right now.

As if Will's failure to respond were an admonition, Eve quickly said, "Don't get me wrong. I know that the honeymoon never lasts. I'm only saying it would be nice if it did. Sometimes I miss that type of attention, the being wooed part." She laughed. "Does anyone say 'wooed' anymore?"

"I certainly don't."

"Well, if Will Matthews from Cheboygan, Michigan, doesn't say it, then I'm reasonably sure it is not said by anyone, anywhere." They shared a smile, but then Eve retreated back into her own mind. "The ironic thing is that when another man pays me the least bit of attention, Sam gets crazy."

Will now regretted that second glass of sake. He could already tell his judgment was becoming impaired, and he worried that the full effects of the alcohol had yet to kick in.

———

Eve asked that Will accompany her back to her place. Will didn't think he could back out of an expected gesture of chivalry, but he was determined that the evening would end in the taxi. He would kiss Eve good night on the cheek, and then tell the driver to take him back to Gwen's place. But when the taxi came to a stop and he delivered his line, Eve shook her head and smiled in a particularly lascivious way.

"I'm not done with you yet, Will Matthews. There's something I need to discuss with you . . ."

For the first time, he thought he heard sloppiness in her speech. She was half his body weight, and had matched him sake for sake. Considering that *he* was certainly feeling it, he could only imagine that the alcohol was hitting Eve that much harder.

"I'm not sure that's such a good idea, Eve."

Her eyes narrowed. "Will, seriously. It's important."

This time she spoke clearly. He weighed rejecting the request a second time, and actually thought the word was going to come out, but instead he said, "Okay, but just for a minute."

Inside the elevator, Eve pressed the button for the fourth floor, but Will's better judgment finally kicked in and he countermanded her, hitting the *P* on the top of the panel.

"We can talk in my place," he said. "I'd like to stay in the fresh air, if that's okay. The sake is making me a little queasy."

In New York City it's never dark enough to see the stars, but it was a clear night, allowing visibility for miles. It was warm too, although Will couldn't be sure it wasn't the sake that had rendered him impervious to the elements.

They sat side by side on the terrace sofa, their legs touching. It felt like a game of chicken, except that instead of two cars crashing, the end result here would be Will and Eve colliding into each other.

"Will, I wanted to tell you something. Something important."

"Okay."

"It's about Sam."

This time Will only nodded. He didn't want to give even Eve permission to say something that Sam might wish had gone unsaid.

"He's not exactly who you think he is."

"I don't know what you mean, Eve. And before you explain yourself, I feel the need to say that maybe I'm not the right person for you to be confiding in. I like you, very much, in fact, but I owe my livelihood to Sam."

Eve laughed. "We all owe so much to Sam Abaddon, don't we?"

"I do," Will said with conviction.

"But what do we owe to ourselves, Will?"

"I . . . don't know what you mean."

"I mean . . ." She hesitated for a moment, as if she was struggling to find the words to complete her thought, and then leaned in to him, placing her lips on his.

Will had what seemed like an out-of-body experience, where he was actually viewing the interaction from above them. He could feel Eve's hand on him, her tongue in his mouth, her weight pushing him onto his back.

He broke their seal more abruptly than was required. "I'm sorry," he said, wondering whether he was apologizing for the force he had used or for rejecting the advance.

"There's nothing to be sorry about, Will," Eve said. She resumed her position inches from him. In her eyes, he saw a sadness he hadn't noticed before.

He could feel his heart beating, more out of fear than lust. Eve leaned in again, but this time angled toward his cheek. Her lips lingered there, and her hand slid into his hair. He could feel her hot breath in his ear.

A soft nibble, on the lobe, and Will's eyes reflexively shut.

He was about to move her off him again when she whispered, "I'm going to go to bed now, Will. Sam is lucky to have someone as loyal as you."

He watched her leave the terrace and then step into the elevator. When the doors closed, he felt a wave of relief at being alone. Then he stood up. He almost made it to the French doors before he vomited all over the terrace floor.

24.

Sam's call woke him—with good reason, given that it was before 7:00 a.m. on a Sunday. Will looked over at Gwen, who stirred a bit but appeared to still be sleeping.

He could still feel the aftereffects of the sake. His eyes and throat were dry, his tongue heavy with a filmy coat.

In the hours since he'd parted from Eve, he'd convinced himself that the outing had indeed been some type of test, likely instigated by Sam. If that's what it was, he assumed he'd passed—although he couldn't be sure. On the other hand, it took a fairly demented mind to put a business associate through that type of hazing to establish loyalty. Perhaps it was all Eve, either seriously or not, seeing how far she could push naive Will Matthews from Cheboygan to compromise himself for a moment of passion with her.

"I thought you weren't coming back until next week," Will whispered into the phone.

"Change of plans," Sam said. "There's some stuff going on, and I'd like to bring you up to speed. Meet me in an hour, at my place."

"Okay. I'll be there."

———

Sam Abaddon was someone who traveled in a suit and tie. Will, on the other the hand, was dressed like it was a Sunday morning, in jeans and a sweatshirt. He immediately regretted his sartorial choice.

Sam didn't seem to care. He thanked Will for coming on such short notice, as if declining had actually been an option.

"I just put on some coffee," Sam said. "Can I pour you a cup?"

Coffee sounded like manna from heaven. "Yes. That would be great."

Despite the urgency in Sam's message, he methodically attended to the coffee, recalling that Will took it with a little cream, but no sugar. He handed a mug to Will without pouring one for himself. Then he led Will into his living room, where he took a seat in one of the two armchairs. He gestured for Will to take the other. Will realized he had seen the same chairs in the Holly Hunt showroom.

"How was your shopping excursion with Evelyn?"

Will's guard immediately shot up. He reminded himself that he'd acted completely appropriate with Eve. For the most part, anyway. He certainly hadn't encouraged her, and he'd stopped her advances almost immediately.

But would Eve agree with that assessment? Would she tell Sam what had happened? Had she already done so?

"It was great. Furnished nearly my entire place. One day."

"Good. I'm glad to hear that. Evelyn is quite a talented decorator."

He was about to ask Sam why he'd been summoned when his phone rang. "Mind if I answer this?"

He assumed it would be Gwen, telling him that she was heading to the office. But it was Eve on the line.

Will had enough experience with the opposite sex to know that these phone calls took one of two paths: apology for drunken action or a request to "talk" about it, which more often than not ended up with the couple picking up where they'd left off.

In this case, the first was unnecessary, and the second was to be avoided at all costs. The more immediate issue, however, was that he didn't want to engage Eve at all while within ten feet of Sam.

"Hi, Eve," he said, looking at Sam while he spoke. "I'm actually with Sam at his place right now. What's up?"

"Really? He's back?"

Will hesitated. Had Sam not shared his travel plans with Eve? Was his return something he wanted to keep secret from her?

He'd already told her that Sam was back, though. Therefore, whatever damage he'd done by speaking out of school was already done.

"Yes. Just this morning."

"Put me on speakerphone."

"What?" Will said. He was stalling, hoping Eve would think better of what she'd just requested.

He then recalled that there was a third way these day-after interactions worked. You just pretended the previous night had never happened. Perhaps Eve actually didn't remember because the alcohol had hit her hard. It was also possible that she remembered every detail but was content to keep it stored away as a secret moment between them.

"Put me on speakerphone. I want to say hello."

"I'm going to put her on speaker," Will said for Sam's benefit. "Eve?" he said after pressing the button on his phone.

"Welcome home, Sam!" she screamed from the phone.

"Glad to be home, Evelyn. I'm sorry I didn't call right away. I assumed you'd still be asleep at this hour. You'll see I texted that I wanted to see you as soon as you awoke."

"That works out perfectly, then. The reason I was calling Will was to tell him that his rugs arrived. Why don't you both come over right now to take a look at them? Will, I promise, you're going to absolutely love them."

Will looked at Sam, hoping he would tell Eve that they had business to discuss first. After all, Will still hadn't heard what was so important that he had to be summoned to Sam's apartment before nine on a Sunday morning.

"That sounds perfect, Evelyn," Sam said instead. "We'll be right over."

———

When the elevator doors opened into Will's apartment, Eve was standing right in front of them, wearing a white linen dress. Will didn't think he'd ever seen her in white before—black was normally her hue of choice. He was struck by how she looked positively angelic. He suddenly doubted she was feeling *any* aftereffects of the sake.

She ran forward and embraced Sam. Whatever concerns she'd expressed about him the night before had obviously dissipated.

Will watched Sam spin Eve around. She seemed like a totally different person today than she had been last night. Maybe everything she'd said had indeed been some elaborate test to determine Will's loyalty. Would he sleep with Eve? Would he badmouth Sam? If that was it, he could relax—he'd passed the test.

After she let go of Sam, Eve said, "So, what do you think?" She was pointing down at the living room rug. "Aren't they everything I said that they'd be? They were just *made* for this kind of light."

Will focused his attention on the enormous Persian rug covering the floor. The background color was a sharp yellow, almost gold, like a sunburst, with blasts of red in the center medallion that reminded Will of fire.

"I hate to play favorites, but the Gabbeh in the bedroom is even more magnificent," Eve added. "The blue . . . I swear, it's like you're looking at the deepest Caribbean water."

Sam placed his hand on Eve's waist. Then, turning to Will, he said, "I need to discuss something privately with Evelyn. It should only take a moment. Do you mind if we use your balcony?"

"Why don't you check out the Gabbeh?" Eve said. "After Sam shares his secret surprise with me, we'll come join you."

"You don't mind, do you, Young Will?" Sam asked. "That I'm going to steal Eve for a moment?"

This seemed uncharacteristic of Sam, asking Will's permission to talk to Eve. He studied Sam's face for some explanation of what was actually going on here: first Sam had urgent news to tell Will but didn't share it; now he had some tidbit that required a private discussion with Eve on his balcony.

"No, I don't mind," Will said.

Sam smiled, bowed slightly. "Shall we, my dear?" he said to Eve.

Sam opened the French doors, then gestured for Eve to precede him outside. Sam closed the door behind him. From the other side of the glass, he smiled at Will. The two men held each other's gazes for a moment, and then Will thought that Sam nodded—although why, exactly, he had no idea.

Part of Will wanted to rush toward the balcony, but he couldn't imagine what he'd say once he was there, other than to reveal the previous evening's events and declare that nothing had happened between him and Eve. But as far as he knew, Sam had no idea that anything other than furniture shopping had occurred.

So Will turned away from the balcony and took a step toward the bedroom.

That's when he heard a loud bang, not dissimilar to the sound of a car backfiring. It was followed a moment later by the unmistakable sound of something heavy hitting the terrace floor.

Everything thereafter happened in a flash. Will reversed course, running toward the terrace. When he made it outside, he blinked hard, trying to make sense of the image before him.

Sam was on the ground, his left arm bent behind him at an unnatural angle, the pocket square that was always folded so perfectly spilling out in disarray. Distantly, Will noted that the handkerchief had red polka dots, which seemed as odd to Will as Sam's state, because Sam had told him to wear only solid colors.

Eve stood over him, gripping a gun with smoke leaving its barrel.

"What happened?" Will said, his mouth dry as sand.

She didn't say anything, but she didn't have to. The answer was self-evident: Eve had shot Sam.

Will dropped to the floor, turning Sam's face toward him. Blood was pooling out of Sam's head, collecting on the cement, and running back toward the apartment.

Oh god, he thought, *they're not polka dots. Splatters of blood.*

As he rose, his sight line returned to Eve. She was standing beside him in her flowing linen. There wasn't a tear in her eyes. In fact, she looked as if she was in a trance. He realized that must be the face of shock, and wondered if he wore that mask too.

"He was trying to throw me off the balcony. And then—"

She didn't finish the sentence. Instead, she threw her arms around him, sobbing into his cheek. They remained like that for a good thirty seconds, until Will ended the embrace and pulled out his phone.

"What are you doing?" she asked. He'd expected her to be crying, but her eyes were still dry.

"Calling the police."

She grabbed the phone out of his hands. "No. Calling the police would be suicide. For both of us. Sam has lots of dangerous friends. If they find out that I killed him, at your house, they'll kill us both."

SUMMER

25.

Each morning, Will awoke wondering if this would be the day. The day he'd learn that Sam's body had been found. The day he was arrested.

But those things didn't happen. Instead, the weeks moved on as they would have had Sam been alive. Will's furniture arrived. He moved into his new apartment. He and Gwen discussed when she would move in too.

Even his work was unaffected by the death of his most important client. Sam had bestowed Will with complete discretion to trade his accounts, which meant that Will was able to buy and sell without regard to the fact that his client would never see a penny of the returns—or lament a dime of loss. At the end of the month, Maeve Grant generated account statements and then electronically transmitted them to the email address Sam had provided. The commissions earned were deposited into Will's account, just as they would have been if Sam were alive.

June 27 began no differently from any of the other days since Sam's death. Will woke up, showered, put on one of his Mario-crafted bespoke suits, and headed to work. He arrived at his usual time and looked up at the Tenth Floor aquarium from the Maeve Grant lobby. He was seated behind his desk by seven, busy examining the overnight trading results on the Nikkei and the trends on the Footsie. All indicators pointed to a strong day in the US markets.

At 10:30, his secretary poked her head into his office.

His office. The thought still made him uneasy. Will would never stop thinking of this space as Wolfe's office. Yet, the day after Wolfe's funeral, Mattismo had told Will that Wolfe's office was now his, along with 25 percent of his former boss's book of business. Maria Murano, Wolfe's assistant, was part of the deal as well.

Will had reflexively declined. It seemed ghoulish. For Mattismo, however, death was simply another line item in the big ledger of life.

"It's not a haunted house, Matthews," Mattismo said. "It's prime New York City commercial real estate. And I'll tell you one thing: we're not turning it into a shrine to Robert Wolfe. That's for damn sure. The way it works is that the windows are given out based on AUM, and you're next in line. You're welcome to pass; then it'll go to Hurley, or maybe Sinclair. And believe me, neither one of them is going to hesitate to take it. That means you'll wait until some other swinging dick dies and hope that you've got the top AUM *when* they kick, or you'll be in cubeland for . . . anybody's guess how fucking long."

"Mr. Matthews, Mr. Billingham asked for you to meet him in his office," Maria said. Then she added, "Right away. He told me to say that."

Will smiled, as if Maeve Grant's general counsel requesting an immediate audience with him was of no moment. In point of fact, nothing could be more disconcerting.

It wasn't until he was in the elevator on the way to the Maeve Grant C-suite that Will was able to assuage his greatest fear: this couldn't be about Sam's death, or Robert Wolfe's either, for that matter. If Sam's body had been found, or even if someone had connected Wolfe's murder to Sam, it wouldn't fall under the jurisdiction of the firm's general counsel. Instead, the NYPD would have come to his apartment—or waltzed right into his office and hauled him off the floor in handcuffs.

Which meant that this was about financial crimes. Not the most silver of linings, of course, but any port in a storm.

The forty-fifth floor occupied the same footprint as all the others, but it contained only enough offices for the CEO, the COO, the CFO, and the GC, and each of their two or three top lieutenants. A few administrative assistants filled the interior space, but huge amounts of square footage were devoted to reception areas, which gave the floor the feel of a hotel conference center.

Billingham's secretary, an older woman with thick glasses who couldn't have weighed a hundred pounds soaking wet, led Will into the general counsel's office. When he stepped inside, he was surprised by the number of attendees.

Seated on one side of a conference room table were six people. Will recognized Billingham from his photograph in the firm's annual report, although he hadn't ever met the man before. To Billingham's left was the head of human resources. Will had met her back when he joined the firm, when he'd needed help completing some insurance forms. The man to her left, and the three people on Billingham's right, were complete strangers.

Will took the middle seat on the opposite side of the table. He offered a weak smile, but his insides were churning.

"Thank you for coming up on such short notice." Billingham sounded almost as if Will had a choice. "I'm Jack Billingham, general counsel of Maeve Grant."

The only African American on the Maeve Grant board of directors, Billingham looked to be about seventy. His scalp was shaved smooth, glistening at the crown. His strong chin and bright eyes were those of a handsome man.

"I'm joined by Laura Johnson from HR and Brandon Sherman, who is also in the GC's office," Billingham said, gesturing to the two people on his left. "I've also asked outside counsel to help us with this matter. From left to right are David Bloom, Anne Steiner, and Claire McKeown, all of Cromwell Altman."

Will didn't know if he was supposed to say anything, so he just nodded. Billingham took a sip out of the water bottle in front of him. That's when Bloom began speaking.

"Will, as Jack said, my name is David Bloom. I'm a partner at the law firm of Cromwell Altman. We've been retained by Maeve Grant to do an internal investigation. Before we begin, I need to go over some ground rules. Okay?"

"Okay," Will said, trying his utmost not to sound scared, and doubting he was fooling anyone.

"As I said, we've been retained by the company. That means we're Maeve Grant's lawyers. We're not *your* lawyers. That's important, because while attorney-client privilege applies to this meeting, it is controlled by the company, and not by you. What that means is that Maeve Grant could choose to share every word of what you say here today with whomever they want. Or the company could choose to invoke the privilege, and thereby prevent anyone from finding out what was said here. The point being that it's totally the company's choice, and you have absolutely no say in the matter. Are we clear about that?"

Will resisted the urge to say "crystal." Instead he nodded, but when Bloom didn't respond to the nonverbal assent, Will said, "Yes. I understand."

"Good. So first thing is that we're going to ask you to sign this document that confirms what I just said."

Steiner, the woman seated to Bloom's immediate right, had a piece of paper at the ready. She slid it to Will. Across the top it read in all capital letters: ACKNOWLEDGMENT AND AGREEMENT OF TERMS FOR INTERVIEW OF WILL MATTHEWS.

Will scanned the seven enumerated items, which were so dense with legalese that he doubted he understood more than half of it. But he got the main point: he was giving up every right imaginable by talking now, and Maeve Grant wasn't giving up a thing.

"What happens if I don't sign this? I mean, it says this interview is voluntary. Does that mean I can decline?"

Bloom smiled. "It is voluntary, but Maeve Grant expects each of its employees to cooperate fully with any inquiry. Therefore, your refusal to answer our questions right now would have . . . negative repercussions on your employment status."

In other words, it wasn't voluntary at all. If Will didn't submit to this interview, he'd be fired.

The last of the Cromwell Altman team, the youngest of them, a woman whose name Will no longer remembered, rolled a pen toward him.

"Should I have a lawyer here?" Will asked. "If for no other reason than to balance out my side of the table?" he said with a chuckle, hoping to break the tension at least a little bit. But apparently none of the faces he was looking at found the comment amusing.

Bloom answered for the group. "I can't stop you from walking out of here and calling a lawyer. All I can do is tell you that Maeve Grant would prefer to hear your answers without a filter, and lawyers are often significant barriers to getting the truth. Also, time is of the essence. Maeve Grant is requesting your full and complete cooperation *now*. Not sometime in the future when you retain counsel. So, once again, although you are obviously free to leave and retain a lawyer if you want, the company would view your refusal to answer our questions at this time to be noncooperation."

"Which could have negative repercussions on my employment status," Will said.

"Yes, that's correct," Bloom confirmed, still without even the hint of a smile.

Will took the pen and signed his name. His signature looked shaky, which was a clear indication that he was making a mistake by not shutting this down right now.

26.

Three hours later, Will walked out of Billingham's office, exhausted. As soon as he returned to his own office, he shut the door and called Gwen. He asked her if he could take her to lunch.

She asked him where they should meet, but he told her he'd like to see her office. If she thought that was odd, she didn't say so. Instead, she ended their call by thanking him for such a pleasant surprise.

When Will stepped off the elevator into Taylor Beckett's main reception area, he was greeted by near life-size oil portraits of Ulysses Taylor and Thomas Beckett. Their full beards and bow ties marked them as men of a bygone era, but the rest of the space was strikingly modern: black-and-white photography on the walls, furniture that would have been at home in a boutique SoHo hotel.

Gwen had apparently been given advance notice from lobby security of Will's arrival, because she appeared even before he could tell the receptionist his name. Will's demeanor must not have betrayed how he'd spent the morning, because Gwen didn't seem to realize anything was amiss.

"Mindy," Gwen said to the receptionist, "this is my boyfriend, Will Matthews. He decided to surprise me with a visit and take me to lunch. Isn't that sweet?"

Mindy confirmed that it was indeed sweet of Will, at which point Gwen led Will down the corridor to her office. On the way, they passed a few of the partners' offices. They were about the same size as Will's workspace at Maeve Grant. Finally they came to rest in a much smaller room, not any larger than Will's cube had been.

"This is me," Gwen said. "It's where all the legal magic happens."

The desk was built-in and industrial. A single guest chair was piled high with binders.

Will shut the door behind them. He reached into his pocket and pulled out a wad of cash. "Here," he said, handing Gwen a one-dollar bill.

Gwen looked at the bill like it was some type of dead bug. "No offense, Will, but I'm not a hooker. If I were, it would take a lot more than a dollar."

He placed the buck on her desk. "I want to retain your legal services, and this makes it legit."

She laughed. "Who told you that?"

"Is that not the way it works?"

"On television, maybe. In real life, not so much. You can keep your dollar and retain me for free. Technically, there needs to be something in writing, but that can be signed later."

Will didn't fully understand whether this meant that Gwen was now his lawyer. "I need to tell you some stuff, and . . . I want it to be within the attorney-client whatchamacallit."

She rolled her eyes, clearly still not appreciating the urgency behind Will's presence. "This is serious, Gwen," he finally said.

"Okay. Poof," she said, making a magician's gesture with her hands. "We are now covered by the attorney-client whatchamacallit. Move the binders to the floor, sit down, and tell me what's so serious."

He did as directed. Once they were both in position—Will in the guest chair, Gwen behind her desk—he began.

"I just came from a meeting with the firm's general counsel, a guy named Jack Billingham. They called me up there this morning. When I got there, in addition to Billingham, there was someone else from the

GC's office, another lawyer, this woman from HR, and some people from an outside law firm."

Gwen now appreciated that this was no laughing matter. Her expression clearly indicated she was concerned.

"What law firm?"

"Cromwell Altman."

Gwen scrunched her nose slightly.

"Is that bad?" Will asked.

"It's not good. It means that Maeve Grant is making a financial investment in the investigation. They wouldn't be so quick to do that if they didn't have some concerns. Do you remember the lead lawyer's name?"

"David Bloom."

This time she nodded. "He's a former Assistant US Attorney. Which most likely means there's some problem that Maeve Grant thinks might be criminal." Then, as if it was an afterthought: "Did they fire you?"

"No . . . at least I don't think so. They didn't take my ID card or anything."

"I think you'd know if you'd been fired."

"I was in a daze for much of the meeting, to be honest. But I don't think they fired me."

Gwen reached for a legal pad near the corner of her desk. "The thing we need to do now is make as complete a record as possible about what they said to you and what you said to them," she said in an all-business tone.

"Mainly it was about how Sam earned the money he invested with me." She scrunched up her nose again, prompting Will to ask, "What?"

"It means they're looking at money-laundering issues. What did you tell them about the source of funds?"

"That I understood Sam had varied business interests, mainly having to do with private equity funds across various sectors. I told them I knew he also had significant real estate holdings, but I wasn't involved in that. I also told them that the payments always came in by wire, and that I vetted them through the Cage. Nobody in Compliance raised any concerns with me, and so I thought it was all good."

"Did they show you any documents?"

"About a million of them. The new-account forms for every account I opened. The incorporation docs for each of the shelf companies. The wire transfers for the deposits."

"And what did they ask about them?"

"With the wires, did I know where the money came from? I told them that I read the wire confirms, but beyond that, I didn't know. Then they'd ask if I knew how the money was earned. I said no. With the companies, did I know who was behind each one? I said that I knew who was on the reported forms. Then they asked if I knew whether this or that company was a subsidiary of another company. I said not offhand, but if it was listed that way on the form, then I did know. That kind of thing."

Gwen nodded along, but the grimness of her expression made clear to Will that this was as bad as he thought. He could only imagine how her face would look if she knew that money laundering was the least of his worries at the moment.

"Did they go through the spiel about them not being your lawyers?"

"Yes. And how I'd be fired if I didn't cooperate. Or if I wanted to retain my own lawyer. They actually made me sign something that said that. And they were pretty clear that I shouldn't discuss what they mentioned with anyone. That if I did, they'd fire me. Can I ask a stupid question?"

"Sure."

"I know that money laundering is taking illegally obtained money and washing it so that people can't tell that it was illegally obtained. I just don't know how I was doing that by what I did for Sam. I thought you did it by buying a cash business and funneling money through it.

Like in *Breaking Bad*. He did it with a car wash. And in *The Wire* it was a photocopy place."

"Those are old-school ways. There's a limit to how much you can launder through a small, all-cash business. If you need to clean tens of millions of dollars, you do it through related-party transactions."

"What does that mean?"

"I had a money-laundering case last year. The way it was done there—*allegedly*—and I cannot stress the *allegedly* enough because this guy is still a client of Taylor Beckett—was that my client owned all these companies and real estate and art and other stuff, and he was working in tandem with another guy.

"They would sell stuff back and forth to each other at inflated prices. So let's say my client has this town house worth four million. He'd sell it to his buddy for eight million. So now my client has a four-million-dollar gain. He ends up paying capital gains tax at fifteen percent on that, but he doesn't care because that's less than a million bucks, and he probably has offsetting losses anyway to avoid the tax. The important point is that he now has eight million in cash.

"When someone—a bank, for example—asks, 'What's the source of those funds?' he says, 'I sold my town house.' And then my client returns the favor and launders the buddy's funds. *Allegedly.* So the buddy sells my client his Picasso—a piece he'd bought for seven million—but my client pays twenty million for it. And they can do that all day long. The buddy might even sell the same Picasso back to my client for thirty million the next year and launder another ten million that way."

What Gwen described fit in with the trading he'd been doing for Sam—moving stocks in closely held corporations with no public trading price from one LLC to another. Will had assumed that the price being paid was fair market value, and that the contra-party was a bona fide buyer or seller. He now saw that neither assumption was probably correct. For all he knew, Sam controlled both the buying and the selling LLC in every transaction.

"Sam might have been doing that with me," Will said. "I never second-guessed the value of the things he bought and sold in his accounts. A lot of it was illiquid positions in private equity funds."

"Even if that's what he was doing, for you to be guilty of aiding and abetting, you'd have to have known that's what was going on. Intent is very difficult to prove. After all, high-net-worth people trading illiquid positions is a big part of Maeve Grant's business. It doesn't always mean criminal activity."

Will took a moment of comfort from Gwen's defense, but that was all it took for him to realize that there was a gaping hole in it. "Damn. What about my apartment?"

"What about it?"

Will's heart was racing. "I'm such an idiot. After the ten million Maeve Grant loan came in, I wired it to Sam's account. *He* handled everything about the purchase of the apartment. So I don't know if he put the purchase price down as nine million, or something much higher."

"Didn't you sign the sale contract?"

"I only saw the signature pages. The seller was an LLC of some type, but the page I saw didn't list the purchase price."

Gwen considered this for a moment. "If he is laundering money, then I think it's likely that the actual sale contract would reflect that you paid twenty or thirty million. Even if you only transferred ten million to his hedge fund friend, Sam could still report that he received the proceeds of the sale by some other transfer—maybe his hedge fund buddy wired him thirty million on that same day—and that would look like clean money he received from you in a bona fide, arm's-length transaction."

Will felt like he was going to be sick all over Gwen's desk. "I'm so screwed, Gwen."

Gwen's poker face wasn't good enough to disabuse him of the notion that she concurred. He was screwed.

"One step at a time," she said. "Maeve Grant didn't fire you. That means they haven't reached any conclusions yet. But I don't want to sugarcoat things either. I'm certain that this is going to become a law enforcement issue, if it isn't already. So this is a very serious situation."

Needless to say, he understood that only too well. Gwen still didn't understand it nearly enough. She still had no idea that he was likely an accessory after the fact to murder, or at the very least guilty of obstruction of justice by hiding Sam's body.

He wanted to share that piece too, so that they finally wouldn't have this enormous secret between them. He was trying to find the words when she continued in her lawyer voice.

"I'm sure Cromwell Altman told you this, but don't tell Sam anything. In fact, you have to assume that any conversation you have with him or anyone connected to him—and that includes Eve too—is being recorded by the FBI. Come to think of it, that's likely why Sam's been so distant lately. He's either already on the run or he's flipped and is now cooperating with law enforcement."

Will took some solace that these seemed like the two most likely scenarios to Gwen. Of course, that was because she'd believed Will when he told her that the reason they hadn't seen Sam and Eve over the past few months was because Sam had a busy travel schedule.

The FBI, on the other hand, knew that they didn't have Sam in custody. That meant their assumptions would be that he was either on the run or dead.

"There's something else, Gwen," Will finally managed to stammer.

She held up her hand like a traffic cop, directing him to stop. Gwen looked back at the crumpled dollar bill on her desk. "I need to give you the speech that all clients get at the outset of a representation." She waited a beat, as if trying to remember the words. "Now that I've been retained, the privilege means that I cannot be compelled by court process—that means a subpoena—to reveal what you said to me, and I cannot voluntarily offer that information to anyone. Similarly, you cannot be compelled to reveal what you told me. However, under certain circumstances, the attorney-client privilege would not apply, and I would be duty bound to reveal what you tell me to the authorities. Ongoing crimes or threats of violence, for example, may not be protected under the privilege."

He wondered if Gwen said this because she knew that Sam was dead, and that was why she was emphasizing this point. But she couldn't know that. It was like she'd said—just the rote speech all clients are given, a prophylactic measure to ensure that she wouldn't be compromised.

Either way, Will ended up in the same place. He'd already said enough. To tell her that Sam was dead would involve her in the crime of obstruction of justice, which would remain ongoing for as long as Sam couldn't be found.

Will would have to figure this out on his own.

27.

Taylor Beckett had 102 partners. Thirteen were women, which oddly enough placed them high on the list of Big Law firms with gender diversity. Of the baker's dozen who had won the ultimate prize, ten were in "soft" departments, the ones that didn't involve true battle: trust and estates, tax, entertainment, environmental, appeals. Corporate had one female partner, and litigation had two. Among the litigators, it had been twenty-seven years between the elevation of Nancy Stein and Kristina Tiernan's election to the partnership, which had happened just two years before Gwen joined the firm.

While Stein's accomplishments were impressive—ranging from first woman at the firm to argue before the Supreme Court to first woman to chair the litigation department to first woman to receive the ABA award for outstanding achievement—she was hardly a role model for the younger set. She'd never married, and as far as anyone knew, she had no life outside the firm.

On the other hand, Kris, as everyone called Kristina Tiernan, had not only a life outside the firm but a picture-perfect one at that. She was married to an English professor at Columbia who looked like a model, judging by the black-and-white wedding photo she kept on her desk. They had three children under ten years old, two boys and a girl. Although it had happened before Gwen's time, everyone at the firm knew that Kris had been elected to the partnership while she was on her final maternity leave. Some said that she was actually told about the vote while she was in labor, although Gwen assumed that was one of those apocryphal tales that allowed the firm to be on the right side of "gender issues."

"You have a second?" Gwen asked as she leaned her head into Kris's office.

Gwen was already aware that Kris *didn't* have a second. The price to be paid for having it all was that you never had a second. It was more the rule than the exception that Kris emailed her team after midnight.

"Sure, Gwen. What's up?"

Gwen shut the door behind her and took a seat across the desk from Kris. Unlike the associates' offices, which were outfitted with built-ins, the partners decorated their offices with an extremely generous budget. For the most part, they were man caves of one kind or another. Dark and foreboding, with aggressive-looking artwork. Being in Kris's office was like walking out of a superhero movie and into a rom-com. Her furniture was light, and her kids' finger paintings were taped to the walls as the office's only artwork.

"I'm sorry to bother you about this," Gwen said, "but it's a mix of business and personal. I need a reality check."

Kris didn't respond to the preamble other than to nod that the floor remained Gwen's.

"I've been seeing this guy for a few months. He's a wealth manager at Maeve Grant. He's got this big client who, between him and people connected to him, has over the past few months given Will maybe . . . I don't know . . . half a billion dollars, probably."

"Will is your boyfriend?"

"Yeah. Sorry. Will Matthews. Anyway, Will just came to see me. He was hauled into Maeve Grant's general counsel's office and interviewed this morning. Maeve Grant retained David Bloom of Cromwell Altman. Bloom handled most of the interview."

Kris nodded at the invocation of Bloom's name. Gwen assumed Kris knew Bloom the same way she assumed that all movie stars knew each other, as if there were regular meetings of the rising stars at big law firms that they each attended.

"It appears from the questions they were asking that they think this client might have been engaged in money laundering. Will swears to me he didn't know anything about this. Still doesn't, actually."

Gwen had said her piece. She watched Kris thinking it through.

"How long has your boyfriend been at Maeve Grant?"

"Two years, about. He started as a trainee."

"So he's about your age?"

"Yeah."

"And some guy has invested a half a billion dollars with him?"

Gwen knew it didn't sound good. She was silently berating herself for being so stupid as to have ever convinced herself that what made no sense to her actually might be legitimate. "Yes."

"How'd they meet? Your boyfriend and his benefactor."

"At a hockey game."

Kris couldn't hide a soft chuckle. "I take it that the investments are made through shelf companies. Lots and lots of them."

"That's what Will told me. He's a director or officer of some of them. But every penny that comes in, every account that he opens, is approved by the firm's Compliance department."

"They always are, Gwen. Otherwise there'd be nothing to invest, because the money wouldn't be there. And you'd never read about big banks paying hundred-million-dollar fines. Because Compliance would have made sure that they'd never done anything wrong in the first place."

"So you think this is a problem?"

"Well, let's be honest. *You* think it's a problem, or you wouldn't be sitting here. And so, yes, it's a problem. Your boyfriend would not have been summoned to give a command performance to the general counsel of the biggest investment house in the world unless there was a problem. And even a place that prints money, like Maeve Grant, doesn't hire

Cromwell Altman unless *they* think they have a problem." Kris paused, and then provided a small glimmer of hope with her smile. "But there are problems and then there are problems. The question is what kind this one is. Is it a 'You've done nothing wrong, but we don't want to be in this type of business' problem? Or maybe it could be a 'We think you should have known your customer better, but you're a young guy so we'll put a letter in your file' problem. Sliding down the continuum, it could be a 'You're fired' problem, and, of course, worst-case scenario would be that it's a 'You're about to be indicted' problem. Based on what you told me, it's difficult to discern which of those it is. Do you have any thoughts on the matter?"

"I guess I was hoping it was the first and fearing it was the last."

"Yeah," Kris said with a nod. "That's where I'd be if I were you too. But the reality of the situation is that Maeve Grant wouldn't have brought in a former Assistant US Attorney to handle the investigation unless they think they have criminal exposure."

"Should Will retain counsel?"

"I assume that's what he was doing when he came to you. At the very least, that's what you should be saying unless *you* want to be a witness before a grand jury. More than that, I consider our conversation to be within the privilege too. We're discussing your client. Right?"

Lawyers, Gwen thought. *Always finding the loophole.*

"Yes. I told Will that I was acting as his lawyer. Do I have to do a conflict check or anything?"

Gwen hadn't thought this through, not fully anyway. Taylor Beckett had a rigorous procedure for taking on new clients, which involved every partner signing off to make sure that the firm's representation didn't run afoul of conflict-of-interest rules. She hadn't done any of that before she told Will she'd be his lawyer.

"Let's put a pin in that because . . . you won't clear conflicts, Gwen. I'm relatively sure that someone here represents Maeve Grant on something, or wants to someday. I don't see any partner willing to go to

Maeve Grant to seek a waiver because of a junior associate's pro bono representation of her boyfriend."

Of course not. Gwen should have realized this too. The powers that be would be furious with Gwen if they ever found out that she'd prevented the firm from taking on lucrative business in the future.

"Let me ask you this." Kris's shift to a softer, less lawyer-like tone made it clear that she was venturing away from strict legal analysis. "How long have you been dating this guy? Did you say his name was William?"

"Will, yes. Since February."

"Is it serious?"

"I don't know."

Gwen said that entirely for Kris's sake, because she had already intuited where Kris was heading. The truth was that she was more than just serious about Will. She was in love. They were about to move in together. After that, get engaged. Married. Kids to fill that second bedroom.

"Okay. Second question. If one of your friends came to you with a story about her boyfriend like the one you just told me, what advice would you give her?"

Gwen had posed this question to herself the moment Will had left her office.

"To run and not look back."

"And that would be good advice."

28.

Will hadn't been back in his office for more than a minute when Brian appeared at the threshold. "Hey, boss. You got a minute?"

Will knew that Brian used the "boss" moniker facetiously. "Sure. What's going on?"

"While you were out, a Chinese guy called. His last name I guess is pronounced Chin—like on your face—or at least that's what it sounded like he said, because the guy had an accent. He said he was looking for you, and Maria transferred him to me. He's a FOSA."

FOSA—pronounced like it was a word—was the internal designation for the accounts related to Sam. It stood for Friend of Sam Abaddon.

"Okay. I'll call him. Email me his contact info."

"Sure." Brian hesitated. "There's something else, though. The guy said something that was . . . strange."

"Yeah, what was that?"

"After he told me his name and everything, I asked him who referred him, and he said that he was a friend of Sam Abaddon's."

"Nothing strange about that, Brian. Ninety-nine percent of our calls are from FOSAs."

"I know. That wasn't the strange part. Right after he said that, he said, 'Not that that matters anymore.'"

Will tried to maintain an even keel. "What's that supposed to mean?"

"No clue. I was so thrown I didn't even ask him why it didn't matter anymore. But it's strange that he said that, right? I thought maybe . . . I don't actually know what to make of it. Is Sam okay?"

Will didn't respond at first. He was deep in thought, trying to simultaneously stay calm and figure out a way to alleviate Brian's concern.

"Maybe you heard him wrong," Will finally said.

"I guess. But if I did, I'm not sure what he would have been saying that sounds like that." He shrugged. "I just thought you should know. Maybe tell Sam about it."

Will tried to think of what he'd say if Sam were alive. "Yeah. That makes sense. Sam's traveling, but when he gets back, I'll definitely raise it."

———

Will had no idea what time it was in Beijing. Nor did he care.

"Wei," he heard a groggy voice say into the phone from the other side of the planet. Apparently it was sleeping time in Beijing.

"Wei," Will said back, fluent in the Chinese greeting for phone calls, which was pronounced *way*. Then he added, "Hello, is this Mr. Qin?"

"Speaking," Qin said, transitioning into English. His accent was not as heavy as Brian had made it seem.

"Mr. Qin. My name is Will Matthews. I'm a wealth manager at Maeve Grant in New York City. I understand that you called looking for me earlier today and spoke to one of my colleagues. He said that you were a referral from Sam Abaddon."

Will left it at that. He wanted Qin to reveal what he knew.

"Yes. That is correct."

Then silence. Will was going to have to push a little.

"Thank you. I'll be sure to thank Mr. Abaddon for the referral."

Qin's response was a low, guttural laugh. Then he said, "Best of luck to you on that, Mr. Matthews."

"Is there something you find amusing about what I said?"

Qin audibly cleared his throat. "No, Mr. Matthews. It is not amusing at all. Quite tragic, if you ask me. Now, I'm sorry, sir. I must be going, as you have called me in the middle of the night in Beijing. I would suggest, however, that you take good care of yourself."

With that, the line went dead.

———

Will left work on the early side the next day and made it to his apartment's lobby by six. In the elevator, after he'd pressed the button for the penthouse, he decided to visit Eve first.

She opened the door looking surprised, although he assumed she'd looked through the peephole, so she knew that it was him knocking. She was wearing a white terry cloth robe. It showed a bare clavicle, leaving it to Will's imagination whether she had anything on underneath.

"I need to talk to you."

He could see in her eyes that she understood his urgency. "Of course. Come in."

She moved aside and walked into her home. Will followed a step behind after closing the door.

Eve lived in a one-bedroom apartment with a dining table in the foyer and a galley kitchen hidden behind the entry. The furnishings were eclectic, looking as if they came from flea markets rather than the high-end designer showrooms where she'd taken Will to buy his furniture.

This was one of only a handful of times they'd seen each other since Sam's death. Even living in the same building, they rarely crossed paths. Will assumed that was by design—that Eve, like him, wished no reminder of what they'd done.

Being in such close proximity to Eve transported him back to the day everything had changed. How quickly he'd agreed to help Eve dispose of the body. Her suggestion that they hide Sam in Will's rug—ironically enough, the Gabbeh that was her favorite. How easy it was for them to carry the rug, first to the elevator, and then down to the garage. Eve was smart enough to pull Sam's car keys out of his pocket before encasing him in the rug. She hid in the back of the Mercedes, leaving Will to drive. He wore a Devils cap pulled down. The idea being that if the car was captured on any surveillance cameras, it would look as if Sam were behind the wheel—and alone.

It was also Eve's idea to head east, toward Montauk.

"Sam has a house there," she explained. "It's not at all unusual for him to drive out there. And I know a place on the way where we can bury him."

Will's heart was beating so ferociously as he traversed the Manhattan streets toward the Midtown Tunnel with a dead body in the trunk that he thought it might burst at any moment. That part of the ride alone took nearly an hour, even though it covered less than five miles. During that time, neither of them said a word. Once they reached the highway, Eve broke the silence.

"There was someone else," she said in a somber tone, clearly still in shock from the events of two hours earlier. "A . . . the details don't matter, obviously. I thought I'd been careful, but Sam found out somehow. I knew Sam knew when he had the man killed. Sam made it look like an accident, but I knew that he'd been murdered. That's when I started carrying a gun."

George Kennefick, Will thought. *It has to be.*

Raindrops began hitting the windshield right about the time they passed LaGuardia Airport. "Where are we going?" Will asked.

"The Long Island Pine Barrens. It's a state park another hour or ninety minutes from here. Lots of desolate acres."

They drove in silence for the better part of two hours, the swishing of the wipers and the thumping of the raindrops on the sunroof the only sounds that broke the quiet. At Exit 70, Eve told Will to take the turnoff and follow the signs toward Manorville.

Every few minutes thereafter, she would tell Will when to turn, until they finally arrived in the park. Will turned the headlamps off and pulled the Mercedes onto a gravel path. He looked into the rearview mirror and confirmed that there was no other sign of life in sight. He continued to drive, now at a snail's pace, until Eve told him to stop the car.

In the glove box, Will found a high-end ice scraper. It was better than using his hands, he reasoned. The rain continued unabated. If anything, it was falling even more steadily now. Guided by the car's headlights, Will used the tool to scrape away the topsoil, and then to break up the dirt below. Eve reached her hands into the hole and threw dirt to the side.

It took more than four hours, which made it past midnight when Will thought the hole was deep enough. He had wanted to go four feet, but had barely gone down two.

They unrolled the rug, and Sam fell onto the mud. They both stared at his corpse.

"We should undress him," Eve said. "If he's found, we should make it difficult for them to identify him. His suit has his tailor's name sewn in the label."

The image of Sam facedown and fully clothed in the rain was disturbing enough. Will shuddered to think about how he'd feel seeing the man's naked body in the mud.

"God help us," Will said when the undressing was done.

After depositing Sam's body in the grave, they spent another two hours covering him with the mud they had just dug out. When it was done, the soil was nearly level.

"I wouldn't be able to tell," Eve said, meaning that it was impossible to discern that this part of the Pine Barrens was now a cemetery. "And the rain is actually a lucky break. It's going to last for a few hours more, so it'll hide the tire tracks."

She looked Will up and down. If he looked anything like Eve, he was a mess. Covered head to toe in mud, with clumps in his hair and on his face.

"Here's what I think we should do," she said. "Let's get back in the car and drive out to Montauk. To Sam's place. I know the security code to get in. That will make a record that he was out there, which is good because the car's license plate will show up at the Midtown Tunnel, if anyone checks. We'll leave the car in his garage but throw the rug out someplace on the way. We'll get rid of his clothes someplace else. We can get back to the city by train. Hopefully it'll be like we were never out here."

It took another hour to reach Montauk from there. The rain had picked up intensity throughout the drive, making visibility difficult toward the end. Will took solace that Eve was right—the tire treads would be washed away by morning.

The sun was beginning to rise when Eve pointed to an extremely large stone house at the end of the street. "That's Sam's house. The garage is on the left side."

It was French château architecture, which made it look out of place among the other beachfront homes, most of which were either modernist or Colonial. Will drove up the limestone driveway and then stayed to the left. Eve opened the console separating the front bucket seats and removed a remote control. She pointed it at the garage doors, which caused them to open.

Will rolled the Mercedes into the five-car garage. Inside was another car. Once they were inside, Eve smiled as if to say that the worst part was over. Will tried to smile back, but he didn't succeed. There were still a lot of worst parts to come.

Now, looking at Eve beside him, Will was thrust back to that night in Sam's Montauk home. Like then, he was scared to death. He took solace in her strength.

"Has something happened?" Eve asked.

He hadn't told her about the meeting with Maeve Grant's lawyers—she had nothing to do with Sam's financial transactions, after all. But if anyone knew Sam was dead, she was in danger too.

"I got a call from some guy in China. Actually, he called when I was out, so he was routed to one of my colleagues, and then I called him back. Anyway, he seemed to know about Sam."

Eve visibly stiffened. "What did he say?"

"I said that I would be sure to thank Sam for the referral. He laughed and said, 'Best of luck to you on that.' So then I asked why he thought that was funny, and he said he didn't think it was funny at all. I think the word he used was *tragic*. Then he said that I should be careful, or at least I think that's what he said, right before hanging up."

Now Eve looked frightened. In an odd way, it brought Will some calm. On the money laundering, he was all alone, but with regard to Sam's death, he and Eve were in it together.

"Just because they know he's dead doesn't mean that they know I killed him," Eve said, "or that we buried him."

"I know. But I feel like it's only a matter of time."

"No, you can't think that way. Sam was mixed up with some terrible people."

"You keep saying that, Eve. *Terrible people.* What kind of terrible people?"

"I don't know, Will. Killers. The kind of people you deal with when you're involved in organized crime."

"If he was mixed up with these terrible people, why were you involved with him?"

"I could ask you the same question."

"And my answer would be because I didn't know. But you did."

She looked at him crossly. But then, in a very calm voice, she said, "I didn't know either, Will. At first, anyway. I mean, there were clues.

Something seemed a little off about Sam. The way he didn't provide specifics about his work. All the money that seemed to come from the sky. But it was so much easier to enjoy it all than to question any of it. Sound familiar?"

Will didn't say anything. His situation was nothing like Eve's. He'd had no idea that Sam was a murderer, and she had.

"And then, when the pieces started to fit together even more, I still ignored them because . . . I just couldn't believe it was true. You know how Sam told you that he was from that town near where you grew up? He isn't. He's got a type when it comes to brokers. Girlfriends too, I'm afraid. Young, Midwestern—*hicks*, he'd endearingly call us—folks who believe that dreams really do come true. We were made to order for him."

"But you stayed after you knew. After he killed your lover. I wouldn't have."

"Well, you weren't put to that test, were you? It's easy to say that you would have walked away from everything, but a lot harder to actually do. What would you have told Gwen? Forget Gwen—what would you have told Maeve Grant? The minute you say you think your client might be a criminal, they launch a full-on investigation and, best-case scenario, you're fired. Worst-case scenario, you wind up in jail. The truth is, Will, that if I hadn't killed Sam, you'd still be doing his bidding—and looking the other way when it suited you."

Will didn't answer. He liked to think that he would have walked away after he realized just how deep he was in. But he hadn't told Gwen the full truth. He certainly hadn't told Maeve Grant the truth. Eve was right that it was easy to say but much harder to do.

After all, he was still in it, and was now in deeper than he could have ever imagined.

29.

An all-hands meeting of the Toolan team was rarer than a blue moon. This was only the second one that Gwen could recall, the last one having been when she was assigned to the case three months earlier.

The meeting was held in the Taylor Beckett boardroom, a space rarely entered by associates. It occupied the entire north wall of the fifty-second floor, providing helicopter views of Central Park. Its interior had a table that sat more than a hundred, so that it could accommodate the full partnership the one time a year they met to decide whether to expand their ranks. The Toolan team numbered less than twenty, which made for a lot of empty chairs for today's gathering.

Gwen sat two-thirds of the way down the table, between fellow third-year associate Steph McCarthy and a first-year, Rob Gardner.

"Any idea what's going on?" Gardner whispered to her.

Gwen almost laughed aloud at the thought that she might be in the know about such things. "No, but we'll find out soon enough."

The meeting was called for four o'clock, but it wasn't until ten after that Benjamin Ethan swept in. "Apologies for my tardiness," he said as he made his way to his seat at the head of the table. "Thank you all for coming on such short notice. You'll be reading in the press later today that the prosecution and I have jointly written to Judge Pielmeier to request a trial date as soon as the Court can accommodate. Precisely when that is going to be is anyone's guess, but I think we're likely to be picking a jury no later than three months from today, and it may be as soon as thirty days. Anyone who's been on trial before will tell you that it's nonstop work. And that begins today. We'll give you this weekend to see your loved ones and feed your pets, but don't expect that luxury again until there's a verdict." Ethan stopped and, after perusing the faces of his team, said, "Now, how was that for a pep talk?"

Everyone laughed . . . the way the press corps does when the president makes a joke.

"Last matter. After this meeting, I'm going to meet with the trial team. The rest of you will comprise the war room, and you'll be on call in the office during the trial days. I know that everyone wants to be in court, but I cannot emphasize strongly enough how critical the war room function will be to the overall defense." He waited a beat. "Any questions?"

Gwen looked around the table. No one raised a hand or said a word, even though she knew that they all had the same question: Who had been picked for the trial team?

Ethan smiled. "Good. Okay then, everybody back to work." Then after a beat, he revealed the winners of the trial-team sweepstakes. "Jay, Doug, and Gwen stay behind. Thank you all."

Steph leaned over to whisper in Gwen's ear. "Oh my God," she said, as if Gwen had just won an Oscar.

As the others scurried out of the room, Gwen noticed that there were suddenly a number of empty seats separating her from the rest of the anointed.

"Come on and join the party, Gwen," Kanner said, motioning for her to occupy the chair beside him.

She could feel everyone's eyes on her as she collected her belongings and transferred them and herself six seats toward the table's head. When she sat down, Ethan began speaking again.

"Congratulations to all of you. And I mean that sincerely. It should come as no surprise to any of you that I selected only the best for this trial team. Your reward for being so outstanding is to continue to be so until Jasper Toolan is acquitted. Now, I know that some of you have been on trial teams before, but I also know that no one has been on a trial like this one before. The media attention is going to be like nothing anyone here has ever faced. And that means that you need to comport yourself as if you are on trial too."

Gwen thought Ethan was pouring it on a little thick. After all, she *wasn't* on trial.

"Your conduct now will directly reflect on Jasper," Ethan continued. "Believe me, reporters will be talking to your friends. They'll be checking to see what you post online. They'll be trying to listen to your conversations in the elevators, at restaurants. The less scrupulous ones will be hacking into your email, if they can, and going through your garbage."

Gwen remained stone-faced through this parade of privacy-intrusion possibilities, although she saw a smirk from Doug Eyland, the most senior associate on the case. Ethan must have seen it too, because he said, "You think I'm kidding, but I'm not. Remember when those idiots representing President Trump were quoted because they were talking about the case in a restaurant? Don't think for a second that if you tell something to a friend in 'confidence'"—he actually made air quotes as he said the word—"the *National Enquirer* or TMZ isn't going to offer that friend ten thousand dollars for the story."

Ethan came to a stop. He made eye contact with each member of the trial team.

"So if there is anything, anything at all, about your inclusion on the trial team that would compromise the defense of Jasper Toolan, you need to withdraw from the trial team right now. Understood?"

Not surprisingly, no one said a word. Instead, everyone nodded that they comprehended, Gwen included. As she did, Gwen wondered if anyone was more compromised than she. She could only imagine what would happen if, in the middle of the trial, her boyfriend was arrested for money laundering.

30.

Will woke up the next day and posted a birthday message to Gwen's Facebook page. He had thought he'd be the first one, given that most people didn't set an alarm for 5:30 a.m., but it turned out that she already had three other messages. Two from the night before, albeit after midnight, and one from a guy who lived overseas.

On his night table was the necklace he'd be giving Gwen that night, encased in its blue Tiffany box. Looking at it now, he wondered if she would think that an engagement ring was inside, even though it was clearly larger than a ring box. If it hadn't been for the uncertainty in his life at the moment, Will would have popped the question on her birthday. So, if Gwen was the least bit disappointed that he wasn't proposing, he could remedy that very quickly.

As his first order of business in the morning, Will ran the same Google search he did each day. What was different this time was that he got a hit.

Will blinked hard and checked the source: New York's *Newsday*. The paper of record for Long Island. Then he double-clicked on the article.

The headline read: BODY FOUND IN SHALLOW GRAVE IN PINE BARRENS.

He could feel his heart rate spike, a hammer now pounding in his chest. According to the reporting, two hikers, a married couple with a dog, had discovered the grave. The victim was unidentified.

Will took a moment to collect his thoughts. He tried to think through what was going on. To be in today's news, the body must have been found last night. His mind conjured the image of a morgue, stark white, men and women in lab coats, with serious expressions, wearing goggles, no doubt.

Then his thoughts turned to Sam. Or at least as much of him as the hikers had found. After three months, not much would be left of him. Animals roamed the Pine Barrens. The elements. Sam couldn't be more than bones by now.

Still, they'd conduct forensic test after forensic test. But what could they really discern? His shattered skull would indicate he'd died of a gunshot, and they'd know the caliber of the bullet. Eve told him that she'd gotten the gun from a friend and that it had been unregistered, which meant that linking the murder weapon back to her was not going to happen.

It was doubtful that Sam's fingerprints still existed, but even if they did, they wouldn't match anything in any criminal database. Will knew this for a fact because Maeve Grant had run a background check on Sam when he opened his account, and it would have been red-flagged if he had a criminal record.

Teeth. He'd still have his teeth. But the police would have nothing to match the corpse's teeth against. Dental records were used to confirm identity, not determine it.

Will breathed for the first time since seeing the headline. No amount of forensic testing would reveal that the dead man in the shallow grave was Sam Abaddon.

———

Before leaving for work, Will detoured to Eve's apartment to share the news about Sam. Given that it was only an hour past dawn, he assumed that Eve would be fast asleep. Through the door he could tell the buzzer was loud enough to wake the dead, but he still expected to wait while Eve rose from bed, put something on, and came to the door.

Instead, the door opened while his finger was still on the doorbell.

Eve was fully dressed, clad in a dark suit. He couldn't recall Eve ever wearing anything but a dress, and more often than not it was something very low-cut. In this morning's outfit, she looked as if she were heading to a corner office. Even more unexpected than the fact that she was awake at 6:00 a.m. and dressed like a banker, she was not alone. Sitting at the small dining room table in the foyer was a dark-complexioned man with a full beard, wearing a suit and tie.

"I'm sorry to bother you so early, Eve. But . . . I need to talk to you in private for a minute."

He wondered if she already knew. Little else would cause Will to ask to speak to her privately first thing in the morning other than something to do with Sam. And it had been only the day before when he'd come to tell her about the Chinese guy who knew Sam was dead. Two visits in as many days, especially after so little contact since Sam's death, should have been enough to create a panic. But Eve didn't show a hint of distress. It was true what she'd said on their first meeting: she was indeed the one who kept her head while all others around her were losing theirs.

"This will only be a moment," she said to the man at the table.

Will tried to get a better look at Eve's guest, but as soon as she stepped into the hallway, she closed the door behind her.

"There's an article in the paper today. Two hikers found a body buried in the Pine Barrens," Will said in a hushed tone. "It didn't identify Sam or state a cause of death, but it's got to be him."

Eve received the information without displaying any emotion. Her poker face was so good that Will asked if she had already heard the news.

"I assumed it was only a matter of time before they found his body. But if we're lucky, they're never going to figure out it's Sam. No one even knows he's dead."

Although she hadn't meant it to, the statement cracked Will's sense of security. Someone *did* know Sam was dead.

"The Chinese guy—Qin—knows."

Eve's face became noticeably strained, her jawline tighter.

"That's what should concern us now, Will. Not the police."

31.

Will's conversation with Eve had put him at ease. *Everything is going to be fine,* he told himself as he walked out of his building.

That optimism was short-lived, however. As soon as Will stepped into the street, he saw two men in dark suits exit a late-model black sedan. They both flashed badges as they approached. It had the effect of freezing Will in place, as if his feet had suddenly become stuck in cement.

"Will Matthews?" one of them called out, not quite a question as much as an identification.

Before Will could answer, the two men were upon him. They were each large, in both directions—six foot two and 275 pounds. By standing in front of Will, the men created something of a wall, blocking any hope of escape.

"I'm FBI Special Agent Thomas Benevacz. My partner is Special Agent Ramirez. We'd like to ask you a few questions."

Nothing the man said registered after "FBI."

When his wits returned, Will knew that the right move would be to end this. He could say that Maeve Grant required that any client inquiries go through the appropriate channels, and while he'd love to help, he would lose his job if he violated firm policy. That dodge would have the added benefit of being true. But he saw the next move too. Maeve Grant would tell him that if he didn't cooperate, he'd be fired.

At least by engaging a little longer, he could get a bead on the FBI's area of focus.

"Okay."

"Do you know a man named Samuel Abaddon?" Benevacz asked.

Despite how confident he'd been a moment ago that Sam would remain a John Doe forever, Will's first thought was that the FBI had already identified his body. But he pushed that aside. There was no way that the FBI could have gotten involved that quickly. A dead body found in the Pine Barrens was a matter for local cops.

Which meant that, just like his meeting the previous day with Billingham, the FBI was here about money laundering. Will couldn't believe that his life was at the point where this constituted good news.

"Yes. He's a client," Will said.

"When was the last time you spoke to him?"

He was careful not to show his relief. The FBI thought Sam was alive.

"I don't remember, exactly," Will said.

"So not recently," Ramirez said.

"No. Not recently."

"A week? A month? Several months?" Benevacz again.

"A couple of months, I'd say. Not sure the exact date, to be honest."

"Is that strange? To go a couple of months without speaking to a client?"

"No. He's out of the country. I don't need to speak to him to handle his accounts, because I have discretion in the trading."

"What did you discuss the last time you spoke?"

Will shrugged. "I honestly don't remember."

"No idea, then?" Ramirez followed up.

"I'm assuming it was about a trade."

"Which trade?"

"Like I said, I can't remember if it even was about a trade. That's my . . . speculation. I trade in his accounts every day."

Benevacz said, "You said Mr. Abaddon was out of the country. Where is he?"

"I honestly don't know."

"You're giving us a lot of *honest* answers," Ramirez said, picking up on Will's nervous tic.

"Can I ask you what this is about?"

"You can ask," Ramirez said, making it clear he was the wiseass in the partnership.

"We'd like to talk to Mr. Abaddon," Benevacz said.

"I don't think I'm allowed to give you his cell number, but I can check with my boss to see if that's okay. Or I can—"

Benevacz interrupted him. "Are you aware of anyone who has spoken to Mr. Abaddon in the last . . . let's say month?"

Will froze, pretending to give it some thought. Obviously no one had spoken to Sam in the last month.

"Mr. Matthews, my partner asked you a question. We're still waiting for your *honest* answer," Ramirez said.

"No. I don't know. I'm sorry."

"You're telling us that"—Benevacz looked down at his notes— "Evelyn Devereux hasn't heard from Mr. Abaddon either?"

The answer should have been a simple no. Instead, Will's silence caused Ramirez to once again pounce on the hesitation. "You know Ms. Devereux, don't you?"

"Yes. I know her. I was trying to recall if she'd told me whether or not she'd heard from Sam. I . . . don't remember."

"You were going to say 'honestly' again, weren't you?" Ramirez said with a cocky smile.

That's enough, Will thought. He now knew what this was about, and he wasn't helping himself by talking to them. In fact, he'd probably done significant damage with what little he'd said.

"I want to help you guys, but I really am not allowed to talk to you about a client without first informing my boss. I'm sorry, but I'm probably going to get into trouble for saying as much as I've already said without firm approval. Would you mind if we tabled this for the time being? I'm going to work now. As soon as I get there, I'll tell the proper people that you want to conduct an interview with me. If you give me your card, either I or someone else from Maeve Grant will get back to you."

Ramirez looked to Benevacz, ceding the next move to him. Benevacz reached into his wallet and pulled out a business card.

———

As soon as Will was in the back seat of a cab and had given the driver Maeve Grant's address, he called Eve. With each unanswered ring, Will's panic went into overdrive. When the call went to voice mail, he hung up.

Agents Benevacz and Ramirez must already be there.

———

Maria got up from the secretarial station as soon as she saw Will approach. "Donna Schwartz was looking for you," she said.

"Any idea what about?"

"No. But she asked that you get right back to her."

Will nodded that he would, but first he needed to reach Eve. If the FBI had visited her right after him, they might have left by now. Unless, of course, they had her in custody.

He went into his office, shut the door, and dialed her number. This time Eve answered right away.

"It's Will, Eve. Is everything okay?"

"Yes. Why wouldn't it be?"

Obviously, she hadn't had the pleasure of the company of Agents Benevacz and Rodriguez, after all.

"As soon as I left you this morning, right outside the building, two FBI agents ambushed me. I thought that they had gone straight from questioning me to you. I tried calling you right away, but it went to voice mail."

"I'm sorry to have worried you, Will. I didn't hear the phone."

Will told himself to get a grip. Why hadn't he thought of that as a possibility rather than put himself through the last twenty minutes of imagining Eve in handcuffs? Why would the FBI even be interested in Eve? They were looking into the financial stuff, not investigating Sam's death.

"When it rains, it pours, I guess," Eve said. "What did the FBI want?"

"They wanted to know the last time I'd heard from Sam."

A momentary silence and then: "What did you tell them?"

"I told them what we agreed on. That I hadn't heard from him in a few months."

"Good. Anything else?"

"Yeah. They asked if I knew if anyone else had spoken to him. That's when they mentioned you."

"And?"

"And I kept to the script. Told them that I didn't know whether you had or hadn't."

He decided not to share with Eve that he didn't think the FBI agents had believed him. Instead, he was fixated on why they hadn't gone to see Eve right after questioning him. Even if they didn't think she was involved in the money laundering, they knew her name. They must have thought she might know how to contact Sam.

———

Will's office phone rang an hour later. The caller ID indicated it was from the Cage.

"Hi, Donna," he said. "I know I owe you a call. What's up?"

"We got a request from the account holder over the phone to transfer funds out of a dozen or so accounts under your name. Total AUM . . . $687 million."

That was everything in the FOSA accounts. And the figure was exact enough that whoever was withdrawing it had to have previous knowledge of the account balances.

"Who called you?"

A momentary pause from Schwartz. "Samuel Abaddon."

Sam Abaddon had not climbed out of the morgue and then, as his first order of business back in the world of the living, called Maeve Grant to transfer out nearly three-quarters of a billion dollars.

"Did you verify that it was Abaddon?" he said. "Because he didn't say anything to me about moving his funds. I . . . thought he was pleased with the performance of the portfolio."

Will knew he was saying things he shouldn't be. Admissions that could come back to haunt him later.

"The caller had the security code," Schwartz said, referencing the password that clients are given just in case they can't reach their brokers and need to execute a trade immediately. "I can put a freeze on it if you think it's suspicious."

Will's career was now over. And that meant that Maeve Grant would demand repayment of his loan—$10 million he didn't have. On top of which, the moment the funds left Maeve Grant, the firm would file a SAR—Suspicious Activity Report—with the Department of Justice. That meant if the FBI didn't already realize his role in all this, they would soon enough.

Still, freezing the account solved none of his problems; it only made them significantly worse. Although the funds would stay at Maeve Grant for a while longer, it was only a matter of time before the firm had to let them go. And by requesting the freeze, Will would be admitting that he was suspicious of the withdrawal. That would be in direct contradiction to everything he'd said to the FBI and to Maeve Grant. It might be enough to impute that he was aware of criminal conduct.

"Am I free to wire it out?" Schwartz asked.

After a deep breath, Will said, "Yes."

32.

Will was surprised he was still employed at the end of the day. He had expected Mattismo to receive a ping on his computer the moment the money was transferred out, and that he'd be fired on the spot. But that didn't happen. At market close, he left for the day as if he were still someone with a future, even though he most certainly was not.

He couldn't even wrap his mind around what had happened. The obvious explanation was that someone had taken over Sam's organization, and that person's first order of business had been to fire Will.

As bad as that was, it wasn't what worried Will most. The question that haunted him was whether the funds had been withdrawn because the "new Sam" knew of Will's involvement in Sam's death. If that was what was going on, being fired wouldn't matter in the least. Dead men don't need jobs.

———

Gwen's birthday dinner was at Baby Moon, her favorite restaurant. It was much more understated than the over-the-top expense-account restaurants that Will was frequenting these days. The place was small, twenty tables at most. There was a wood-burning oven in the back, out of which came the thinnest-crust pizza that Will had ever had. Each table had a starched white tablecloth and a single candle burning in a silver holder.

Will asked Angelo, the manager, to seat him even though Gwen had not yet arrived. Once there, Will ordered a very nice bottle of her favorite champagne. Angelo himself attended to filling the two flutes and then placed the bottle in a silver ice bucket beside the table.

Although it was a tall order, Will was determined to put today's events behind him and focus all his mental energy on Gwen. No amount of obsessing was going to make the FBI go away or reveal who'd contacted the Cage today with Sam's password. But if tonight went well, perhaps at least one thing in Will's life wouldn't be a complete and utter disaster.

He arranged the blue Tiffany box atop the white china plate on Gwen's side of the table, placing the card in an unsealed envelope beside it. Looking at it now, Will wondered how on earth he was going to pay his American Express bill when it came due.

"Tiffany's!" Gwen said as she approached the table and saw the box.

Will stood and kissed his girlfriend on the lips. "Happy birthday, sweetheart."

"Do I open the present first or drink the champagne?"

"Neither," he said. "Give me a second just to look at you."

She blushed. "I guess that means the present first."

She reached for the box, slid off the white satin bow, and removed the lid. Then she gasped upon viewing the diamond-and-sapphire pendant inside. It was the reaction the sales clerk at Tiffany's had said he was guaranteed to receive.

"Oh my God. Will . . . It's beautiful."

Gwen removed the necklace from the box and dangled the chain from her fingers. The light danced off the stones, shimmering like the blue at the top of a flame.

Then her eyes caught the key that he'd placed underneath the necklace. "It's time," Will said. "You can keep your place if you'd like, but I think we should make the move-in official."

She smiled at him. "Your apartment doesn't have a key."

He laughed. "It's symbolic. Although, truth be told, there is a key to the elevator, but I couldn't find mine to copy that one, so I just put a random key in the box. I think it's to my old place, actually."

She laughed. "Well, I love both my gifts. Thank you."

"Let me put the necklace on you."

Gwen unclasped the gold chain she was wearing. After putting it in her purse, she handed Will the Tiffany necklace. Leaning over her, he pushed her hair to one side and slipped the necklace around her throat. After locking the clasp, he brushed his lips against the top of her spine and saw the goose bumps rise.

When he returned to his seat, he got a good glimpse of his gift. As he stared, Gwen placed her hand over it, as if concealing it out of modesty.

"Thank you again, Will."

"Not every day you turn twenty-nine."

"That's true. In fact, this is going to be the only one."

Will raised his champagne flute to eye level. "I love you, Gwendolyn Lipton. I'm humbled and grateful to be with you at the start of your twenty-ninth year."

She laughed. "Thirtieth, actually. The first year is zero."

"Right. I should have known that."

"Well, I know you're not very good with numbers . . . I have some very exciting news to share that's not birthday related. You're looking at the newest member of the Jasper Toolan trial team."

Will knew that had been Gwen's professional goal since they'd met. He reflected on the oddness of the timing, wondering whether Gwen had been told about her selection at the same moment he had been informed of the withdrawal of nearly all his AUM, effectively ending his career.

"Amazing, Gwen. And not just for you either. That Jasper Toolan is as good as a free man now."

She laughed. "Let's not get too ahead of ourselves here. I'm just going to be taking notes and pulling documents for the more senior people at the counsel table. But, yeah, I'm really excited about it. I've always admired how you're so passionate about what you do. About everything in your life, really. I like to think that some of that be-like-the-dog philosophy has rubbed off on me. So thank you for that. And for my presents too."

———

When the alarm clock went off the following morning, Will was momentarily confused. He threw his arm onto Gwen's side of the bed—only to have it hit the mattress. She never woke up before him. Lawyer days started at the extremely civilized time of ten. He looked to the bathroom, figuring that was where she was, but the lights were off.

"Gwen?" he called out.

Nothing came back. He rubbed his eyes, hoping that they'd adjust quickly to the breaking daylight. When they did, he wished that they hadn't.

Dangling from the table lamp on the nightstand was her sapphire-and-diamond Tiffany pendant. Beneath it was the key.

Will rolled over to the table, assuming there must be a note accompanying the returned gifts. But there wasn't.

He reached for his phone. Before he could ask Siri to call Gwen, he saw her text.

I know that breaking up by text is the coward's way. I'm sorry. I just couldn't work up the courage to tell you. I didn't want to ruin the evening, which was truly lovely. And for that I thank you. I also thank you for the last four months. I've loved every minute of it and . . . I love you too, Will. I truly do. I'm sorry. I wish only good things for you. G

She didn't cite a reason. The lawyer in Gwen, careful not to leave a paper trail. But she didn't have to document why she'd ended it. There was only one explanation that made sense: Gwen was running away. From him. From what she saw as his future. A future she was smart enough not to want any part of.

He could hardly blame her. He wished running away from himself were an option for him too.

———

Will stayed in bed the rest of the weekend. He emerged only to eat some cold cereal for lunch, and then to help himself to another bowl for dinner.

He resisted the urge to call Gwen and ask for another chance. To promise that her fears wouldn't come true.

But he couldn't say that. At least not honestly. Not while Sam Abaddon's body sat marked John Doe in a morgue in a drawer. Not while the FBI wanted to know the last time Will had spoken to him. Not while someone close to Sam was withdrawing hundreds of millions of dollars from Maeve Grant. Not while the NYPD was still investigating Robert Wolfe's death.

Will wasn't the kind of man who talked to his father aloud. He'd been so young when his father passed that he couldn't even remember what the man looked like from his own memories. Instead, when he thought of his father, the image that came to mind was one depicted in a photo that had sat on the piano in his home in Cheboygan. In it, his father was wearing a white, short-sleeved button-down shirt and skinny black tie, as if he were a 1960s NASA employee, even though the picture was likely snapped in the late 1980s. Will didn't even know what occasion would have had his father wearing a tie, which he'd rarely done.

Nonetheless, at this moment, when his life was caving in on him, Will was overwhelmed with the need for paternal advice. He ventured out onto the terrace, as if being outdoors would improve the connection to his father. All that did, however, was bring his sins to the fore.

He was standing almost precisely on the spot where Sam Abaddon died. He had scrubbed the blood out of the cement thoroughly with bleach—on more than one occasion—but he was certain he could still see its outline, even though he repeatedly told himself that it was all in his imagination.

"Aren't you proud of me, Dad?" Will said with a chuckle. "I obviously didn't take to heart the life lessons you imparted about what truly mattered. Do me a favor, will you? If it's at all possible, try to shield Mom from what I've done. I . . ."

And with that, Will began to sob.

33.

Gwen couldn't recall the last time she had felt so alone. As if she was starving and at the same time was sick to her stomach.

It was a far different sensation from when she'd ended things with Peter. Then she'd held the self-righteous moral high ground. "How *could* you?" she kept yelling at him, and there was really nothing for him to say, which was probably why she kept yelling it at him.

But Will had never been anything but a loving and supportive partner. What made matters even worse was that a part of her felt she shared some of the blame for Will's predicament. She knew that a shrink would tell her that Will made his own choices. Yes, he had information that she wasn't privy to, but Gwen had been with Will in real time as his relationship with Sam progressed. She hadn't raised a red flag with Will—not when Sam made his initial deposit, not when the *Pretty Woman* shopping spree occurred, not when he entrusted Will to manage hundreds of millions of dollars. No, she did not say anything until she learned how Sam had engineered the purchase of Will's apartment. And even then, she wasn't Paul Revere, shouting from the rooftops about the coming danger. Instead, she had accepted Will's explanation at face value, putting aside the voice in her head that told her that everything was not as it seemed.

One of the things that Gwen loved about Will was that he was such a romantic, and at a time when that type of unbridled belief that good things would happen to those who worked hard seemed not only quaint, but downright mad. He believed that fate had touched him at that hockey game and was rewarding him for the hard work he'd put in every second of every day until that moment.

The cruelest blow of all was that the cynics were proven right. Will's dedication and perseverance hadn't paved the way to success. Instead, his dreaming had blinded him to the cold reality that dreams *don't* just come true, and there is a Sam Abaddon around the corner, lying in wait for anyone who thinks otherwise.

Sadly, that wasn't even the cruelest part, after all. It was that Gwen, knowing that Will was pure of heart, cut him loose anyway. As much as she wanted to be one of the romantics, she had proven herself to be a cynic too, in the end.

———

Gwen would have preferred to wallow in self-pity, but she had a 10:00 a.m. with Jasper Toolan. So she pulled herself out of bed, showered, and within the hour was sitting in a conference room at Taylor Beckett, awaiting her client's arrival.

Toolan had been granted his own building pass and key card, so Gwen was not provided any warning that he had arrived; he simply opened the conference room door. It was the first time she'd be seeing him in the flesh. The image she had in her mind was one from his Wikipedia page, which she'd nearly committed to memory, but in the photograph Toolan was dressed in formal wear, most likely at an awards ceremony or premiere. Today he was in jeans and black suede loafers, a black collared sweater, probably cashmere, and a sports jacket of almost the exact same hue, likely also cashmere. His hair was long and shaggy, but not quite touching his shoulders, and his beard was at three-day-stubble length.

In other words, he looked exactly like an A-list director suspected of murder meeting his attorney on a Saturday morning. The one part of the picture that didn't exactly mesh was that he was holding a shopping bag.

"My mother taught me never to come to any meeting without food, so I brought us some breakfast and coffee. I didn't know how you took yours, so I also have some milk and assorted sweeteners."

Gwen had assumed that Jasper would live up to his reputation as a charmer. Although he was out of her age range—fifty, at least according to Wikipedia—he was certainly handsome, and there was a confidence in his bearing that she knew drew people in.

She came to her feet and extended her hand. "Thank you for breakfast, but you didn't have to. We can order in food in the future."

"I figure I'm paying for it either way, so might as well get out from under the delivery fee and tip."

Gwen smiled. She was sure he knew that the delivery fee and tip might have saved him ten dollars at most, and his quip, plus the time he was taking to arrange the breakfast pastries in an appetizing way, would cost him seventy-five in billable lawyer time.

Gwen accepted a coffee with milk, no sugar, but declined the pastry. Meeting clients was a little like being on a first date; it was best if they didn't see you eat.

"Thanks for coming in on a Saturday, Mr. Toolan."

"Jasper, please. And may I call you Gwen?"

"Of course. Thank you for coming in on a Saturday, *Jasper*. Benjamin thought it was best if we did this on weekends to eliminate any rubbernecking."

"One of the perks of being unemployed is that every day is a weekend for me," Toolan said. "So I should be thanking *you* for coming in on a Saturday."

"My pleasure. Let's start, shall we? Benjamin told me that my assignment was to go over with you the testimony that you would give, if you testify."

"Not *if*. *When*," Toolan said.

Gwen hadn't ever worked on a trial team before, but she knew from other people's war stories that clients always wanted to testify. And generally speaking, that was good defense strategy too. There was no better way for the defense to put on its case than by letting the defendant give it straight to the jury.

"That's why I'm here," she said. "To prep you for testimony. I thought it was best to start on the day that your wife died. You should use all of your professional skills to paint the fullest picture of that day. No detail is too small. We'll hone the story and cut what seems superfluous, but it's important that the jury feel like they're in that room with you and your wife."

Gwen usually took copious notes in meetings, but it often meant that she wasn't truly present, acting more like a scrivener than a lawyer. Of course, that usually didn't matter because there was always someone more senior present. Today, however, she was the senior lawyer in the room.

"Where to begin . . ." Toolan said, largely to himself. "I had just come back from location. It was six months in Morocco. I had never been so happy in my life. Paradise. Truly. And the moment I walked into my house and saw Jennifer, I . . . just knew I couldn't go back to my old life again."

He broke from the narrative. At first Gwen thought he might cry, but that turned out not to be it at all. Instead, he focused on her with much greater intensity than he had just a moment before.

"Can I ask you a question, Gwen?"

"Okay . . ." she said tentatively, already having the sense that it would be something personal.

"Have you ever been in love? I mean, really in love?"

"Yes," she said, and left it at that.

"So imagine, if you would, the best moment of that relationship. The peak feeling of being in love." He paused a beat, as if he was conjuring it in his own mind. "Do you have it?"

"I do," Gwen said, thinking about just last night.

"Imagine that feeling, and then imagine what it would feel like to never feel it again."

Gwen didn't have to imagine. She was living it—right now.

"That's why I decided I had to tell Jennifer. I could have just remained silent and kept on with my life. Except . . . and you know this if you've truly been in love . . . I couldn't do that. I had to be with Hannah. It was a matter of survival for me. Nothing less than that. And that meant I had to tell Jennifer that I was in love with another woman, that I was going to leave her to be with Hannah. I couldn't wait. I had to do it *that second*."

He was good. Gwen had to give him that. The man could tell a story and make you hang on the words. A jury would eat this up.

"So I told her."

"What, to the best of your recollection, did you say?"

"I said, 'Jennifer, I have something very difficult to tell you. And I'm very, very sorry. While I was on location, I fell in love with Hannah, and I need to be with her.'"

He stopped and wiped his eyes. Gwen made a mental note to tell him not to do that in the future. A little too over the top.

"Go on," she prompted.

"I told her that I wanted a divorce. And I remember saying that she could have whatever she wanted—the house, of course. And I'd provide for her, so that wouldn't be an issue. I didn't want us at each other's throats. I said, 'I'll give you whatever you want, and I won't fight you.'" He again made eye contact with Gwen. "I didn't care about the money, or anything other than being with Hannah. I don't think I said that to Jennifer, but I might have."

"Did you mention the movie?"

Toolan looked momentarily confused. Almost as if he wasn't certain what movie Gwen was referencing.

"Oh, *Beautiful Agony*. No. I know that there's speculation that Jennifer would have held up distribution in a divorce, but I didn't even care about that. I mean, it's a movie. It's not the cure for cancer. What difference does it make if it comes out this year or next? Or never?"

"And then?" Gwen said.

"And then, it all happened . . . at first in regular time, then in slow motion, and then all at once. Jennifer didn't respond to what I'd just said, or at least I don't remember anything she said, but she walked over to the closet. I couldn't see what she was doing, but the last thing I would have imagined was that she was getting a gun. I had a permit for guns, and actually had a small collection. Occupational hazard of being involved in so many shoot-'em-up movies from when I started out directing. But I wouldn't have thought that Jennifer even knew the guns were there. Also, I was kind of emotional. I had just had this epiphany about Hannah and had unburdened myself to Jennifer. I was thinking about how I was going to leave the house right then and jump on the next flight to LAX and ask Hannah to marry me. I don't think it even registered with me that Jennifer didn't seem upset. She hadn't screamed or cursed or said anything. That should have been a warning to me that she wasn't responding in a rational way to what I'd just told her. But I was . . . I know this sounds bad, and we'll need to figure out a better way for me to say it at trial, but I was just thinking about myself at that point."

Gwen was hanging on his every word. "And then?"

"That's when she turned from the closet. She had the gun, and she was pointing it at me. This is the part where time, I swear, literally stopped. I'm staring at the barrel of the gun, and I'm in disbelief. Not even a second ago, I'm thinking about my life with Hannah and I'm deliriously happy. Now I think I'm about to be murdered. The one thing I do remember thinking about quite vividly at this moment, and again, you and Benjamin will have to tell me if this is something I should say or not, but I remember thinking that if she killed me,

Hannah would never know that I had been willing to give up everything to be with her."

Gwen, of course, knew how the story ended. Still, she wanted him to tell it.

"How long did she have the gun pointed at you?"

"I don't know. It felt like a long time, I'll tell you that. But my guess is it was seconds, at most."

"Did you say anything to her?"

"I don't remember. I really don't. I don't think so. And if I did, it wasn't anything noteworthy. Maybe *Don't*. Or I called out her name. But nothing to try to convince her not to kill me."

Toolan turned slightly, away from Gwen, so he could take in the view. "That's when everything sped up to hyperspeed. She moved the gun so instead of it pointing at me, it was against her temple—I've wondered if that was intentional. You know, temple . . . Hannah Templeton. Then she pulled the trigger."

34.

The moment Will arrived at his office on Monday morning, even before he opened his door, Maria told him that Mattismo was looking for him. Will decided he'd best get it over with immediately, rather than wait for Mattismo to come to him. He made the death march down the corridor to Mattismo's office.

Mattismo's assistant, a woman named Kylie, had just begun working at Maeve Grant. She looked a lot like his prior assistant, which was to say that she was twenty-three and pretty in a girl-next-door kind of way. The fact that she was a newbie to Maeve Grant, and to being in Mattismo's employ, meant that she had a bright-eyed look that Will fully expected to vanish in short order.

Even before Will said a word, Kylie reached for the phone. "He's here." Then a moment later, she said to Will, "You can go on in."

He opened the door, expecting to see Mattismo sitting at his desk. Instead, his boss was standing in the center of his office. The furniture had clearly been rearranged for this meeting. Mattismo's two guest chairs were now facing away from his desk, toward the sofa. David Bloom occupied one of the chairs, and the same two women from Cromwell Altman that he'd met before sat on the sofa, notepads at the ready.

"Shut the door and sit down, Will," Bloom said.

The chair beside Bloom was vacant, but Will knew that it was reserved for Mattismo. Will took the seat on the end, which meant that everyone was looking right at him.

Will resisted the urge to ask what this was about. Nothing would be gained by his saying anything. Besides, he already knew what it was about. So he sat in his chair and waited to hear Bloom say it.

At least the wait was short. Small favors.

"I'm going to get right to it," Bloom said. "The firm has decided to terminate your employment. Effective as of right now."

"I know this is disappointing news, Will," Mattismo said. "But I told these guys that you were a professional and there was no need for a big scene with a bunch of security people coming up here. There's one guy waiting outside the door, and he's going to escort you out of the building."

Bloom added, "And, of course, by virtue of your termination, your note becomes immediately due."

Bloom sounded like he expected Will to pull out his wallet and pay the $10 million on the spot. Will stuck to his plan, however, determined not to utter a word in response. An awkward few seconds passed, and then Mattismo stood. This caused Bloom and his flunkies to do likewise. Will stayed put, however, as if he could somehow keep his career if he didn't let the meeting end.

"So, shall we?" Bloom said, gesturing to the door.

Will took a deep breath and considered his options one last time. It didn't take long for him to realize he didn't have any.

As Mattismo had said, a single security guard was standing on the other side of the door. "After you, Mr. Matthews," the guard said.

Will walked to his office, looking straight ahead, trying his best to block out the stares from his coworkers. His peripheral vision caught enough, however. It was a walk of shame. Had he been in handcuffs, it wouldn't have been any less dignified.

Once he was outside, after his escort had turned and reentered the building, Will craned his neck to the sky, peering up at the full height of the Maeve Grant Tower. He knew he'd never be inside again.

———

Eve was sitting on Will's living room sofa. The fact that she had once again entered his home when he wasn't there should have been disconcerting, but after being sacked by Maeve Grant, he found an odd comfort in not being alone.

Still, he had to ask. "What are you doing here?"

"I figured that you might want someone to talk to," she said.

"I don't understand."

"I assumed that you got some bad news at work."

"How'd you know that I was fired?"

"Isn't that the logical assumption when someone suddenly withdraws nearly seven hundred million?"

He looked at her through narrowed eyes. What she'd said didn't make the least bit of sense. *How in the hell does Eve know about the withdrawal?*

"I needed you out of Maeve Grant, Will. Enough time has passed since Sam's death. It's time to get back to work."

It was as if Eve were speaking in a foreign tongue. Not a word of what she'd said made the least bit of sense.

"Haven't you figured it out yet?"

He really hadn't. In fact, he didn't have the first clue what she was talking about.

"I want you to assume Sam's duties. Managing my affairs."

"That's not funny, Eve."

She wasn't smiling. In fact, he couldn't ever recall her looking more serious.

"I don't understand."

"Of course you do, Will."

"I really don't, Eve. And you're kind of scaring me. I'm really not in the mood for it."

Eve smiled now, but it was nothing like the come-hither expressions he'd seen before. This one was more akin to the way Robert Wolfe had sometimes bared his teeth.

"In short, everything you thought Sam was, *I* have always been. *His* money is really *my* money. *His* friends are really *my* friends. *His* business is really *my* business. And it's time for me to get back to work. But before I can, I need a new Sam. And, lucky me, you need a new job."

Could this even remotely be true? That Sam was nothing more than a figurehead? That Eve was the one laundering funds? That she was the one with the dangerous friends?

Will's mind whirred with things he must have missed.

He replayed every scene and was struck by the realization of the role she was playing. It was truly brilliant. There was no better to protect yourself in the criminal underworld than setting someone else up as the head of your organization. Better than having a double or a bodyguard. No one would ever think about killing Eve as long as they assumed Sam was the one in charge and she was little more than arm candy.

Except Sam must have known.

Now Sam's murder made more sense. He hadn't tried to throw her off the balcony in a jealous rage. She hadn't killed him in self-defense. Sam's death was a cold-blooded hit, mob style. Eve likely also killed Kennefick. Not because he was her lover, which he probably wasn't, but over some power struggle or business dispute.

Eve had withdrawn the money from Maeve Grant. She had the pass code. After all, it was her money all along.

Will looked at Eve, as if for the first time. She was still just as beautiful, but now far more dangerous, more evil, than he could have ever imagined. How had he failed to see that in all the times they'd been together?

"No," he said. And then, when he wasn't sure if he'd actually said it aloud or merely imagined himself refusing the offer, in a louder voice he cried, "No!"

She smiled, but now she looked downright sinister. A predator baring her teeth.

"Will, this is not an offer. You don't have any choice in the matter. Unless you think that living in a jail cell for the rest of your life would be preferable to the very luxurious accommodations you have here in the penthouse."

"Why would I be going to jail? All it would take is one phone call from me, and *you'll* be under arrest."

She smiled again, this time actually looking amused. "Come now, Will. Do you think I'd give you that leverage over me?"

He didn't answer, which meant he didn't.

"As you, I'm sure, now are well aware from the FBI's role in all of this, for the past several months, *you* have been engaged in the laundering of hundreds of millions of dollars," she said calmly. "The source of those funds were illegal ventures, the financing of arms deals mostly, but I also have an interest in several heroin operations in Central America."

"I didn't know any of that," Will said, trying to sound defiant.

"You knew that Sam was dead when you agreed not to call the police and to bury him, Will."

"Because you told me that he tried to kill you. You told me that his associates—your associates—would try to kill *me*."

"I don't think the police will believe that story. And, just in case you found a sympathetic ear, I took the liberty of making sure that if they did find Sam's body, and they were ever able to identify him, they'd find the carpet fibers that I very meticulously stuck under his fingernails. Those will tell them that Sam last came in contact with a very expensive Gabbeh rug. A one-of-a-kind, actually." She waited a beat. "The FBI will want to know what happened to that lovely Gabbeh you bought, Will. It was forty thousand dollars, after all. And I took the liberty of insuring it. That way, if it were ruined for some reason and it had to be thrown out, you could have made an insurance claim. Did you do that when we rolled Sam's body in it?"

Will could feel the walls closing in. Eve was more than a step ahead of him. That stood to reason, as she had been planning this for months, but he still couldn't believe he'd been such an idiot.

"What motive would I have to kill him?" Will said. "I owed everything to him."

"Me too," Eve said. "But people do have these business disputes. I'm certain I can convince the FBI that Sam told me that you were demanding a higher cut. Words must have been exchanged, and you shot him. Happens all the time, or at least that's what I'm told. Besides which, Sam's been dead for three months and you haven't missed a beat, have you?"

She was right. If she was willing to say that he had killed Sam, and the evidence supported that, why would anyone believe that he hadn't?

"If they have the rug fiber, why haven't they already figured it out?"

"Oh, Will. Think. I'm sure that the CSI folks know that this dead body out in the Pine Barrens must have come in contact with a fancy yarn whose color came from the type of vegetable dyes used in only certain regions of Iraq, and which dated from before the fall of the Shah."

Will covered his face with his hands, still in disbelief at this turn of events.

He'd always believed that he was a good person. Perhaps not the type who would never bend a rule, but certainly someone who tried his best to do the right thing whenever possible. Even his decision to cover up Sam's death had, at the time, been motivated by the belief that it was the right thing to do under extreme circumstances. In his mind, it was no different from stealing bread to avoid starvation. Calling the police would have resulted in Eve's death at the hands of Sam's criminal associates. He had had no choice.

Of course, he now knew he had been completely wrong. About Eve's peril and much more than that, it turned out. At every turn, what he thought he was seeing had not been real at all. It had been arranged solely for him to witness it. A lavish production for an audience of one.

And yet he could not deny that at least some of the warning signs had been there, in plain sight. Red flags flapping in the wind. And he blew by them without a moment's hesitation. To slow down and take heed would have diverted him from the destination he so desperately wanted to reach. Sam Abaddon had promised to make his dreams come true, and Will's greatest mistake was not his inability to see Eve pulling the strings, or to realize that Sam's murder had been in cold blood, but his belief that his dreams could actually come true.

"It's going to be okay," Eve continued. "You'll see. The two of us will make a great team. Much better than Sam and I, even."

FALL

35.

Will's arrangement with Eve had become as straightforward as it was uniquely strange. He continued to live in his penthouse. She dutifully made the payments to the condo board and provided him with a modest amount of spending money. She even told him that she would repay the Maeve Grant $10 million loan, although she wanted some time to pass before cutting that check, so as to not raise too many suspicions. Will recognized this as just another way for her to have power over him.

Not that she needed it, of course. He was, for all intents and purposes, her prisoner. Even the fact that he was allowed to come and go mattered little—he rarely left the apartment unless it was to perform some task that Eve required.

Not a day went by when he didn't think about running. As far away from New York, and Eve, and his mistakes, as he could get. It was the one time that his lack of family was an advantage. He could be gone in a moment and vanish without anyone missing him.

He wondered if he could do it, disappear into the ether in a way that Eve couldn't find him. Or would he leave some crumb for her to follow? And if Sam's experience was any guide, Eve would not be merciful if she did find him.

But it wasn't fear of what Eve would do to him that kept him there. Rather, it was the threat she'd made to him that day, when she told him who she really was and how he fit in to her plans for the future.

"It's only natural for you to think about a way out from under all of this, Will," she'd said. "But remember: even if you don't value your own life, I know where Gwen lives."

———

That evening's assignment found Will outfitted in the tuxedo Mario had crafted, accompanying Eve to a $50,000-a-table charity function at the Hayden Planetarium. The cause was to raise funds for glioblastoma, a rare form of brain cancer found in children.

The gala took place outside the theater. Guests were free to mingle in the Rose Center for Earth and Space during the cocktail hour, then were ushered to a sit-down meal to hear speeches describing the great strides being made by medical research, followed by an appeal for donations so that more good work could be done. Once the hat had been passed around, Kesha would perform a few songs for the well-heeled crowd.

The guests were each assigned to tables where name cards designated their seating assignments. Will was the titular benefactor of their ten seats, and although buying a table entitled the purchaser to invite the other nine guests with whom he or she would dine, Will had generously donated that right back to the foundation—with the exception of a single ticket in addition to his and Eve's.

"Will Matthews," Will said, extending his hand to the man who pulled up the chair beside him.

"Timothy Paulson," the man said, fingering his name card, which read the same thing.

Timothy Paulson was almost exactly as Will had imagined: in his midtwenties, which made him the youngest person at the event and likely the only person younger than Will, and wearing a tuxedo that Will was certain had been rented for the occasion. The fact that he was wearing it with regular business shoes all but confirmed that conclusion.

The most disturbing aspect of his appearance, however, was that he was obviously thrilled to be there. A night with the rich and powerful of New York City was clearly a rare exception in his worker-bee life.

"So nice of you to support the cause," Will said. "Do you have someone in your life touched by the disease?"

"No," he said. "It's a very good cause, and I'm happy to support it, but I'm here somewhat by happenstance. I'm in wealth management over at Harper Sawyer. They had one ticket available for tonight, offered first come, first served. I'm a big fan of Kesha, so I replied to the email. I never win those things, but I suppose the stars were in alignment this time, because here I am."

"A man of faith who also makes his own luck," Will said. "I like that. I'm that way too. I find that it's rare among people of our generation."

"And how did you come to your ticket . . . Will, is it?"

"Yes. Will Matthews. I purchased the table."

Will saw the switch flip in Timothy's eyes. As if it were a reflex, he sat up straighter, assuming a business-meeting posture.

"If I'm not out of line saying this, I think it's rarer for people of our generation to be able to afford a $50,000 table at a charity event."

Will smiled. "Not out of line at all. Honest. Another attribute I value." He turned to Eve. "My dear, allow me to introduce you to my new friend, Timothy Paulson. Timothy, this is Eve Devereux."

Eve extended her hand. It might as well have been a hook. The moment their fingertips touched, Will knew that Timothy Paulson was a goner.

He imagined it was precisely the thought Sam had at the hockey game. And wondered if Sam had also been dying inside, like he was, at the prospect of luring an unsuspecting idealist into Eve's orbit.

36.

As was the case for *Beautiful Agony*, the *People v. Jasper Toolan* was a Jasper Toolan production in every way. People came to see the star. In both instances, that was Hannah Templeton.

By virtue of her age and gender, Gwen had the most firsthand familiarity with Hannah's work. She had been an avid watcher of *Murder High*, Hannah's star-making television role. Even when Gwen was in college and Hannah's character had supposedly been in her seventh year of high school, *Murder High* had been must-see TV for Gwen.

Then came the rom-coms. Gwen had seen them all, and she doubted that the men on the trial team were really as ignorant of them as they claimed. Given that they all had wives or girlfriends, they must have been dragged to at least one of her films, *The Fabulous Felidia*, if no other, as seemingly everyone had seen that.

There was a hush in the courtroom when the prosecutor called Hannah as her final witness. As the woman of the hour walked down the center aisle toward the witness box, Gwen had the feeling she was watching a bride. For the briefest flicker, she actually felt surprised that everyone in the gallery hadn't stood.

Hannah Templeton looked nothing like the femme fatale that she'd been in *Beautiful Agony* and usually was in real life. Instead, Gwen could almost hear Hannah's stylists saying "rich librarian" to describe her ensemble: cream-colored pants and a dark-blue sweater set. The hair that had launched a thousand teenage copycats was pulled tightly into a simple ponytail. No jewelry other than modest pearl studs. The pièce de résistance? Oversize black-framed glasses that caused Gwen to wonder whether they had any prescription in them at all.

Hannah had ended her relationship with Toolan after his arrest. According to news reports, she was cooperating fully with the prosecution, lest anyone think that she and Toolan had conspired together to kill his wife. Not surprisingly, she had refused to meet with the defense.

It had been Gwen's job to coach Toolan on how to deal with his former lover's testimony. They were aided in the effort by various jury consultants, all of whom were in agreement on the central points. Be respectful, which meant no facial gestures indicating disbelief, such as head-shaking or mouthing "no." A well-placed tear wouldn't hurt when she described their relationship.

When she and Toolan were alone, however, Gwen gave him different instructions. "Be yourself, Jasper. I've spent so much time with you over the last few months, I know that if you just react honestly to what Hannah has to say, the jury will get it."

As it turned out, Hannah wasn't the only one who had dressed up for this big scene. Carolyn Vittorio was also clad in her courtroom best—dark suit, dark shirt, serious hair. She stood behind the podium as she guided her witness through the "on-set sexual affair," which was the term she constantly used.

"Who was the initiator of this on-set sexual affair?" Vittorio asked.

"Definitely Jasper."

"Did you know that he was married at the time?"

"I did, but given the way he pursued me, I assumed that this was his usual MO with his leading ladies."

Gwen felt that punch land. The prosecution was going to try to show that Toolan wasn't actually in love, was nothing more than a philandering husband preying on a young woman. It didn't matter that Toolan had told Gwen in no uncertain terms that he had never before been unfaithful, and that with Hannah he'd felt as if he was no longer in control of his own actions. The prosecution's theory that it had been Toolan who had manipulated Hannah into a relationship and then killed his wife rather than lose his mistress better fit the narrative that most people attributed to the movie business, and to men in general.

"Were you in love with Mr. Toolan, Ms. Templeton?"

She sighed, and then showed a glimpse of the smile that Gwen remembered as the expression Hannah had whenever she solved a case on *Murder High*. Looking right at the jurors, she said, "I can't deny that, at the time, I thought so. I know that's terrible, and I'm so sorry that I let myself get swept up in . . . all of it. But you have to understand, we were spending months on location in Morocco, and I'd never been on set or away from my friends and family for that long. Jasper was my only real connection to other people."

"What about the other people working on the movie?" Vittorio asked.

"The role of Lily was really intense. Nothing like I'd ever done, and to be able to capture that on-screen, Jasper encouraged me to try to feel like she might all the time. I don't think he did it in a malicious way. I'm not saying that at all. He wanted to get my very best performance out of me, which I think he did. That's why Jasper is such a genius. But the collateral consequence of me living 24-7 as this repressed monster was that my costars, not to mention the PAs and other folks on set, really everyone but Jasper, kept their distance. It was the loneliest I'd ever been. I think Jasper saw that. Looking back on it, he used it to gain my trust."

Gwen wanted to provide some comforting gesture to Toolan, but the jury would misconstrue any touch as evidence of another young woman who had fallen under the Great Man's spell. So, like her client, she remained stoic as Hannah spewed her self-serving lies.

"Are you still engaged in a sexual affair with Mr. Toolan?"

"No. Of course not. It ended . . . when the shoot ended, actually. Same day. We packed everything up, I flew home to Los Angeles, and he went back to New York. But in the airport, before we boarded our planes, I told Jasper that I didn't want to be the other woman."

"And what did Mr. Toolan say?"

"That he loved me."

"Did he ever say anything about his wife, Jennifer Toolan?"

"That day, or ever?"

"Let's start with ever."

"Yes, of course. I knew he was married, as I said. He told me that the marriage had been over for a long time, but he'd stayed with her because of the cost of a divorce. That they hadn't had sex in years. That he didn't love her anymore."

Gwen got the distinct impression that Hannah had been told similar things by scores of married men. The way she rattled them off with ease, as if she were reading items from a menu.

"And on that last day?"

"He begged me not to end it. I told him that I just couldn't be with him while he was married, and so he had a choice to make."

"And he made that choice by killing her, didn't he?"

"Objection!" Ethan shouted.

"Sustained," Judge Pielmeier said. "Ms. Vittorio, you know better."

"Apologies, Your Honor," she said, looking anything but sorry.

———

With every other witness, Ethan had shown a sniper's precision, asking only a handful of questions, each one striking at the core of the witness's testimony so as to shake the foundation of what had been sworn to previously. Ethan's very first question to Hannah followed that script.

"Ms. Templeton, I take it that Mr. Toolan never once suggested that he might murder his wife."

"Of course not."

"And in the course of his telling you about his marriage, did he ever mention that his wife suffered from severe depression?"

"I don't know if he said it was severe, but I do recall him saying that she was on medication, yes."

"And did Mr. Toolan also tell you that he was very concerned, given his wife's mental state, about how she would react to the news that he was in love with you?"

"I don't know if he said it like that, but—"

"Let me ask you this, then," Ethan interrupted, a master at keeping control of the witness. "You knew that if Mr. Toolan told his wife that he was in love with you, that would not make her happy, right?"

"No one wants to hear that their husband is in love with another woman."

"And you also knew that Mrs. Toolan had not filed for divorce, correct?"

"Yes. They were still married."

"So you must have presumed that hearing that Mr. Toolan wanted a divorce would be very upsetting to Mrs. Toolan."

"Yes."

"If I understand your testimony, on the day that Mrs. Toolan died, you told Jasper Toolan that if he wanted to continue a relationship with you, he had to ask for a divorce. Is that your sworn testimony, Ms. Templeton?"

She exhaled deeply. "Not exactly. I told him that I couldn't continue a relationship with him while he was married."

"But you also said that you would continue a relationship with him if he were not married, correct? Or at the very least, isn't that what your words suggested?"

"Objection!" Vittorio shouted, seemingly more to break the rhythm than for anything else.

"Basis?" Judge Pielmeier asked, because she also didn't grasp what was wrong with the question.

Vittorio hesitated. "Compound question."

"Rephrase, Mr. Ethan."

"I believe you previously testified that, at the time you were having your discussion at the airport with Mr. Toolan, telling him that you did not want to be the other woman any longer, you believed you were in love with Mr. Toolan, correct?"

"Yes."

"And you wanted to be with him, but only if he wasn't married, correct?"

"But he was married."

"That was not my question, Ms. Templeton. Do you want me to ask the court to have my question read back, or do you remember it?"

"I remember. If Jasper had not been married, we would not have broken up at that time. That's true."

"And you believe that Mr. Toolan knew that too, correct?"

"I told him that his being married was the reason we were breaking up. So he would have assumed that if he were not married, we wouldn't have broken up, yes."

"You wanted Mr. Toolan to ask his wife for a divorce, didn't you?"

"I don't—"

"Come now, Ms. Templeton. You say you were in love. You say you would have stayed together if he wasn't married. Are you really saying that you didn't want him to get a divorce?"

"I . . . I didn't want to be involved with a married man."

"And there are two ways for him to be not married, correct? Mrs. Toolan could die, or he could get divorced. But you never, even for a moment, thought that Mr. Toolan would murder his wife to be with you? Did you?"

"No, of course not," she said, sounding convincing for once.

"That's right. What you *thought*—what you *wanted*—was for Jasper Toolan to walk into his house and tell his wife that he wanted a divorce. Wasn't it?"

Hannah appeared to now realize that Ethan's cross-examination was like quicksand—the more she struggled, the more she went under. It was better for her to just give him what he wanted.

"Yes."

"And you have no idea that this isn't exactly what happened after he left you, correct? That just as you expected, and as you wanted, when he left you, Mr. Toolan went into his house and asked his wife for a divorce so he could be with you. Is that right?"

"I don't know what went on in their house. I wasn't there."

"Right. None of us was there, that's true. But you had just spent months with Mr. Toolan on location. Is it fair to say that you believed you knew him very well?"

"Yes. I thought so."

"Ms. Templeton, you never thought—not in a million years—that Mr. Toolan was going to then kill his wife so that the two of you could be together, right? That thought never entered your mind for a split second. Because if it had, you would have done something to prevent that from happening. Isn't that right?"

"Yes. I never thought that Jasper would hurt his wife."

———

Judge Pielmeier ended the court day as soon as Vittorio rested her case. After the jury left the courtroom, Toolan's face lit up in a broad smile.

"That was amazing," he said to Gwen.

"It was," she agreed. "I think Benjamin completely neutralized Hannah as a witness."

"You want to know what a sap I am, Gwen?" He didn't give her time to respond. "I still love her. Can you believe that? After all this time, after hearing that she doesn't love me anymore, that she thinks I took advantage of her in some way, I am still in love with her."

"I don't think that makes you a sap, Jasper. It makes you a romantic."

He laughed. "You always know the exact right thing to say, Gwen. I take it that's because you're a romantic too."

Even though Gwen had had very limited client contact in her career, she knew that being a lawyer was like being a therapist. It was all about the client, all the time. You didn't bring in your own life, even to make a point. So she smiled but didn't otherwise respond to Toolan's comment. She was saved from having to do so by Ethan's approach to discuss the evening's agenda.

If she had responded, however, Gwen would have told Toolan that she didn't recognize him as a romantic because she was one herself. To the contrary, she was the least romantic person she knew. After all, she'd given up the love of her life because she was afraid it might hurt her career.

She had a flashback of Will's smile.

What is he doing now? Does he ever think about me? All the time, like I think about him? Does he miss me? If he does, is it the way I miss him?

37.

The next day, Will received a call from a blocked number. His heart jumped, but the "Hello, Mr. Matthews?" he heard when he answered was clearly not the voice of the late Sam Abaddon.

"Yes, this is Will Matthews."

"Mr. Matthews, my name is Jessica Shacter. I'm an attorney. I have been asked by Maeve Grant to represent you."

"About what?" Will said.

Jessica laughed. "Yes, I should have made that clearer. Apologies. My specialty is white-collar criminal defense. My understanding from speaking to Maeve Grant's lawyer is that there is a criminal investigation involving some of the accounts you were handling when you were employed by the firm. The firm's lawyers cannot represent you because that would represent a conflict of interest. As a result, it is fairly common procedure for the firm to retain someone like me—at their full expense, I might add—to represent you. I'll go over all of this again when we meet, but the key point is that I'm going to be your lawyer—assuming you agree to retain me, of course—but Maeve Grant will pay my fees."

This time Will laughed. "That sounds like a Maeve Grant type of arrangement. No conflict of interest that way, right?"

"I understand your skepticism. But let me suggest we proceed in this way. Come meet with me. There is some urgency, so I suggest today at two o'clock. My office is right next to Grand Central, at 230 Park Avenue. At that time, we can go over everything."

Will didn't say anything. His silence was not because he was seriously contemplating turning down the offer of free legal counsel, but more to reflect on the urgency Jessica referenced. It could really only mean one thing: he was on the verge of being arrested.

There was a time when Will could not have conceived of anything worse than a federal criminal indictment. But now, being indicted seemed like the least of his worries.

The silence lasted long enough that Jessica said, "Mr. Matthews, are you still there?"

Will shook the thoughts of a bloody death at Eve's hand out of his head. "Yeah, I'm here. Okay. I'll see you at two."

———

The office of Jessica A. Shacter did not appear on the building's directory. Because Will didn't know what floor she was on, he had to ask the security guard. Unfortunately, the guard had no idea who Jessica Shacter was, which didn't exactly inspire Will's confidence. Jessica must not get many visitors, then, which meant that she didn't have many clients.

"Could be the law offices on fourteen," the security guard said with a shrug. "A bunch of lawyers up on that floor."

"Thanks," Will said as he headed for the elevator.

Another directory appeared opposite the elevators on the fourteenth floor. This one had Jessica's name, albeit in a font different from the others, indicating that she was a new occupant of the floor. Hers was one of half a dozen names listed as occupying suite 1401.

He followed the signs around the corridor, but when he finally arrived at suite 1401, the glass doors were locked. There was no receptionist inside. Will pressed the buzzer.

After a minute or so, a young man probably not much more than a year out of college, if that, wearing jeans and a button-down shirt came to the door. Will would have sooner imagined this guy almost anywhere else other than working in a law office.

"What can I do for you?"

"I'm here to see Jessica Shacter," Will said.

"Who?"

"Jessica Shacter. She's a lawyer."

"Okay," the man said, acting as if he didn't believe Will, although Will was not sure which lie the man thought he'd told—that Jessica Shacter worked there, or that she was a lawyer.

The man retreated back behind the glass doors, and Will waited another minute before they opened again, this time by the hand of a woman who looked to be in her early fifties, with large brown eyes and an inviting smile that seemed somewhat unlawyer-like. Will flashed on the thought that Gwen was a lawyer with an even better smile.

"I'm Jessica Shacter. Are you Will Matthews?"

"Yes."

"Nice to meet you, Will. I'm sorry it's under these circumstances, of course. Please follow me. We can talk about everything."

The space Jessica led him through looked about as much like Taylor Beckett as his high school gym resembled Madison Square Garden. The hallway was dark, with a threadbare carpet. The small conference room they entered was an interior space, and empty aside from a nondescript table and six chairs.

"The way I like to begin is to explain the arrangement we're about to enter into. As I'd be the first to admit, it seems a bit unorthodox for the uninitiated," Jessica said once they were seated and he'd declined her offer of something to drink. "For people in my line of work, it's very, very common, but I've never met someone who hears about it for the first time and doesn't think there's got to be something improper about what's happening. So I always think a good place to start is to tell you why it's all totally on the up-and-up. Okay?"

Will nodded. Nothing was okay about any of this, but he was willing to hear his new lawyer out.

"Good. A large part of my practice is serving as what is called *conflict counsel*. What that means is that I'm hired by companies to represent their employees. The reason the company's lawyers can't represent the employee is because there is a conflict of interest, and professional rules prohibit the representation. Now, the obvious question, and I'm sure the one you're just too polite to ask, is—if the company's lawyers can't represent you, how is it that the company can pay for someone else to represent you?"

Will was thinking that very thing. It wasn't good manners that kept him from asking, however. He assumed Jessica would address it on her own.

"That comes down to an issue of trust in me," she said. "I am *your* lawyer. I'm not Maeve Grant's lawyer. I have a professional duty to represent your interests, and your interests alone. I keep your secrets. If Maeve Grant wants to know what we've talked about, I tell them to go to hell. If Maeve Grant wants you to . . . for the sake of argument, take a plea deal, I tell them to go to hell. Or, on the other hand, if they want you to turn down a plea deal, I tell them to go to hell. That—and every other decision—is yours and yours alone to make. And the advice I give you to help you make that decision is rendered solely based on what I think is in your best interest. The bottom line is that the one and only time I don't tell Maeve Grant to go to hell is when they ask me where to send the payment for my services. Then I say, 'Thank you very much,' and give them my wire instructions."

Will considered he'd done well in the lawyer lottery. Jessica not only had an easy way about her, but she could also tell a story and drive home a point. He figured that she must be pretty good in court, while at the same time hoping that he would never have to test that assumption.

"The truth of the matter is that I wasn't really selected by Maeve Grant anyway," she continued. "Cromwell Altman recommended me to Maeve Grant for this assignment. And the reason they did that, at least I like to think this is the reason, is because they know that I'm going to represent you well. To them, that means that I'm not going to do something that will hurt Maeve Grant, because I'm smart enough to know that I can't hurt them without hurting you much worse. Lots of people sitting where you are now don't appreciate that. I know that Maeve Grant fired you. And I know that you owe them ten million bucks, and I'm going to take a wild guess that you don't have it."

Will nodded. He couldn't explain his relationship with Eve to Jessica. Not in a way that wouldn't make her run screaming from the office. Better for her to think that he was like all the other clients she had represented.

"Yeah. That ten million is a problem," he said.

"I've seen it all before, Will. Too many times to count, in fact. And more than enough times to know that what you want more than practically anything else is to throw gasoline all over everything and everybody at Maeve Grant and set it aflame. But believe it or not, they do not want you to go to prison either. Not because they really care about you, of course. That's my job. Not theirs. The reason Maeve Grant doesn't want you to go to prison is because that would be bad publicity for them."

Prison. That was where this was heading. Will could hardly wrap his mind around what that would mean.

"Now, if there was a way that I could get you out from under all of this by turning on Maeve Grant, you need to know that I would do it in a heartbeat. I've done it before as conflict counsel. Maeve Grant knows that I'm not doing my job if I act otherwise. All they ask in that case is that I give them a heads-up, and sometimes I don't even give them that if I think it's not in my client's best interest."

Will had long ceased believing in things that were too good to be true, but he still had to ask. "Is that possible for me? Turning on Maeve Grant to get out from under this?"

"Right now, I don't see it, unfortunately. Not unless you tell me that you were instructed by people above you to engage in the activity at issue. Or you alerted them to the possibility of criminal wrongdoing and they told you to be quiet. I'm assuming that none of that happened, or else you would have told that to the Cromwell Altman lawyers when they interviewed you. Am I right?"

"Maeve Grant's Compliance department approved everything I did. Right up until they fired me."

"I understand, but that's a different defense. If you were going to cooperate against Maeve Grant, you'd have to admit that what you did was wrong—and that you knew it was wrong—and they ordered you to do it anyway. What's often called the Nuremberg defense, so named after the German soldiers in World War II who were accused of war crimes and claimed that they were only following orders. By contrast, I understand you told Cromwell Altman in your interview that you didn't think anything was wrong, and you based that assumption, in part, on the fact that Maeve Grant Compliance and your supervisors didn't raise any concern."

He nodded. That was his defense.

"What crimes do they think I've committed?" he asked.

"I'll tell you what I've been told. But keep in mind that I'm getting this from David Bloom over at Cromwell Altman, and he was relaying what the US Attorney's Office communicated to him, so there's room for confusion because of this game of telephone. On top of that, the US Attorney's Office might have withheld critical information from David, and David might have done the same with me. Anyway, with all those caveats, he told me that the focus of the investigation is your client"— she looked down at her notepad for his name—"Samuel Abaddon. Now, it seems that this Abaddon fellow is something of a mystery to the US Attorney's Office. So much so that they can't even locate him. In fact, Maeve Grant wanted me to find out from you if you had any idea where to find him."

Will considered the question. It was hardly a surprise that would be the first order of business.

"I already told the FBI that I didn't."

"Is that what you're telling me too? Like I just said, I'm not going to share this information with anyone, including Maeve Grant. But I can only do my job if I get the truth from you. Otherwise, you might as well represent yourself. You may not know the law, but at least you know the truth. And I swear to you, that's the more important of the two in terms of keeping your freedom."

Lying to his lawyer right off the bat was not the best approach. On the other hand, admitting he'd already lied to the FBI wasn't much better. And, of course, given that Eve had planted evidence linking him to Sam's murder, the last thing he wanted was for the FBI to learn that the John Doe in the Suffolk County morgue was Sam Abaddon.

"I don't know where he is."

Jessica nodded, but in a way that conveyed she believed there was more to the story than Will was letting on. Will felt a perverse sense of comfort that his lawyer could tell when he was lying to her, as well as some shame that he was lying even to people who were professionally obligated to keep his secrets.

Jessica didn't call him on it, however. Instead she said, "Well, if you *did* know where to find him, that would be a good card to play. In fact, the only path that I can see for you to truly get out of this is to cooperate against Abaddon. So if you come across that information in the future, please be sure to tell me."

Will nodded that he would. Jessica took a moment to read his expression, as if she was trying to memorize his tells, and then went on.

"David Bloom also *said* that Maeve Grant's side of this is strictly financial. Money laundering. But he got the distinct impression the investigation went far beyond that. That's hardly a surprise, though. Money laundering is always the midway point to criminal activity that throws off cash that needs to be laundered in the first place. So, the real Holy Grail for the prosecution is evidence that leads to the crime being committed that generated the dirty money."

"Sam was always pretty cagey with me about how he made his money."

"I don't doubt it. David told me that the Assistant US Attorney wouldn't even tell him what they suspected. But the FBI agents working the matter are out of antiterrorism."

"Antiterrorism," Will said, not so much a question as just repeating the statement to make it seem real.

"FBI agents move around, so it doesn't definitely mean there's a terrorism angle, but that is the safe assumption. Your friend Sam Abaddon was probably either supplying arms to enemies of the United States or, more likely, financing those people so they could buy their own weapons. Either way, some seriously bad stuff."

"Jesus," Will said. "I had no idea."

"I'm sure you didn't. But if you did, my job would be a hell of a lot easier. Like I said, if you help them make a case against Abaddon, you have something to trade, which puts you on track to get a reduced sentence or even an immunity deal. The more you have, the better the deal I can strike. On the other hand, if the FBI thinks you *could* help them but you *aren't*, they'll squeeze you until you do by threatening a very long prison term. And if you don't eventually offer up someone else to serve that term instead? Well, guess what? It's all yours."

Will could barely manage a sigh. "And let me guess. They think that I can give them Sam?"

Jessica nodded. "According to David Bloom, the FBI is convinced you can lead them right to him—and provide enough evidence that they can lock him up and throw away the key."

Will considered his options. Telling Jessica that Sam was dead meant he'd have to explain how Sam died. That would mean involving Eve, which meant that Will would likely be dead soon too.

"I can't," Will said, concluding it was his only way to stay alive. "Sam was just a client."

Jessica frowned. "You can't tell them what you don't know. But in that case, you better buckle up good and tight. This is going to be a very rough ride."

38.

"We only have about twenty minutes, Jasper, so I'm going to have to make this quick," Ethan said.

He was standing, his palms flat on the table. Toolan sat before him, Gwen to his side. The venue for this discussion was the witness holding room, which was not much larger than a walk-in closet with a small round table. It lacked any windows but had two doors: one leading out to the hallway, the other into the courtroom. It was empty now because the defense had only one witness left to call: Jasper Toolan.

"It's my strong advice that we should rest now—and do so without you taking the stand."

Gwen could tell from Toolan's expression that he was not going to be so easily persuaded. He was shaking his head vigorously.

"I need to tell them my side of the story, Benjamin."

"That's my job. During closing argument. And I know this is hard for you to accept, but I can do it much better than you can because I'm not going to be cross-examined about it afterward."

"It's not the same if they hear it from you. You know that."

"I know you want to testify, Jasper. All defendants do. But trials are fluid, and the strategic decisions have to reflect the real-time realities on the ground. Judge Pielmeier let us get in everything we needed about Jennifer's mental state—the medication, the depression diagnosis, the prior suicide attempt. Hell, I even got her doctor to say that he didn't think suicide was out of the question. And you know that Hannah's testimony went better than we dreamed. But everything we've done so far goes away in a heartbeat if you take the stand. The moment you're sworn in, the trial becomes about one thing and one thing only: Do those twelve men and women think *you're* telling the truth?"

"And you don't think they will?" Toolan said, challenge in his voice.

"No. I'm not saying that at all, Jasper. I'm saying there's a risk they won't. Testifying will be difficult and emotional for you. It doesn't matter if everything else has been laid out perfectly for them. If your testimony contains a single lie—even about something relatively insignificant—that lie is like a drop of cyanide in an otherwise-gourmet stew. It'll make the entire dish toxic. And my point is that this is a risk you don't have to take. Think of it this way: You're ahead on points in the last round of a boxing match. You're asking me if you should go for the knockout, and I'm telling you it's too risky. I'm not saying I don't think you can do it; I'm saying why even try?"

The speech seemed to do the trick. At least to the extent that Toolan stopped arguing his case.

"At the end of the day, it's ultimately your choice," Ethan said. "If you insist on it, you can testify. I'm duty bound to let you. But remember that you're paying me a pretty penny to maximize your chances of acquittal, and it is my very strongly held view that you should not take the stand."

Toolan looked over at Gwen, and she offered a confirming nod. Ethan had briefed her on what he was going to say—and reminded her that her job was to support him.

She understood the instructions, but she didn't agree with Ethan's advice. After hours upon hours of rehearsing with Toolan, she firmly believed that what Toolan had told her was true. And as much as she was in awe of Ethan's ability to sway a jury, there was simply no way he could convey that sense of being so hopelessly in love that nothing else mattered but being with that person, which meant that he couldn't sufficiently capture the despair that Jennifer Toolan must have experienced upon hearing her husband confess that another woman was his soul mate.

The knock on the door was so sudden that it startled Gwen. Kanner stuck his head in. "Sorry to interrupt, but Carolyn has an issue she needs to discuss about today's schedule."

Ethan nodded. "Okay. I'll be right out." After Kanner closed the door, Ethan said, "Think about it for a few minutes, Jasper. Talk it through with Gwen. But when I get back, I need an answer. I suspect that's what Carolyn wants to know too."

The moment they were alone, Toolan caught Gwen's eye. "Et tu, Gwen?"

"Yes. I'm sorry, but Benjamin is right. Testifying has too much risk for you."

He smiled. "Well, if I've lost you . . ."

"You haven't *lost* me, Jasper—"

She was about to tell him that it was still his choice, that if he wanted to testify he could. Maybe even say that, deep down, she thought he should. But then she saw a smile come to Toolan's face.

"There's one bright side to my not testifying, at least," he said.

"Aside from being acquitted?"

"Yes. It means that I can stop lying to you," Toolan said.

It was the very last thing that Gwen wanted to hear. In that moment, she realized that she had held on to the belief that he was innocent as much for her sake as his. She desperately needed to be on the right side of justice for once, not just a hired gun helping a wife abuser get away with murder.

Jasper Toolan was now going to take that away.

"Being with Hannah was like nothing I'd even contemplated was possible," Toolan said, almost as if he were delivering a soliloquy to a packed house rather than speaking to Gwen in a cramped room. "I'd be the first to admit that I've had more than my fair share of happiness. But being with Hannah was like nothing I'd ever experienced before.

I thought I knew what being in love was like, but this wasn't remotely comparable. Being with Hannah was . . . a perfect drug high."

"I wouldn't know about that," Gwen said.

Her voice snapped him back to her. A smile curled around his lips. "Trust me, Gwen. It's euphoric. I would have given my life to be with Hannah."

Gwen put aside her normal bedside manner. A murderer didn't deserve it.

"But instead you gave up your wife's. Not really much of a personal sacrifice, was it?"

"I didn't do it for myself. The part I told you about asking for a divorce, not caring about the money? That was all true. I only cared about being with Hannah."

Toolan's expression narrowed. He seemed more thoughtful than Gwen had seen him before.

"You have no idea what goes into a decision to take another life. I suspect that only people who have made that decision have any conception of it, and it's easy to say that you would never do it when you've never had any reason to do it. Don't get me wrong. I'm not saying I should be rewarded for it. But Jennifer would never have let me be with Hannah. Not in a million years. She would have done anything and everything she could to poison Hannah against me. So you see, I really had no choice. It was kill Jennifer or never be with Hannah."

39.

As best Will could tell, Eve presided over a criminal enterprise comprised of a confederation of partners, each engaged in their own operations. Her role was to provide protection and financing, and in return, they kicked back a percentage of their revenue. As far as anyone of them knew, Will Matthews had replaced Sam Abaddon as the Godfather of it all. Each and every one had been told to kiss his ring or suffer the consequences.

Eve had made a point to tell him that they had not missed a beat in the transition. As long as the resources they needed continued to flow, the others in the organization were indifferent to whether their financing and protection were dispensed in the name of Sam Abaddon or Will Matthews.

Will's days were spent mainly in his apartment, which he now equated with a very luxurious prison. Whenever he made that connection, however, he quickly reminded himself that actual prison would be much worse than his self-imposed exile from the world in a Manhattan penthouse. How much worse he wasn't sure, but he was terrified he'd find out soon enough.

More than he wanted them to, his thoughts went to Gwen. What was she doing? Was she happy? Had she forgotten about him? Was there another man in her life?

Hardly a day went by when he didn't think about reaching out to her. But he could never play out the conversation in his head so that, at the end of it, he was happy to have initiated contact. Gwen had ended things because she didn't see her life moving forward with him. With all his complications. And since then, it had only gotten worse. Much, much worse.

At eleven that night, Will heard the familiar knock at his door. By this point, late-night visits were more the rule than the exception. Just like when he was at Maeve Grant, saw a blocked caller ID, and knew it was Sam on the line, these knocks on his door meant Eve was calling.

Tonight she was dressed as if she had attended some sort of function. Her little black dress was slit up the leg, and her high heels made her a good two inches taller than Will. For his part, Will was wearing pajamas.

"Did I wake you?" she asked when he opened the door.

"No," he said coolly.

He had long since stopped acting like he enjoyed these visits. In fact, when he reflected on his life, he couldn't help but note the irony that once upon a time he had thought Robert Wolfe was the worst boss imaginable. But the Wolfe had never threatened to kill him.

Eve made herself at home on his sofa. She looked around the space, a smile coming to her lips.

"You know, I like this place even better than Sam's. His was . . . I don't know . . . too over the top. You know what I mean? Your place has a warmth that I never quite achieved with his. Probably because you have a warmth that he lacked, Will. Plus, I really like having you in such close proximity. Letting Sam live in another building was a mistake that I don't intend to repeat."

Even after two months, Eve's world was still mostly a mystery. She was barely thirty, and yet somehow had achieved the role of criminal mastermind, engaged in money laundering and financing who-knew-what for God-knew-whom. At the same time, she worked behind a straw man—first Sam, if he even had been the first, and now Will. She made sure that they looked the part and lived the life of a Bond villain while she lived in a small apartment, as if her only income derived from interior-decorating work. Will wondered if somewhere Eve had a home that befitted her status—an island compound somewhere in the South Pacific or a mountain retreat in Gstaad. Even in her role as kept woman, she could have played Sam as the kind of sugar daddy who would buy her an expensive apartment. Eve never mentioned money around Will, other than in the context of making more of it. It was as if earning it—illegally, that is—was more important to her than spending it.

As Will sat down on the armchair across from Eve, he wondered if she knew about his meeting today with Jessica Shacter. Was that the reason she was here?

Eve would not be pleased that Maeve Grant had provided him with a lawyer. She undoubtedly would offer to pay for someone else, a lawyer who would report back to her directly about the investigation. And while he still didn't completely trust the arrangement that Jessica Shacter had with Maeve Grant, he was reasonably sure that neither his ex-employer nor his new lawyer had any interest in seeing him dead. He couldn't say as much for Eve.

"So where do things stand with our favorite Kesha fan, Timothy Paulson?" Eve asked.

Will breathed a sigh of relief. Eve must not be following him, or else she would have known that the Midtown office building he'd visited today was not the Harper Sawyer building where Timothy Paulson worked. But perhaps this was Eve's way of lulling him into security. The doorman could have told her that today was one of the rare times Will had left the building.

"I spoke with him today," Will lied. "It'll take a few more meetings, but you'll be able to do business with him."

After the gala at the planetarium, Eve had said that bringing Paulson aboard was a priority. It made sense that Will would have reached out to him the next day to discuss setting up some accounts at Harper Sawyer.

Will considered the irony that Paulson was probably sitting in his cube cold-calling, cursing the fact that Will hadn't yet made contact.

"*We'll* be able to do business with him, Will. You're part of this. It's disconcerting to me when your language doesn't reflect that."

"I didn't mean to imply otherwise, Eve. Is that why you're here? To check on the progress with Paulson?"

"No. The reason I'm here regards another of our mutual friends. Jian-Ying Qin."

It didn't take long for the name to compute. "The guy who called me when I was still at Maeve Grant? The one who knew Sam was dead?"

"The one and the same. He controls quite a bit of our distribution in the Far East. When he was told about the change of leadership at the top, from Sam to you, he insisted on a face-to-face with you."

"So you want me to meet with him?"

"Yes, but I also want to warn you about what you'll be walking into with Qin. I've been concerned about him for some time. I think that he finds his role a bit limiting and feels he's in line for a promotion. Remember how right before Sam's unfortunate demise he was out of the country?"

Will nodded that he did, recalling the early morning phone call and the meeting at Sam's apartment.

"I believe that Sam was meeting with Qin."

"About what?"

"That I'm not sure, but I have my theories. Given that it wasn't a meeting Sam told me was happening, I can only assume it was about Qin's ambitions and how Sam could help him. Although I could have it backward, I think Sam had sought out Qin to see how to improve his own position. Either way, I'm of the view that Sam and Qin were plotting something. I think Sam might have also fallen into equating the position he held in name with his actual importance. My very strong advice to you, Will, is that you not become victim to the same faulty logic. It won't end well for you. Believe me on that."

Will certainly believed her. Eve had never explained how Sam came to his role, but Will had assumed it was similar to his own ascent. He already knew that Sam fit the bill of an orphan—if that part of the backstory was even true—and even though Sam wasn't actually from Michigan, Will could certainly believe that he had come to New York from someplace else with a dream, just as Will had. And Eve had somehow exploited that dream, just as she'd done with Will. Just as Will was doing now to Timothy Paulson.

"What am I supposed to do at this meeting?"

"Nothing. Just listen to what Qin has to say and report back to me."

"Okay. Where and when?"

"Tomorrow. At the Central Park Zoo. A little too cinematic for my taste, but it was his selection. On a bench on the west side, across from the sea lion tank. Qin will be wearing a San Francisco Giants baseball cap. Meet at 3:45 p.m."

"That's an odd time, don't you think?" Will said.

"The sea lions are fed at 3:45. He figures that there will be lots of people around. He thinks it'll be safer that way."

Will didn't like the sound of that at all. Murder was part of Eve's business—Sam, George Kennefick, and maybe even Robert Wolfe had taught him that. But he didn't like the idea that he might be setting Qin up for a hit.

Eve must have read Will's mind, because she laughed. "Relax, Will. It's not like the movies. I'm not going to have a sniper waiting to take Qin out. I need him as much as he needs me. That's why I'm asking you to meet with him. If I wanted him dead, I wouldn't ask you to meet with him—I'd just kill him."

40.

Ethan returned to the witness holding room a minute after Toolan's reveal. Gwen was still speechless, uneasy being so close to a man who had murdered his wife, and furious at herself for all the comfort she'd provided him until that moment.

"So, are we decided?" Ethan asked.

"If you think it's best. I'll follow your advice, Benjamin," Toolan said.

"I do. It's the right call, Jasper. Trust me on this."

Toolan smiled. For the first time, Gwen saw the cruelty behind it.

She followed Ethan into the courtroom, leaving Toolan behind. Ethan started making his way toward Carolyn Vittorio, no doubt to tell her that the defense was going to rest without calling any other witnesses.

"Benjamin, can I talk to you for a second?" she said from a step behind him.

He stopped and turned. "Sure." And then, noticing her demeanor, he added, "Are you feeling okay, Gwen? You look . . . like you've seen a ghost, frankly."

"Yeah . . ." She looked around. There were too many people within earshot for her to share her news. "Can we go somewhere private? It'll just take a second. I need to tell you something that Jasper just told me."

Gwen looked for some hint of recognition from Ethan. After all, the list of things that Jasper could have so quickly imparted that would have made Gwen blanch were surely limited to the one thing that he'd actually said. But Ethan didn't flinch.

Does that mean he already knows? Or does he always have this cool demeanor, even when about to be told something truly shocking?

Ethan's eyes surveyed the courtroom. They had just come from the only place where they could truly be afforded privacy, but Jasper was still there. Everywhere else was a public space.

He led her over to the twelve seats in the jury box, all of which were now empty. He sat in the seat reserved for juror number seven—the one in the back row farthest from the judge's bench. That gave them a twenty-five-foot buffer from the nearest other person.

Without any prompt, Gwen leaned in toward Ethan and whispered in his ear. "Jasper just told me that he killed her."

Ethan displayed no visible reaction. Gwen wondered if it was because they were in plain view, but she had a sinking feeling that wasn't the reason at all. He already knew. Maybe even from day one.

In a conversational voice, Ethan said, "Then we're making the right call keeping him off the stand."

"That's *it*?" Gwen said.

"What more is there, Gwen?" Then, more *sotto voce*: "I understand that this is disturbing news, but it can't have taken you completely by surprise. I mean, the man is on trial for murder. The thought he might actually be guilty must have entered your mind."

"But *you* said he was innocent. I believed you. I believed him."

He looked at her sternly, the way her father sometimes did. As if *she* were at fault for this turn of events. Gwen held his stare, however. She had done nothing wrong except believe that they were representing an innocent man.

"Gwen, now is not the time for this type of discussion. I'm sorry, but I need to prepare our closing."

———

When Judge Pielmeier took the bench, before the jury was summoned, Ethan stood and announced that the defense was resting, without calling Toolan to the stand.

"Is that correct, Mr. Toolan? You have chosen not to take the stand in your own defense?"

Toolan stood. "Yes, Your Honor. On the advice of my counsel."

"Did your counsel also advise you that it's your choice, not his?"

"Yes."

"Please confirm on the record that you are aware that you have the right to testify in your defense, but you are freely relinquishing that right."

"That is correct." Then he added, "On the advice of counsel."

When Toolan sat down again, he smiled at Gwen, as if to say he was glad that was over. Or maybe he was looking for her to smile back, as she had so many times during the trial.

This time, however, she looked away.

———

If Benjamin Ethan had any qualms about representing a guilty man, his closing argument didn't betray it. He spoke for more than an hour about the injustice that convicting Jasper Toolan would be.

"Jasper Toolan is an artist the likes of which the world has far too few. And as an artist, he feels things very deeply. It is because he can plumb the depths of his own emotions that he can bring them to the screen and make each of us sitting in the audience feel them just as deeply. Can there be any doubt that when he told his wife of eight years just how much he loved Hannah Templeton, she too felt that those words were true? That in those moments, she realized the utter loneliness that would follow her, since she had irretrievably lost the man she had always believed she would grow old with? And you heard the evidence that Jennifer Toolan was already suffering from depression, already under a doctor's care. That she had attempted suicide once before. I know she did not leave a suicide note, but you heard from experts that only a small percentage of suicides—something on the order of fifteen to forty percent—leave behind a note. It's certainly reasonable that Jennifer Toolan was one of the vast majority who did not. Besides, her one loved one was her husband, and Jasper Toolan knew exactly why she had taken her life.

"Ladies and gentlemen of the jury," Ethan said, his voice booming in a closing crescendo, "there is no possible way—none—that you could find *beyond a reasonable doubt* the prosecution's version of events to be true. Would Jasper Toolan, a man who could have easily afforded whatever division of marital property or alimony a court provided, have sooner murdered his wife than simply file for a divorce? There is a far more plausible scenario: that Jennifer Toolan, already depressed, already suffering, took her own life when she heard the news that her husband was leaving her for a younger woman. And if you are saying to yourself that either scenario is possible and you just don't know, then reflect on the one thing that *is* beyond doubt." He waited a beat for emphasis. "When you just don't know, or even if you *think* it happened one way but recognize the other way is still reasonably possible, the law requires you to acquit."

The prosecutor got the last word, and Carolyn Vittorio used that opportunity to rebalance the scales a bit. She couldn't mention the prior abuse, of course, thanks, in part to Gwen's winning argument on that point. Still, she did her best to bring the jury back to the idea that Jennifer Toolan had been murdered by her husband's hand.

The jurors left the courtroom to deliberate. Gwen truly had no idea which way they'd decide. She was far more certain, however, about the verdict *she* wanted to hear.

41.

As Will walked into the zoo, he could hear an amplified voice.

"These amazing creatures are California sea lions. Fully grown males weigh in at more than six hundred pounds. They can eat five to eight percent of their body weight in a single meal. Just imagine how many Big Macs that would be for a human."

It was crowded, just as Qin had expected. Earlier in the day, the sky had looked threatening, but now the sun was out in full force.

The sea lion tank was the focal point of virtually everyone in the zoo—other than Will. His eyes zeroed in on the Chinese man sitting on the bench, wearing a San Francisco Giants baseball cap.

Despite the sun, there was an autumnal chill in the air. Qin was bundled in a heavy shearling coat and dark sunglasses to deal with the glare. His feet only barely reached the ground from the bench. Given the way Eve talked about him, Will had expected, if not someone the size of a sumo wrestler, at least an average-height individual. By the expression on Qin's face, Will did not think that Qin was any more impressed with him.

Will sat down beside him on the bench, but he didn't offer to shake hands. Instead, he made the quarter turn to look at Qin. Then he offered the subtlest of nods. "Mr. Qin. My name is Will Matthews. I was told that you wanted to discuss some matters."

Although Will had never had much interest in the performing arts, he had come to realize that being the new Sam was akin to playing a part. He could summon a steely resolve and Clint Eastwood–like squint that told the other side he meant business. If only, he sometimes thought, he were more like *this* Will Matthews in his real life. Perhaps he wouldn't have ever found himself playing this role at all.

"First things first," Qin said. "Please confirm what I have been told: that Mr. Abaddon is no longer with us."

"He's dead," Will said in a tone meant to convey that a similar fate might befall Qin if he didn't get with the program. He was in full New Sam mode, completely in character. "I have taken control of the organization, which I know you've already been told. I also know that you've been similarly informed that you are to treat me as you would Sam. Which is why I was disappointed that you asked for this meeting before we could resume doing business together."

The barking of one of the sea lions momentarily distracted Qin. Will followed his line of sight to the tank. They watched as the handler dangled a fish to get the animal to bark again before allowing him to receive his prize.

"You put up a good front, Mr. Matthews. Evelyn has taught you well."

Qin's mention of Eve meant that her suspicions had been confirmed. He must have been working with Sam, because no one else could have told him that Eve was actually in charge. Not to mention that, to Will's knowledge, no one else ever called her Evelyn other than Sam.

And if Qin knew that Sam had been under Eve's thumb, he had likely also surmised that Will was in a similar predicament.

Perhaps, Will thought, *Qin could be my ally? As he was Sam's?*

As if he was reading Will's mind, Qin said, "Sam came to me, asking for my assistance. He knew that, sooner or later, what ultimately happened to him was the only ending Eve could allow. If you're half as smart as Sam, you know that too. Which means that I'm your only hope of salvation, Mr. Matthews."

Will surveyed their surroundings. All he saw were happy families clapping at the display in the tank. One of the sea lions was barking, asking for even more fish. The trainer wagged a finger at him in mock anger.

"Everyone," the seal handler said through her megaphone, "that's our show for today. On behalf of our California sea lions, Flip, Whiskers, Cecil, and Phineas . . ."

Out of his peripheral vision, Will spied a man moving briskly through the crowd. He knew he recognized the full black beard, although it took him a moment to connect the face to a place. And then it was all there.

This was the man he'd seen in Eve's apartment. The day that he'd read that Sam's body had been discovered.

He turned back to Qin, who had slumped over. A knife was sticking out of his back.

Whatever coolness Will had managed to summon to play his part with Qin vanished. He launched into full-fledged panic mode.

He jumped up and began to walk away, moving briskly enough that anyone following would have to stand out in order to keep pace but not so quickly that he was jogging himself. Once he reached the zoo's exit, Will finally turned around.

That's when he heard a woman's scream.

———

Eve was waiting in a black Suburban parked at the planned rendezvous point on Fifth Avenue.

"All in all, that went rather well, I think," she said as Will joined her in the back seat. "I usually prefer something a bit subtler—a road-rage incident or a car accident, for example—but sometimes a message needs to be sent. A knife to the back tells everyone in no uncertain terms to toe the line, don't you think?"

"So that was the plan from the beginning?" Will said. "You were never actually interested in hearing what he had to say."

"One thing that you should know about me, Will . . . I'm not at all interested in doing business with anyone who thinks he's smarter than me. There's a lesson there for you, but I assume it's one you've already grasped."

42.

The jury had been out for five days.

On the morning of the second day, they had asked to hear back the testimony of Sharon Lerner, one of Jennifer Toolan's friends. Lerner had tried mightily to tell the jury that Jennifer had confided in her about her husband's abuse, but Ethan had been able to block that testimony at every turn. The passage the jury wanted read back to them had to do with one of those exchanges.

"I think it's a good sign that they want to hear it again," Kanner had said to no one in particular when the trial team discussed the development. "It suggests that they want to confirm there's no evidence of abuse."

Gwen knew the jury was more likely confirming their suspicions that Lerner knew of abuse but couldn't mention it because of Ethan's "lawyer tricks"—a term that Carolyn Vittorio used from time to time as something of a dog whistle for the jury. She was clearly trying to convey that there was more to the story that she couldn't tell them. Or maybe that was just Gwen's wishful thinking.

There had been quite the fight before Judge Pielmeier about what portion of the testimony should actually be read back to the jury. Ethan insisted that Judge Pielmeier read the testimony only, omitting any reference to the questions he had objected to and the judge's ruling on those objections, nearly all of which had been sustained. Vittorio argued just as vehemently that the objection colloquies were helpful for the jury to understand the rhythm of the Q and A and therefore to effectively put them back in the position they were in when they first heard the testimony.

Judge Pielmeier sided with the defense, which meant that the entirety of what the jury was read back consisted of this:

On direct examination:

Vittorio: Did you ever observe Mrs. Toolan act in a way that suggested to you that she might be fearful of her husband?

Witness: Yes.

On cross-examination:

Ethan: You testified on direct that you observed Mrs. Toolan act in a way that suggested she was fearful of her husband. Please re-create the way you observed Mrs. Toolan act that gave you that impression.

Witness: I don't know if I can. It was like this [witness makes a gesture].

Ethan: Thank you.

On the afternoon of the third day of deliberations, the jury asked to see the crime-scene photos. Kanner once again had a positive spin: "This is good for us, because the pictures don't suggest anger."

Gwen kept to herself that it was not a plus for the defense for the jury to be focusing on the image of Toolan's beautiful wife with a bullet hole in her head and blood pooling beneath her.

Yesterday, the jury had asked to see the murder weapon. Kanner thought that this was also good news. By now, Gwen had learned to tune out his analysis.

Finally, the court bailiff informed them that the jury had reached a unanimous verdict. Gwen was surprised to find herself so calm at the news. When the trial had begun, Gwen imagined that waiting for the verdict to be read would feel like being blindfolded and awaiting execution in the firing line. That sense of finality was about to come true, but with the added wrinkle that the guns might not fire, and the condemned would be set free.

But now Gwen was armed with the truth, and that changed everything. She no longer feared a guilty verdict. In fact, she'd welcome one.

———

With the close of evidence, the witnesses who had previously been prevented from being in the courtroom during testimony were free to return. The reporters still took up most of the seats, identifiable by the pads in their hands—electronic devices were not permitted in the courtroom. Jennifer Toolan's family—her sisters and her mother—were in the front row, holding one another's hands.

Hannah Templeton was not there, however.

Toolan must have known of her absence, because he never even turned around. He did, however, reach over to take Gwen's hand. Into her ear, he whispered, "No matter the outcome, I can never thank you enough for the support and friendship you've shown me. I hope that, if we get the result we want, you'll let me show my appreciation."

His words sent a chill up her spine. She felt almost as low as when he first confided in her that he had murdered his wife. She didn't want to be providing friendship or comfort to Jasper Toolan now, and she certainly didn't want to be on the receiving end of his "appreciation" later.

Thankfully, she was spared having to respond by the bailiff's cry: "All rise."

Everyone stood, and Judge Pielmeier entered through the door to her chambers. As was her invariable practice, she waited until she was in her seat before saying, "Please be seated, everyone." She managed to use an inflection each time that suggested she hadn't meant to keep them standing so long and had merely forgotten that they would not sit until she so directed.

"My court clerk has alerted the parties that the jury has sent a note that they have reached a unanimous verdict. Before I bring the jury in, does either the prosecution or the defense have anything that they wish to say?"

Carolyn Vittorio stood. "Nothing for the prosecution."

Gwen thought she sounded confident. She knew, however, that Ethan would too.

"The defense is ready as well," he said a beat later, with every bit of the assurance Gwen had imagined.

"Very well, then," Judge Pielmeier said. "Mr. Jackson, please bring in the jury."

All eyes turned to the door from which the jury entered and exited the courtroom. Before they could begin to file in, the judge's court officer had to walk the hundred or so feet from the bench to the back of the courtroom and summon them. A moment after he did so, the first of the jurors appeared. They promenaded in single file into the courtroom.

It was almost like watching a parade. Each juror deliberately made his or her way down the center aisle of the courtroom, then turned to enter the jury box. They marched in the reverse order of their seating assignment, with juror number twelve entering first and then taking her seat in the second row, closest to the bench.

Kanner had previously shared his views about reading a jury just before it issued the verdict. They made as much sense as any of his other pronouncements. This time it was the cliché that if they make eye contact it's because they're going to acquit—the idea being that they won't look a man they've just condemned in the eye.

Gwen knew that was crazy talk. After all, the jurors might be looking at Toolan out of disgust, or maybe just because they were being polite, or because they thought his tie was an interesting color. Her theory was obviously close to the mark, because the jurors showed no pattern of consistent behavior upon their entry, despite the fact that their verdict had been unanimous. Juror twelve assiduously avoided eye contact, and juror eleven looked as if he was trying to memorize Toolan's face because he would be called on to describe it later. Gwen's tally had it at four to four. Three others were too difficult to ascertain, and one she thought was checking her out more than looking at Toolan.

It took less than two minutes for them all to enter the courtroom and be seated, but the process felt interminable. Finally, the silence was broken by Judge Pielmeier.

"Ladies and gentlemen of the jury, I understand that a unanimous verdict has been reached. Mr. Foreperson, is that correct?"

The juror in the first row seated closest to Judge Pielmeier rose. He was one of two African American men on the jury. During voir dire, each prospective juror had filled out a questionnaire. Among other tidbits of information, the questionnaires had included what each person did for a living and the highest education level they had achieved. Thinking back, Gwen couldn't remember if the man now standing was the middle school science teacher or the retired pharmacist, but he looked to be over seventy, which made it more likely he was the retired pharmacist. Not that it mattered, of course. She recognized that she was distracting herself so she would think about anything other than what was about to happen.

"It is, Your Honor," the jury foreperson said.

Gwen was pleased that the foreperson spoke clearly and with decent amplification. She had heard that was sometimes a problem, especially when an older person was selected to read the verdict.

"Mr. Jackson, please retrieve the verdict form from the foreperson."

The bailiff left his perch beside Judge Pielmeier to make the six-foot trek to the jury box. Juror number one handed him a slip of paper, and Jackson made the return trip back to the judge.

The paper wasn't folded, but try as she might, Gwen couldn't see what was written on it. Judge Pielmeier took a moment to look at it. Without saying a word, she returned the slip to Jackson, who then retreated the ten or so steps to the railing enclosing the jury box. Juror number one took the paper out of his hand and waited for Judge Pielmeier's next prompt.

"The defendant shall please rise," Judge Pielmeier said.

Gwen got to her feet a beat after the men to her right stood, although it took Toolan a second more to rise. At the prosecution table, Carolyn Vittorio and her number two remained seated. A not-so-subtle reminder that only Jasper Toolan was truly on trial.

"This is a one-count indictment, with the only charge being premeditated murder not involving a peace officer, which in New York State is charged as murder in the second degree," Judge Pielmeier said. "Will the jury foreperson please read the verdict?"

A second elapsed, almost as if the foreperson had forgotten that this was his job. Finally, in a steady voice, he delivered his line.

It took another beat for it to register with Gwen.

Have I heard that correctly? Does the jury actually believe that Jasper Toolan is innocent?

Her internal monologue was interrupted by the man himself. He threw his arms around her and pulled her into him.

"This is because of you, Gwen," he said. "I couldn't have made it through all of this if it weren't for you."

Gwen was dying inside. This was what her life had become. She had devoted all of her efforts to helping a wife murderer go free.

43.

After watching Qin die beside him, Will spent the rest of the day alone in his apartment, getting drunk. He ended up passing out sometime around midnight.

When he woke, his head ached and his throat was dry. He tried to remember if he'd vomited the night before, but couldn't.

It was when he checked the time on his phone that he realized he had a voice mail waiting. He hadn't heard his phone ring, even though it had been right beside him.

Even in his sorry state, his heart lifted when he saw the caller: Gwen.

He took a deep breath, then hit "Play." He could hear the raucousness of a party in the background, or perhaps Gwen had made the call at a bar. He'd read the news online the previous day concerning Jasper Toolan's acquittal, and so he already knew the cause of the celebration. The irony was not lost on him that at the exact moment that Will had sunk to his lowest, as a knife plunged into Jian-Ying Qin's back, Gwen had realized her greatest career achievement.

"I'm so sorry for . . . everything, Will. I love you. Is there any way you can forgive me? Any way we can be together again?"

"Off the phone, Gwen-o-veer," a man said in the background. "Come do a shot with me."

Will knew the man wasn't Benjamin Ethan. This guy sounded younger, and he recalled Gwen's stories about the junior partner on the case. Canned something-or-other—that was the guy's name. Will remembered because whenever Gwen referenced him, Will thought of canned vegetables, usually a variety he didn't like.

Gwen didn't say goodbye. She just broke the connection.

But what would she have said next if it had not been for canned peas?

Then again, what more *was* there to say? She wanted them to be together again. That was everything.

He reached for the phone and considered what he'd say to her. But his thoughts were quickly invaded by the prospect that she had been drunk and most likely now regretted leaving the message—or perhaps didn't even remember doing so.

Besides, even if she had meant what she said, what difference did it make? She had decided she wanted no part of him when he was a Maeve Grant employee under investigation for unwittingly being involved in money laundering. Why on earth would she want a future with someone who had gone completely over to the Dark Side?

He put down the phone. Then he got an answer to his first question of the morning. He hadn't vomited last night, because he was about to be sick now.

———

Will spent the day drinking more. All the while spying his balcony, considering whether tossing himself off it might be the smartest decision he could make.

At 8:00 p.m., Will heard the dreaded knock at his door. But when he opened it, Eve was not there. Instead, he saw Gwen.

He blinked hard, thinking at first that this was some type of mirage. That he had drunk so much he was hallucinating.

"I'm sorry that I asked George not to announce I was coming up. I wanted to maintain the element of surprise, I guess. I figured you didn't call me back for a reason, and I was afraid that if I buzzed up you wouldn't let me visit."

He wasn't sure if it was the alcohol or his genuine shock, but he couldn't formulate any response. He just stared at her, worried that if he looked away, she might vanish.

"Can I come in, Will?"

He stepped aside and motioned for Gwen to enter. They sat down on his sofa, facing each other. Will felt as if he were being pulled in opposite directions. His heart told him to be thrilled by the prospect of Gwen's reentry into his life, and that he should immediately declare his love for her in no uncertain terms before she changed her mind. But his head knew the reasons that she'd left in the first place, and those hadn't changed. To the contrary, they'd grown exponentially worse, and Gwen had no idea.

So he said nothing and waited for Gwen to speak. To fill in the silence with the reason she had come.

"I've been fantasizing about this for so long," Gwen said, looking as if she was trying to hold back tears. "About seeing you again. About what I was going to say, and what you'd say in response. And I'm not going to lie. A very big part of me wanted to say nothing and just yank you into bed."

She stopped, as if she was asking him to concur. But as much as that sounded like heaven, he couldn't.

Gwen must have sensed his reluctance, because after a beat she said, "But I know that we have a lot to talk about. So I figure we should do that first."

He was still mute. He wondered if he could speak even if he had something to say. He could only imagine that he was a sorry sight. Although he had managed to shower and change into clothes at some point during his bender, he still looked and smelled like a man who had been drinking for the better part of the last twenty-four hours.

"I need to apologize before we talk about anything else," she said. "What I did, the way I did it, was just awful. I'm so sorry. At the time, it made sense to me. I had just been selected for the Toolan team, and I knew I wasn't going to have any time for you. And . . . I was afraid. Benjamin Ethan told us that the press would be investigating the lawyers on the trial team, and possibly also their friends and family. And . . . I don't want it to sound like I did it for you, Will. I know that it was the most selfish thing I could have done, but there was a part of me that thought that you'd be better off too by it being over."

She was now losing the battle to contain her tears. She rubbed her eyes, moving the evidence away.

"It wasn't," he said, surprised by the sound of his voice. It came out croaky, but he continued. "Better for me, I mean. I was devastated."

"I'm so, so sorry. And all I can do now is tell you that I meant every word of what I said on the voice mail, Will. I love you. I know we can be happy together. Have a future together. And that means for better and for worse. I'm so ashamed that I abandoned you when you needed me. The first sign of 'for worse,' and I ran away. But I promise you that it will never happen again. Please forgive me and say that we can try again."

Part of him just wanted to end it there, to take Gwen in his arms, and into his bed. But the better part of Will knew that he had to come clean with her, so their new life together would be free of the secrets he was keeping. Of course, he also knew that by sharing those secrets, it was much less likely that they'd *ever* have that life together.

He leaned in and kissed her, which brought out a soft, tentative smile. He mirrored one back.

"I love you too, Gwen. So much. I think you have no idea. And I have loved you from the first moments we were together. Like I said, I was really devastated when you ended things. I can't lie about that. But I understood why you did it. Believe me, I understood—"

"Thank you," she interrupted. She kissed him on the lips.

"I'm not done yet," he said, pulling back. "There's more. A lot more, unfortunately. It's the reason I didn't call you back. And I think I need to tell you everything, even though I'm really afraid to do that, because I don't want you to leave again."

"I won't. I promise, Will. I won't."

"You can't make that promise, Gwen. You don't know what I'm going to tell you."

She sat up straighter. "Then tell me, Will. I'm listening."

Despite the fact that he'd been rehearsing this speech in his head for months, when he was finally called on to deliver it, he didn't know where to begin. And then it just came out.

"Sam is dead. Eve killed him. I . . . was there. I helped her bury the body."

She looked at him in abject terror—eyes wide as saucers, mouth open. She even covered it with her hand. He wondered if she could take any more, and realized that there was so much more he had to say.

"Do you want me to go on? If you've already heard enough, I understand. But there's more."

She nodded. Now it was as if *she* was too scared to speak.

In a rush, Will told her everything. As the words came out, they sounded absurd even to him. How the meeting at the hockey game had been a setup. That Eve was actually a criminal mastermind, and Sam worked for her. That he'd lied to Gwen about Sam's death because, at the time, Eve said that she'd killed him in self-defense, that Sam was enraged by jealousy and had tried to throw Eve off his balcony, and Will had believed her. He'd also believed that Sam's business associates would kill Eve, and maybe him too, if they learned of Sam's death, which was why he'd agreed to help her bury the body.

Gwen didn't say a word in response. Her usual approach would have been to cross-examine him on every point, or at the very least ask questions for clarification. Her silence was so pronounced that he wondered if she even understood what he was saying. But once he'd started his confession, he couldn't stop.

"I was fired from Maeve Grant. Eve withdrew all the money in Sam's accounts. Then she said that I had to work for her, take over Sam's role. That if I didn't do what she said, she'd kill me. If I ran to the police, she'd tell them that *I* killed Sam. She put a fiber from one of the rugs that I bought on Sam's body when we buried him. So once his body is identified, it'll link back to me as his murderer. And if I tried to run, she said that she'd go after . . . you."

He took a deep breath, filling his lungs enough that he knew he could have gone underwater for a long time. He wished that were an option.

"It's okay if you want to go now," he said. "I'll understand. I was heartbroken to have you leave my life before, but I understood then too. I know that if I had originally put on my dating profile 'broke, awaiting indictment, still engaged in criminal activity, possibly soon to be murdered,' you wouldn't have swiped right. But the one thing I ask of you—not even ask, but beg—is don't stay now if you're going to leave me later. I just can't go through losing you again."

44.

Gwen woke to the sweet sound of Will snoring lightly.

The light outside was still faint, suggesting that it was only shortly after daybreak. She smiled at the thought that she could spend the entire day with Will, and that he'd share her bed again tonight. After so many nights apart, she felt like a freed prisoner, thankful for every moment that they had together.

Looking at Will, there was no doubt in her mind that she was hopelessly, head over heels, in love. That feeling, which she'd always wondered whether she'd truly recognize, was finally here. She couldn't say with certainty that it would last forever. Or even that someday she might not look upon this feeling and give to it a different name. But lying in bed beside him right now, she was experiencing something new. And she was equally certain it wasn't any of the emotions that had previously led her to wonder whether she was in love: lust, or friendship, or longing.

These happy thoughts were shunted aside by the dark events Will had recounted the previous evening. She had no illusion that his problems were any less serious than he had made them out to be.

Even so, one of the things she loved about Will was his sense that anything was possible. The cynicism and suspicion that seemed to define every other person she knew were completely foreign to him. She had reveled in the fact that his sunny outlook was rubbing off on her, convinced that it was Will's voice inside her head that made her so angry about Jasper Toolan when Benjamin Ethan had no qualms about representing a guilty client.

Will's father would have been proud: his son was more like the dog than anyone she'd ever met. And maybe he was right to be. Maybe he—they—could still have a happy ending.

Will stirred, then turned onto his back. He opened his eyes and smiled as if he were looking at her face for the first time.

"Good morning," she said.

"Thank God. I was worried that I was dreaming last night."

"Maybe you were. Tell me what you remember, and I'll tell you if it actually happened or not."

"It went a little bit like this," he said, and then put his lips on hers.

"Yes. I remember it now too," she said, kissing him back. "Although it still seems a bit unreal to me."

"Then let's not ever wake up," he said, rolling Gwen onto her back.

———

Gwen called in sick that day. She had no work to do anyway, not until George Graham assigned her a new case. She might as well take advantage of it.

Besides, she *was* sick. In the light of day, she was beside herself with worry over what Will had shared the previous evening. Although she had promised him that she would never leave, could she really stand by him through this?

She so desperately wanted to believe that happily ever after wasn't just in fairy tales. That it was possible for regular people too. That the moral of the story could not be that those who believed amazing things could happen for them were destined to be defeated in the end by those who take advantage of that belief.

Which meant that she needed to help him figure a way out of this. That was the only thing that mattered now.

And she had a plan.

The first part of which was for her and Will to meet with his lawyer.

———

Later that day, Gwen and Will were sitting in the same windowless conference room at Jessica Shacter's office as Will had occupied during the first meeting. Jessica appeared a moment later. She had a coffee mug in one hand and a red file folder with papers sticking out of it in the other.

When'd he asked for this meeting on such short notice, Will had told Jessica that there had been an important new development he needed to discuss with her right away. He'd also said that Gwen—whom he described as a lawyer and his girlfriend—would be joining them. "The more the merrier," Jessica said.

"Nice to meet you, Gwen," Jessica said as the women shook hands. "I was surprised when Will said you were at Taylor Beckett that you'd be given permission to help out on this. The big firms almost never like to appear adverse to the big investment houses."

"I got dispensation from Benjamin Ethan. I was on the Toolan team, so I guess he was feeling generous."

This wasn't true. Gwen hadn't asked anyone for permission to be there that day. Will had said that he didn't want Gwen risking her career for him, but Gwen had waved away his concerns. "It's far less risky than what you're going to do," she'd said.

That was right, but also beside the point. Will had to stick his neck out to save it. Gwen, on the other hand, was putting herself at risk solely for him, for their future.

"Before you get to what you want to share with me, I have some news of my own to report," Jessica said. "I just got off the phone with the US Attorney's Office. The headline is this: you're not the focus here. Obviously, that's not a big surprise, but it's still nice to hear. As we had already surmised, they believe that Sam Abaddon is the head of a very large criminal enterprise. They wouldn't tell me what the underlying crimes are, but what they said was consistent with what David Bloom told me, which is to say that it is something relating to terrorism or at the very least the financing of terrorism. In other words, very serious stuff."

Jessica looked down at her notes. She closely considered what was on the first page, but merely skimmed the second and third pages, running her hand down the center as if she was speed-reading.

"They said that your current designation is *subject*, but I find the whole witness-subject-target classification system to be virtually meaningless. In my experience, everyone is a subject until they're told they're a target—and that's usually at the exact same time that they're told they're being indicted."

"I'm sorry, what does all that mean?" Will said.

Gwen answered. "The Department of Justice has three categories. 'Witness' means just that. There's no cause for anyone in law enforcement to believe the person has committed a crime. That's obviously the best one. I think of those people like bystanders who see a shooting. On the other end of the spectrum are the targets. The DOJ has a definition that applies to them, which is that there's a present intention to indict. Or that they have enough information right now to bring an indictment. Once you become a target, the DOJ is supposed to tell you that, which is why they technically label virtually everyone a subject until they're ready to indict."

"And that's what I am? A subject?"

"Yes," Jessica said. "As we discussed the first time, it seems pretty clear that Sam Abaddon is the target. Although they didn't come right out and say that, it's a reasonable extrapolation of what they *did* say, and what they want from you. Like I said, not much of a surprise. He's the top guy, so of course that's who they want to bring down."

Will looked over to Gwen, to remind her that there was so much that Jessica did not yet know. Gwen provided a subtle nod, confirming her complicity in keeping Jessica in the dark that Sam was dead, and that he had been anything but the top guy even when he was alive. As well as the fact that the top guy was, in fact, a woman.

"So what do they want from me?" Will asked.

"To tell them where they can find Sam Abaddon." Jessica waited a beat, and then added, "It's just too bad you can't help them with that. Because if you could, I might be able to get you out from under all this."

"What if he could?" Gwen said. "What if Will could deliver Sam Abaddon to the FBI? Do you think that would be enough to get him immunity?"

This was exactly the plan Gwen had shared with him. The reason they were meeting with Jessica now. Will would give the FBI Sam's whereabouts in exchange for immunity—after that was granted, he would also claim to be the one who'd killed Sam, leaving Eve completely out of the narrative. Once that was done, Eve would have no leverage over him regarding Sam's murder.

"She could still kill me," Will had countered when first hearing the plan.

"But why would she?" was Gwen's response. "You'll just tell her that you want out, and in exchange, you'll keep her secrets. She can't go to the police about you killing Sam, because you'll have immunity. And you'll tell her that if anything happens to you, you've given a lawyer instructions to deliver the FBI a statement revealing everything you know."

Jessica silently considered this turn of events. In their last meeting, Will had told her that he had no idea where to find Sam. Now Gwen was implying otherwise.

"Just telling them where to find Sam Abaddon won't be enough for immunity," Jessica said. "They'd need him to flip for that to be of any real value. So there are two things they'll expect from you if you want immunity, Will: Sam's present location and evidence from you that he committed some crime. Can you provide them both?"

Gwen had anticipated that merely providing Sam's location would not merit immunity. But the rest of the information they were more than happy to divulge, since it all related to Sam and nothing on the paper trail mentioned Eve at all. It was Gwen's idea that Will should make Jessica work to extract each piece, however. "That's how it always works with clients," Gwen told him. "They lie to you at every turn. It's only at the end, when they can see the finish line, that they begin telling the truth."

Jessica's tone made clear that she had been onto Will's lie from the get-go. He doubted that he was the first of her clients to lie to her face, but he nevertheless felt ashamed that even as he professed to tell her everything now, he would still be lying.

Nonetheless, Will stuck to the plan. He doled out information to Jessica slowly, but only as much as was necessary for him to get immunity.

"What about the fact that I already told the FBI I didn't know where he was? Isn't lying to them a crime?"

"It won't be a problem," Jessica said. "I'm certain that they'll be more than willing to let that go as part of the immunity deal. In fact, they'll likely conveniently 'forget' that you ever said it. Now, what about that other part? Can you also tell them about any crimes Abaddon committed?"

Will looked at Gwen to once again confirm that this was the road that they should be traveling down. She nodded.

"Yes," Will said.

"Well, that is good news." Jessica said this with a smile, as if the fact that her client was actually a criminal, and not just someone wrongfully caught up in someone else's crimes, was cause for celebration. "Tell me what evidence you have of his criminal activities, so I know what we're getting into here."

"For one thing, I'm almost certain that Sam was laundering funds when I bought my apartment. He told me that the purchase price was

$9.2 million, but—and I didn't know it at the time, but I'm near certain now that he was the seller—I think he actually put down the purchase price as a much higher figure. And then there's all the trades that I did for him. I'm betting that many of them were related-party transactions too, where he was just buying and selling stuff to himself at inflated prices to hide the fact that he was using criminal proceeds."

"Anything else, Will? I need to hear all of it."

"Tell her about George Kennefick," Gwen said, playing her part. "And Robert Wolfe too."

"I think Sam murdered them. I don't know the particulars, but he told me that he thought something was going on between his girlfriend and Kennefick, and the next thing I know, Kennefick is dead and I'm going to replace him on the board of some shelf company."

"How'd this Kennefick guy die?"

"Car crash, Sam said."

"That does happen sometimes, Will."

"My old boss, Robert Wolfe . . . I think he was also murdered. The police think it was a road-rage incident. But they don't know that right before it happened, Wolfe told me that he had concerns about Sam's trading. He said that he wanted to discuss Sam's accounts with Sam directly. I had told Sam that Wolfe was threatening to go to the Maeve Grant Compliance people, or maybe even to Legal. That's why Sam had him killed."

Will was reasonably sure that Jessica's practice was white collar only—embezzlement, tax fraud, money laundering, insider trading. But if this was the first time the word *murder* had been uttered in Jessica's conference room, she didn't show it.

To the contrary, she smiled broadly. "This is exactly what the US Attorney's Office is going to want to hear, and it should be more than enough to get you immunity. Let me propose that we do this: I'll see if I can get a meeting with them for first thing tomorrow. I'm going to give them an attorney proffer, which means I'm going to tell them everything that you just told me. I'll also tell them that we're looking for an immunity deal. If that's not on the table, then we'd all be wasting our time."

Will looked again to Gwen, who nodded her confirmation. This was exactly the way they had been hoping this would turn out.

"Okay," Will said.

"But before I make this call, I need to know that you know exactly what it means to start down this path. Simply put, there's no turning back. You need to tell them everything they ask about. And you need to answer truthfully. One lie, one omission, even one misleading statement, and the whole deal goes to hell."

"I understand," Will said. "I'm not going to lie to them. I promise."

Will looked at her when he said this, determined not to betray that he was lying to her.

45.

Will was so nervous he had to remind himself to breathe. As if she could sense his unease, Gwen reached for his hand. Jessica sat on his other side in the waiting area of the US Attorney's Office, her hands in her lap.

Their hosts were running late. Or at least that was the excuse they'd given Jessica when the trio had been told to cool their heels. Will thought it was a power play, to bring about the very heightened sense of anxiety in him that he was now experiencing. When he said as much to Jessica, she replied with a more likely explanation. "Sometimes they run late, Will."

After fifteen minutes, Will saw a man he recognized, although it took him a moment to register from where. It was Agent Benevacz, who had ambushed him in front of his building months ago. The agent waved for them to come forward.

After they navigated the metal detector, Benevacz introduced himself to Jessica and Gwen. To Will he said, "Good to see you again, Mr. Matthews."

Will found the meeting anything but good.

The sign on the door on the fifth floor said TERRORISM AND INTERNATIONAL NARCOTICS UNIT. Another set of metal detectors guarded the entry. Benevacz walked around it, no doubt because he was armed. He instructed the others to place any metal they had in the plastic bin.

After clearing the checkpoint, they were delivered into an interior conference room that was even more depressing looking than the one at Jessica's office, which was something Will wouldn't have previously thought possible. The others were already in place on the other side of the table. They stood, almost in unison, upon their guests' arrival. The man in the center reached for Jessica's hand.

"Thank you for coming," he said.

"Always a pleasure, John," Jessica replied, in a way that might have been sarcastic, although Will wasn't sure. "This is my client, Will Matthews, and my co-counsel on this, Gwen Lipton."

"Mr. Matthews, I'm Assistant United States Attorney John Yoo," the man said.

Yoo wore eyeglasses that were a touch too large for his face, but he was otherwise dressed as if he cared about his appearance—dark suit, crisp white shirt, and solid-blue tie. On his lapel, he wore an American flag pin.

"You have met FBI Special Agent Benevacz," Yoo said. "The rest of our team includes Assistant US Attorney Lynn Nielson and Howard Goldberg, who is the deputy chief of this unit."

Of the two other lawyers, the woman was obviously junior to Yoo, probably no older than Will and Gwen. Goldberg, however, was in his forties, a bald man with a swarthy complexion and already exhibiting some five o'clock shadow despite the fact it was still morning.

Jessica said, "I didn't know you'd be in attendance, Howard."

"I wanted to hear what your client had to say before we considered whether to give him the golden ticket of immunity."

Jessica smiled. "Well, the more the merrier, I always say."

She directed Will to sit to her right. She took the middle seat, which separated Will and Gwen.

When they were all in place, Yoo turned to Will and said, "The understanding we've reached with your counsel is that you're now going to share with us information relating to facts of which you have first-hand knowledge and could competently testify about in a court of law. The representation made by your counsel was that those facts would implicate Mr. Samuel Abaddon in criminal conduct. In addition, you will be able to provide us with information that will lead directly to our being able to bring Mr. Abaddon into custody. Is that your understanding too, Mr. Matthews?"

"It is," Will said.

With that, Yoo slid a page across the table. Will couldn't help but remember the same thing happening when he'd first met with Maeve Grant's lawyers.

"This is the letter immunity agreement you asked for, Jessica," Yoo said. "It's our standard agreement, so you've seen it before. And I know you know this, but I say it so your client understands, there's no negotiation on its terms. Take your time to review it if you'd like. We can give you the room, but you need to sign it before we go any further."

The understanding that had been negotiated between Jessica and the prosecutors was that this meeting would be covered by letter immunity. Jessica had explained that it was a limited form of immunity, preventing the government from using any evidence against Will that they obtained from what he said, or that derived from what he said.

"Think of it like a path," Jessica had explained. "So long as the prosecutors follow the evidence you give them, no matter how many twists and turns that path may take, they can't use any evidence against you that they acquired along that path. So, if, for example, you lead them to Sam and he gives them evidence of crimes that involved you, they can't use that evidence against you because it derives from the evidence you gave them. Same thing if Sam gives up someone else, and that person testifies against you. It's all what's called 'fruit of the poisonous tree.'"

This sounded good to Will, but like everything in the law, he'd come to realize, there was a loophole.

"But, and this is a big but," Jessica continued, "they are still free to prosecute you in two circumstances. First is if you lie to them. In that case, all bets are off, and they can use whatever you say against you. Second is if they later discover evidence of your own criminal conduct that has nothing to do with what you tell them now. Continuing my path metaphor, imagine if they're following a different path that does not connect with your path, and somewhere along their path they come upon evidence of your criminal conduct. To get out from under that, you would need what's called *full transactional immunity*. That's the *get-out-of-jail-free* card, but you don't get that without Department of Justice sign-off, and only then after you give a detailed proffer of everything you have to provide. So, right now, letter immunity is the best we'll be able to do."

"No, you can stay," Jessica now said to the prosecutors on the other side of the table. "I went over the terms with Will already. Just give me a few minutes to read it to make sure that it's the same agreement he and I discussed."

They all sat there silently while Jessica read the two-page agreement. When Jessica's eyes lifted off the page, she signed at the bottom. Then she pushed the pages to Will.

"It's the same as we discussed," she said. "You sign below me."

Will took the pen out of Jessica's hand. Without saying anything, he signed and handed back the paper and the pen.

"Good," Yoo said. "To put in colloquial terms what you just signed, Mr. Matthews, this meeting affords you certain protections, but not complete immunity from prosecution. Do you understand?"

"I do," Will said.

"One more thing," Goldberg said. "As I'm sure Jessica has explained to you, no agreement will ever protect you from criminal prosecution if you are untruthful to us. Is that also clear?"

"It is," Will said.

"Good. So now that the rules are agreed upon, the floor is yours, Mr. Matthews," Goldberg said. "Tell us what we're all here to learn about Mr. Abaddon."

The narrative Will delivered had been drafted by Jessica. Will had practiced it numerous times, as if he were an actor about to give a performance. He began with the meeting at the hockey game, discussed the party at Sam's apartment, the trading accounts that he'd opened, and the money that flowed into those accounts.

Nielson, the young Assistant US Attorney, was scribbling furiously as Will spoke, as was Gwen. The others, however, stared right at Will.

"I received a retention loan from Maeve Grant," Will said. "Ten million dollars. Sam suggested that I buy an apartment with it, and even offered that he knew of a unit that he thought I'd like. He arranged for me to see it right away and said he'd finance the purchase, so long as I used the proceeds of my Maeve Grant loan to invest in a private equity fund his friend ran. I cleared all of this with Maeve Grant, and they signed off. What I didn't know at the time, but have since learned, is that the seller of my apartment was a company that was owned by Sam, and that the amount I was paying, which I thought was $9.2 million, was not the actual purchase price that was listed on the sales contract."

"What was the actual purchase price?" Yoo asked.

"A little under $29 million."

"And how did you learn that?"

"I later saw that in the actual sale documents."

"Later?" Goldberg said, obviously in disbelief.

"Right. When I signed, I only saw the signature pages. The price wasn't included among them."

"You signed them without checking the price?" Yoo asked.

"Sam told me the price. I trusted him."

Jessica chimed in. "I recently took the opportunity to pull up the deed of sale from the Department of Buildings." She reached into her briefcase and pulled out the document. "As you'll see, the sale price is listed as $28.9 million. Also, you'll see that the seller is Highline Property, a New York corporation. A little more digging revealed that Highline is wholly owned by a company called Drogo Inc., which is a Cypriot entity. Mr. Abaddon has a penchant for naming his holding companies after *Game of Thrones* characters and incorporating them in tax havens. We can't be certain that Drogo is owned by Mr. Abaddon because I don't have access to Cypriot records, but we assume you could easily ascertain that with a subpoena."

Will proceeded with the script, telling the prosecutors about the other questionable trades, and then ending with his suspicions about the deaths of George Kennefick and Robert Wolfe. When he finally finished, there was a momentary silence. Out of his peripheral vision, Will saw Jessica nod, her way of saying that he was doing well. He turned more fully to see Gwen smile—*that* was the confirmation he needed.

The other side of the table was engaged in cupped-ear whispering. First between Yoo and his boss, and then between Yoo and Benevacz.

"Okay," Yoo said when their secret discussions were completed. "We can definitely work with this. But as you know, it's meaningless without our being able to find Mr. Abaddon. So . . . where is he?"

Will looked to Jessica, who nodded. She still didn't know the answer. She'd asked, but on that point Will had made it clear that she didn't want to know. Although Jessica had said she didn't like to operate in the dark, she had relented because Gwen assured her that she had advised Will to remain vague.

"He's dead. You can find his body in the Suffolk County morgue."

Yoo and Goldberg looked at each other. Then, turning back to Will, Goldberg said, "How'd he get there?"

Will steadied himself. It was all leading up to this.

"I killed him. He wanted me to do something that was illegal. I told him I wouldn't. That's when he revealed who he really was and everything he had done. When I told him I was going to call the police, he came at me and tried to throw me off my balcony. Lucky for me, I was armed. Otherwise *I'd* be the one lying in the morgue now. After he was dead, I buried the body. I wasn't worried about the police. I knew I'd acted in self-defense. But if word got out that I'd killed Sam, I knew his people would kill me."

This time Will assiduously avoided looking at Jessica. He could only imagine the daggers she'd be shooting him after he'd kept this explosive detail from her. Instead, he watched another ear-cupping whisper exchange between Yoo and Goldberg. When they broke their huddle, Goldberg was smiling.

"Let's now talk about the truth, Mr. Matthews," Goldberg said.

Jessica put her hand across Will's chest like a mother protecting her child when she has to slam on the brakes. "Are you saying that you believe what Mr. Matthews just said is untrue?"

"No. I don't *think* that," Goldberg said. "I *know* that what he told us was untrue. You didn't kill Mr. Abaddon, Mr. Matthews."

The jig was up, and yet Will had no choice but to play out the string.

In for a penny, in for a pound, he thought.

Given that he'd already lied to them, lying more wasn't going to make his predicament any worse.

"I did. You might even find evidence of a carpet fiber somewhere on his body. It'll be from my rug, which is how I transported him from my home. It's a one-of-a-kind rug."

"Is *that* what Ms. Devereux had over you?" Yoo said. "The rug fiber?"

"Who?" Jessica said, trying to keep up.

"She's Sam's girlfriend—or was," Will said. "They broke up."

Goldberg chuckled, making an odd sound, as if he rarely laughed and didn't quite know how to do it. "That's one way of saying it. *They broke up.* Another is that she murdered him and disposed of his body, I'm assuming with your help, Mr. Matthews. Still another is that she's murdered more than half a dozen people, including Mr. Kennefick, as you mentioned. Also, Jian-Ying Qin, who I believe you're also very well acquainted with. So, now that you know what we know, Mr. Matthews, let's put an end to story time, shall we?"

Gwen's carefully constructed plan to get Will out from under Eve's control had officially gone to hell.

Will hadn't been playing them; *they'd* been playing *him*. They already knew Sam was dead. And they knew Eve had murdered him.

Eve was their target. Not Sam.

The only thing they hadn't known was where to find Sam's body. That's why they'd given Will immunity. And now that he'd lied to them, he'd squandered that.

"Does the name Maximilian Devereux mean anything to you?" Yoo asked.

Will shook his head. From what he could see of Gwen's and Jessica's confused expressions, the name didn't ring a bell with them either.

"He was the head of one of the largest criminal enterprises the antiterrorism task force had ever seen. We were getting close to him, and then . . . three years ago, he vanished. As if he'd never existed. That's when his only child, his daughter, Evelyn, took up the family business. But she installed Mr. Abaddon as the face of it, a lightning rod, as it were. Until she and Mr. Abaddon had a falling-out, one that involved the aforementioned Mr. Qin. After killing Mr. Abaddon, Ms. Devereux also took it upon herself to murder Mr. Qin, as you well know."

"This is the first I'm hearing of any of this," Jessica said, alarm in every word.

"Mr. Matthews, do you care to bring your lawyer up to speed?" Goldberg said.

"That's not how we're going to do it," Jessica said. "Give us the room so I can consult with my client, please."

———

After everyone cleared out, and it was just Jessica, Gwen, and Will, Jessica read them the riot act.

"What the hell, Will? I told you on day one that you might as well be your own lawyer if you're going to keep me in the dark. So now you *don't* have immunity in connection with whatever you did concerning the Abaddon murder, and you've lied to the FBI, which is a crime in and of itself. On top of all that, you're now quite likely viewed as an accomplice in this guy Qin's murder."

Will was having difficulty meeting her eyes, like a chastised child.

"Gwen, how in the hell could you have let him walk into this type of trap?"

"She didn't *let* me do anything," Will shot back. He could see that Gwen had tears in her eyes. "It was my call. I was hoping to get immunity from being an accessory to Sam's murder. Then, once I told Eve that Sam's murder case was closed, she would no longer have the threat of pinning it on me. She would let me go. I'm sorry to have lied to you, but if I'd played it any other way, Eve would have killed me. And maybe Gwen too."

"That was a pretty fucking stupid plan," Jessica said. "So now let's fix it."

46.

The new plan was dictated by the FBI. It was simple enough. To avoid a lengthy prison sentence, not to mention Eve's making good on her threats, Will needed to get Eve to admit she had killed Qin. With that, Yoo and Goldberg believed that they'd have enough to get Eve to ultimately take a plea. Without Eve in charge, they were certain that the rest of the organization would disintegrate. If that happened, Will's role in bringing it down would merit immunity, with the added incentive that he'd be able to go on with his life without constantly looking over his shoulder for someone ready to plunge a knife in his back.

His only other option, as the FBI so effectively pointed out, was to go home and wait for Eve to kill him. They now knew where to find Sam's body, so the moment they confronted Eve with their suspicions about his death and Qin's murder, she'd know that Will had turned and could link her to both crimes. He'd be dead within twenty-four hours.

Which was why Will was now standing in front of Eve's apartment door, scared to death. Following the FBI's playbook was the only chance he had to stay alive and out of prison.

"Can I come in?" Will said as soon as Eve opened the door. "I need to talk to you about something. It shouldn't take very long."

He could feel the recording device on his chest. It seemed almost as if it were fighting against his heart.

They made their way into Eve's living room. Will sat on the sofa, Eve in the chair opposite him. If she knew what he'd come to share, she didn't show it.

"What's on your mind, Will?"

"The other day with Qin . . . That was more than I bargained for in any of this. You told me that I'd only be doing financial things. I don't want to be part of any more murders."

Eve did not visibly react. Not a twitch or a blink. The silence between them lasted a good ten seconds, during which time Eve never took her eyes off him. Her stare was so intense that Will was forced to look away, only to see that Eve had not wavered when he resumed eye contact.

"I have no idea what you're talking about, Will," Eve finally said. "Who is this Qin person? And what on earth do you mean by murder?"

The look in her eyes contradicted her words. They were like lasers, piercing through Will.

She wasn't confused at all.

Eve knew he was wearing a wire.

Will looked to the door. It was less than fifteen feet away, but he'd never make it there if Eve wanted to stop him.

He turned back to Eve, fully expecting her to brandish a weapon. But she didn't.

Instead, she stood and said, "I think you should leave now."

Will followed her to the front door. As he exited, he looked back at Eve and saw an expression that confirmed without any doubt that he was now a dead man.

———

A black van was parked around the corner, waiting for him. It was outfitted just like the ones he'd seen on television: electronic equipment on all sides.

"Now what?" Will said when he climbed into the back.

Yoo removed his headset and ran his hand through his hair. "That was fucked. She knew you were wired."

"How?"

"No idea. Some people have a very refined survival instinct. Or maybe it's as simple as her having you under surveillance, so she knew where you'd spent your morning."

"Then why didn't she kill me?"

"With us listening in? She's too smart for that."

———

When they were back at the US Attorney's Office, Will was reunited with Jessica and Gwen, who had been waiting for his return. From the look on her face, Gwen knew the plan had failed before anyone said anything.

"We need to regroup on our end," Yoo said. "Will can fill you in on the shit show we were just part of."

When Yoo cleared out of the room, Will said, "Eve knew I was wearing a wire. She claimed she had no idea who Jian-Ying Qin was, and then told me to leave. The look in her eyes, though. She's going to kill me. First chance she gets."

"I've been talking to Howard about what the next step is if it played out this way," Jessica said.

"And?" Will asked.

"I've asked for witness protection. No guarantees, but he said that it was definitely a possibility. Provided, of course, you're willing to testify against Eve on this Qin murder."

"How does witness protection work?" Will asked, although he already knew the most important part: he'd never see Gwen again.

"There are a lot of steps to it, actually," Jessica said. "It's not like in the movies, where tomorrow you're living under a different name. They need to do a thorough psychiatric evaluation. There's a lie detector test. While that's going on, they put you in a safe house. But the one part that the movies get right is that you're cut off from contact with anyone from your former life."

"Including me?" Gwen asked.

"I would think especially you, Gwen. If Eve thought that she could get to Will through you, that would put you at risk."

"Is it forever?" Will asked.

"It should be, if you want to stay safe. But it's really up to you. It's not prison. You can leave it whenever you want. Subject, of course, to the same risks that made you go into it in the first place."

No one said anything for a good twenty seconds. Jessica was watching Will and Gwen. She seemed to intuit what they were not saying.

"This is not a very difficult call, Will," Jessica finally said. "Not really. Eve now knows that you're cooperating with the FBI. There's no way she's going to let you live. And I know that you don't want to leave Gwen, and I'm assuming, Gwen, that the feeling is mutual. But allow me to inject a little bit of earned wisdom that comes with age. Life isn't *Romeo and Juliet*. I don't doubt that you two love each other, but believe me on this: given time, you'll both find happiness with other people. So much so that I guarantee that you'll look back on this moment and wonder how you could ever have considered sacrificing your life for a person who . . . you can't even remember exactly what they look like anymore."

"Can we at least say goodbye?" Gwen asked.

"Of course," Jessica said. "Let me give you two the room. Come on out when you're ready."

———

As soon as they were alone, Gwen embraced Will tightly, and then she began to cry. At first slowly, as if she could hold back the emotion welling inside of her, and then with abandon, recognizing the futility of the endeavor. Will was left with no choice but to hold it together. He didn't want her last memory of him to be of someone bereft.

As he held her, her tears spilled onto his shirt and her hands dug into his back. He lost himself in the embrace, wishing that his life would end right there, because he could not fathom ever being happy again.

"I'm so sorry, Gwen," he said into her ear.

"Promise me that we will see each other again," she said. "That somehow you'll tell me where you're moved, and I'll be able to get to you."

"If I can, I will," he said.

"Promise."

"I promise."

47.

It had been three days since Gwen and Will had said their goodbyes. Three days after she had made Will promise not to lose hope. Three days after she had sworn to him that they would see each other again.

They had been the worst three days of her life. The kind of days that Gwen couldn't imagine enduring much longer.

She left her building at midnight. The moment she ventured outside, she was careful to scan the street in every direction. There was no sign of anyone watching. Not that she'd necessarily know if they were, of course. She assumed that if Eve had her under surveillance, it would be at a distance.

Even at that late hour, the number 6 train at Thirty-Third and Park was still relatively crowded. She allowed two trains to pass without boarding as a way of making sure that no one was on the platform solely to follow her. Then she boarded the downtown train, getting off at the City Hall stop.

She walked into the Oculus—a post-9/11 structure that resembled a bird with outstretched wings. It too was crowded. This time Gwen would have preferred having fewer people around, so she could make quick judgments about whether anyone posed a threat. She moved quickly through the space, leaving most of the tourists when she entered the entrance to the PATH train—the rail connector to New Jersey.

Like with the subway, she let the first PATH train go and waited on the platform alone for the next one. It arrived ten minutes later. It took another ten minutes to reach her intended stop in Jersey City, but she stayed put when the doors opened, traveling all the way to the end of the line at Newark. New passengers boarded for the trip back to Manhattan, and Gwen traveled with them. On her second pass, she got off in Jersey City.

Once aboveground, Gwen again surveyed her surroundings. There was no one in sight; she quickly strode toward the large apartment complex on the corner of Marin Boulevard and Eighth Street.

As she entered the building, Gwen once again looked in every direction. All clear.

Or at least she thought it was.

———

Two hours later, Gwen reversed course. This time there was no need for subterfuge. Whereas her initial trip had taken ninety minutes, returning home took less than half that.

It was slightly after 4:00 a.m. when she arrived back at her building. At that late hour, the streets were empty, which made the ten-minute walk back to her apartment building particularly nerve-racking. With each step, she heard the sound of her own heartbeat. She tried to block out the thumping so she might hear if someone else was approaching. But no one else materialized. She entered her lobby and hurried up to her apartment.

She couldn't sleep, however. So she lay in bed, restless.

She was uncertain how much time had elapsed, but it occurred so suddenly that she didn't even have time to scream. A large man was upon her, his beefy hand over her mouth.

Eve stood beside him. The man removed his hand from her mouth but kept his other hand firmly on the back of Gwen's neck. The deterrent was unnecessary, however. Gwen was not going to scream.

All it took was a subtle nod from Eve for the man to punch Gwen in the face. The pain was excruciating, like nothing she'd ever experienced before. Her first reaction was to wonder if she still had all of her teeth, and she was surprised when her tongue alerted her to the fact that she did.

"We saw you go to Jersey City," Eve said. "We know you can get a message to him. So you tell him that if he testifies, you're dead. I told him before that if I ever couldn't find him, I'd kill you. You need to remind him of that."

Gwen was crying now, but trying to regain her wits. Forcing herself to ignore the throbbing in her jaw, to focus. She extended her hand under her pillow and grasped the cold steel she'd hidden there.

In a single motion, she withdrew the gun, pointed it at the man who held her neck, and pulled the trigger. She had been aiming for his chest, but the bullet struck dead center of his forehead. He fell back immediately, shaking the bed as he hit the floor.

It was now just the two of them. Eve was already reaching into her bag, but Gwen didn't hesitate.

She fired twice. The first shot went into Eve's torso, the second through her neck.

All that time playing *Call of Duty* hadn't been a waste after all.

———

Jasper Toolan had been right. You don't know if you're capable of taking a life until the situation is thrust upon you.

Gwen was quite certain that her killings would be ruled justified. She also knew that hers was as premeditated a murder as Toolan's.

She had no idea where Will was being held. The FBI had been crystal clear about not revealing that information and about denying Will any means to contact her. Of course, Eve wouldn't have known that.

So Gwen had engaged in her subterfuge of making it seem as if she knew how to get to Will, suspecting that Eve was watching. And when the ruse was done, she waited with the Glock, which she had secured courtesy of her ex-client Jasper Toolan, under her pillow.

———

Agents Benevacz and Ramirez found Gwen sitting in the living room. It hadn't taken very long for them to arrive, less than half an hour from her call, but she had rehearsed several times what she was going to say. It had the benefit of being the truth. Well, mostly.

"I got a gun because I was scared," she said. "I kept it under my pillow, and they just broke in. It happened so fast that I couldn't even reach for it until the guy had already hit me. I didn't want to shoot Eve, but she was reaching for a gun."

There was indeed a gun in Eve's handbag. Gwen had checked before she called the police.

She had also deliberately decided not to ice her jaw, so the FBI would see her wounds in all their glory. Being struck had not been part of the plan, although she realized it was fortuitous, buttressing her claim of self-defense.

Benevacz and Ramirez listened attentively to Gwen's narrative. She told them she got the gun on the dark web. Although there might have been some justice in putting Toolan in harm's way, he had done her a favor in securing it, so there was no reason to involve him.

The possession of an unlicensed firearm was illegal in New York City. Technically, as a first-time offender, Gwen could receive up to two years in prison. As a practical matter, however, she was confident that the steepest penalty she would face was the payment of a fine. If that. After all, how could anyone punish her for protecting herself, especially when her fears turned out to be well founded? Had she waited the required period to obtain a gun lawfully, she'd be dead.

"We think you should see a doctor about your jaw," Ramirez said. "It may be broken. And we're going to need to discuss with the DA about the gun charge, so you should put on some clothing and let us take you to the precinct."

Gwen nodded, and then winced from the pain in her jaw. "Can I call my lawyer to meet me down there?"

"Sure," Benevacz said.

Gwen reached for her cell phone. She had Jessica Shacter's number on speed dial.

48.

Will's safe house was in Queens. A one-bedroom apartment in the back of a low-rise apartment complex near JFK Airport. It was clean, but the decor was at least thirty years old. Will couldn't recall the last time he'd seen a non-flat-screen TV.

Since his arrival, he'd been completely cut off from the world around him. The agents had taken away his phone and not allowed him to have access to a computer or to even leave the apartment. Two heavily armed guards sat in the living room at all times.

The knock was coded. Three quick raps, followed by two slower ones. Still, the guards always unholstered their weapons before opening the door.

It was Agent Benevacz, but he was not alone. Beside him was Gwen.

She rushed forward and into Will's arms. It almost seemed like a dream to him, but the scent of her hair was not something he could conjure with his mind alone. She was actually there, in the flesh.

Agent Benevacz offered the explanation. "We figured that we could save the taxpayers a little money by protecting Gwen here with you. Assuming neither of you objects, of course."

Will took a step back. To Gwen he said, "I don't understand."

Gwen looked over her shoulder at Benevacz. "Be my guest," he said.

"Eve's dead," she said. "She broke into my apartment last night. She thought I knew where you were. And I shot her."

"Are you okay?"

"I'm fine. A little shaken, and my jaw hurts. The guy with her hit me pretty good. But all in all, I'm fine. And it's all over now."

———

The logistics were all worked out by the FBI. Gwen's family was told that she was safe. She resigned from Taylor Beckett, and the FBI explained to Benjamin Ethan that Gwen had been instrumental in convincing her boyfriend to cooperate with them, and through that cooperation they had dismantled one of the largest organizations responsible for financing worldwide terrorism.

Ethan had asked for them to relay back that he was proud of her, and that there would always be a job for her at Taylor Beckett if she wanted it. When Gwen heard the news, she laughed. The last place she ever wanted to be again was at Taylor Beckett. She had already decided that if she was going to practice law again, it would truly be on the side of the angels.

The FBI confiscated Will's apartment—as well as his possessions—and sold them all at auction. The proceeds were used to pay off Maeve Grant's loan, part of the negotiated deal Jessica had struck. It was the least the government could do, she'd argued, considering Gwen had nearly been killed.

Gwen and Will were transported to Arizona and kept under lock and key there. Gwen likened it to a honeymoon, and Will agreed. They wouldn't have wanted to leave the hotel even if they were in Hawaii or Bora Bora.

Agent Benevacz predicted that, although it would take time, everyone in Eve's syndicate would soon be behind bars. When that happened, he told them, they could come out of witness protection and go back to their old lives.

Will didn't have an old life to go back to, but Gwen would welcome being able to see her family again.

In the meantime, they had each other.

And Will knew that was all he really ever needed.

ACKNOWLEDGMENTS

What did you think of *A Matter of Will*? Email me at adam@adam-mitzner.com with your thoughts. I truly love to hear from readers and will definitely respond. Also, if it's not too much trouble, please post a review. It doesn't matter where—Amazon, Goodreads, Facebook, Instagram, Twitter—but I would greatly appreciate any help I can get in spreading the word.

A Matter of Will is my seventh novel, and as was the case with each one before it, I am indebted to a great many people who helped it come together. This is my time to thank them, although what I write here truly cannot capture how grateful I am for their support and friendship.

I begin with my agent, Scott Miller, which is fitting because my writing career began with Scott's discovery of my work. Thanks also to all those who work with Scott at Trident, especially Kristin Cipolla.

To the wonderful people at Thomas & Mercer, especially Liz Pearsons and Caitlin Alexander, both of whom provided invaluable notes that improved the book. A special shout-out to all those people at Thomas & Mercer whom I've never met but who worked on the book, from the people who create the cover to proofreaders to those in marketing. The same heartfelt appreciation goes to the people at Audible Studios, who record my books.

To my partners and colleagues at my law firm, Pavia & Harcourt, for allowing me to have two careers, and especially to George Garcia, Elizabeth Acevedo, and Jennifer Fried.

My friends and family provide much-needed support throughout the writing process. Loyal readers will note that most of these names are listed in the acknowledgments book after book: my sister, Jessica Shacter, who lent her name; Kevin Shacter; Clint Broden; Jodi (Shmodie) Siskind; Matt Brooks; Lisa Sheffield; Jane and Gregg Goldman; Bonnie Rubin; Ellice Schwab; Debbie Peikes; Sue McMurry; Margaret Martin; Ted Quinn; and Lily Icikson.

My parents, Linda and Milton Mitzner, never had the opportunity to read my books, but I know that if they were alive, they'd be among my first readers, and I thank them for that and so much more.

This book, and my life, are dedicated to my family. My daughter Rebecca inspires me with the dedication she shows to her craft; my stepson Michael reminds me of the importance of good hair and also getting your facts right; my stepson Benjamin remains the only one of my children who reads my books, and I look forward to his "constructive complaints" with each one; and my daughter Emily, by all accounts, is the master storyteller in our family.

My wife, Susan, reads each of my books three times in draft: once early on to make sure the beginning makes her want to read more, a second time when the first draft is complete to make sure I didn't mess up the ending, and a final time to make sure it's perfect before I submit it. In between reads she talks with me about the characters as if they're a part of our family. As invaluable as all that is, I thank her mostly because she helps me "be like the dog." Without her, I most certainly would not come close.

My last thanks go to each and every one of you who reads *A Matter of Will*. It is humbling beyond words to know that, through my writing, I am able to spend time with people I've never met and likely never will. Thank you.

ABOUT THE AUTHOR

Photo © 2016 Matthew Simpkins Photography

Adam Mitzner is a practicing attorney in a Manhattan law firm and the author of several acclaimed novels, including the #1 Kindle bestseller *Dead Certain* and its sequel, *Never Goodbye*; *A Conflict of Interest*; *A Case of Redemption*; *Losing Faith*; and *The Girl from Home*. *Suspense Magazine* named *A Conflict of Interest* one of the best books of 2012, and in 2014 the American Bar Association nominated *A Case of Redemption* for a Silver Gavel Award. Mitzner and his family live in New York City. Visit him at www.adammitzner.com.